GRACE LIKE A RIVER FLOWS

R MARSHALL WRIGHT

DEDICATION

Dedicated to Lynn, my wife of fifty years and who continues to refuse
to give up on me.
The particular reason for this dedication is that we lived in "Glencoe"
and many of the things that take place in the book were a part of our
lives together in this small town. PS, she is not Prudy.

INTRODUCTION

Grace Like a River Flows comes from the age old advice given to new authors--write about what you know. I retired from active duty in 1986 and accepted a call to a church in eastern Ohio. It was a wonderful experience being their pastor and if I have one regret in my ministry, it was that I left this congregation to pastor a larger, more prominent church. The church in this story is not the church I pastored. Well, the building is, but the congregation is not. I am not Reagan Lamb and Prudy is not Lynn, who was as active in every church we served as I was. My disclaimer: No real resident of Glencoe, living or dead, was harmed by the writing of this book.

Glencoe is a beautiful little town and my description is fairly accurate except for the Oaks which are both real and made up. Readers who reside in the town of "Glencoe" will recognize the location of many things. They will understand much of what I describe and perhaps remember many of the fictional characters based on former residents.

I have blended parts of myself into characters and situations throughout the book. It will be up to you, the reader, to determine truth from fiction... I'm not telling. I will give you one freebie. I have a Miata named Molly. I would have loved driving her on the winding roads of Washington County.

One of the characters in the book, and the most important to me, was very real but did not live in 1992. His name is Beasley and he was my adorable blond Cocker Spaniel. Everything I have written about him is true and don't be surprised if Beasley shows up in every book I write.

CHAPTER 1

Thursday, May 17, 1992. It isn't the part of town you would call rural, but it's near the outskirts of Glencoe where the houses are far apart and people mind their own business. People in the Oaks care little about how their property looks. They only have two concerns... their privacy and their welfare check. You can be sure that behind each door is a pit bull and a semi-automatic rifle. If you are brave enough to go on their property without permission, you are likely to meet one or the other. Behind one of these doors is a man named Billy Maddox. How to describe Billy....What was the song, "meaner than a junkyard dog"?

When you walk along these streets, you never know what you might hear or see. Kids yelling and screaming, dogs barking, rusted out cars with loud mufflers or no mufflers racing through the neighborhood, and husbands and wives yelling at each other. They don't care what they say, and they don't care if you hear...there's a code here. Everyone knows you never saw or heard anything.

"Martha, bring me another beer, now!"

"In a minute."

"Not in a minute. I said now! And when I say now woman, it means now and not a minute from now. Move your butt, now!"

"You stupid broad, how can you burn spaghetti? Dang. You're so dumb you could even burn the water. How can you burn spaghetti? Don't tell me. I don't even want to know."

"Helen, if you don't shut up that miserable mutt, I'm gonna shoot it. I swear, I will. I work all day and when I get home, I want peace and quiet!"

"Charlie, you're not the only one that works."

"You gonna try to tell me standing behind the counter at the Seven Eleven for four hours a day, three days a week is work? Woman, you need to get a real job and then you can complain."

So it goes, in house after house. Story after story. Each one is different, but they are all the same. Poor choices, in almost every case, led them to the Oaks or has kept them here. Lots of people have never married the person they live with. It's strictly a "marriage of convenience." Others got married because they "had" to get married. For most of the rest, somewhere along the line, the wedding vows of "to love and to cherish, for better or for worse, in sickness and in health until death do us part," vanished, and it became everyone for themselves.

They have neglected the sidewalks in this part of Glencoe for years. In fact, there's a lot that's been neglected on this side of town. It's not the part of town that moves to the top of the priority list for the town council. So, you best keep your head down and watch where you step.

The town was prosperous at one time. Both oil and coal were in abundance and by the 1920s Glencoe was prosperous. In the 1950s the oil dried up and by the 70s, most of the mines had closed. By the

1990s the town was about half the size it had been during the boom years. Young people now go off to college and never come back. But for those who live in the Oaks, life probably wouldn't be any different anywhere else.

There are two obvious sections of Glencoe and they've always been like night and day. The old Victorian homes line the main street, and almost all of them are well maintained. The oil barons and mine owners formerly owned them. On the side streets are the lesser but still stately homes owned by the oil and coal executives, lawyers, doctors, bankers, and business owners of that glorious time in Glencoe's history.

Down near the long-abandoned railroad tracks that once hauled mile-long trains filled with coal and oil out of Glencoe, is where the Oaks begins. At one time it was a working-class neighborhood, but now there are few here who bother to work at all. Many of the homes were row homes, where only the home on each end has three outside walls. Often there were ten two-story homes in the row. The mine owners built these as company housing and rented them out to the workers.

Some other buildings had been fairly nice single-family homes. Years ago someone converted them into slumlord apartments with the more prominent people in town being the slumlords.

Shotgun style bungalows make up most of the Oaks, along with single-wide trailers. The trailers have had multiple additions built on with no permits and they go in every direction and angle.

Shotgun style house means that the door was on the left or right side. There was a hallway from front to back and you could open the front door and the back door, fire a shotgun, and the buckshot wouldn't hit anything on the way through. Most of the Oaks is pretty run down and the occasional homeowner who still takes pride, is the exception. Grandma used to say "maybe you can't do anything about being poor, but there's no excuse for being dirty... soap and whitewash are cheap."

～

Brad was out walking his dog. He rarely walked in this part of Glencoe, but tonight he let Beasley decide where to walk. Brad wanted to walk uptown, but Beasley insisted tonight they needed to go to the Oaks. Beasley usually got his way. He was pretty spoiled.

Walking with Beasley was always an adventure. Beasley was an adorable little Cocker Spaniel, the runt of the litter and he weighed fifteen pounds full grown. Brad adopted Beasley from the Humane Society when he was about seven years old and made his new forever home the best years the little guy ever had.

A walk with Beasley was always slow. He sniffed every blade of grass, every tree and every fire hydrant. He'd lift his leg and cover the old scent with his own. After about fifteen leg lifts nothing came out, but that didn't stop him from stopping, lifting and trying.

As they rounded the corner onto Maple Lane, Brad heard yelling and screaming like someone was being killed. Not unusual here. Likely, if you asked their next-door neighbor about it the answer you'd get is, "What screaming? I didn't hear nothin.'" Even Beasley, who was almost deaf, looked around for the noise. They walked further down the street and it got louder. Brad noticed that the sounds were emanating from a house that had once been a yellow clapboard-sided bungalow, but now there were only a few faint spots of yellow. The front porch was missing its column on one end and the porch roof was hanging six inches lower than the other end of the porch. It looked like it rotted years ago. An old coon dog lay on the porch, oblivious to the racket coming from inside. Brad approached and two young children ran out the door with the screen door slamming behind them. They scrambled up an old apple tree in the front yard. The tree looked like it hadn't produced apples in twenty years. They climbed up the tree as high as they could go until they were nearly out of sight.

From inside the house, there was the crashing of dishes and a string of vulgarity like you have never heard.

"Billy, I'm sorry. I didn't mean it. Billy, please it won't happen again. I'll be a good wife. Please Billy, no more." Yup, that's Billy Maddox.

"Heather, I ask so little from you. I took you and those rotten brats off the street. All I ask is that you clean the house in return. Cook decent meals. Take care of your brats and keep them away from me. And get me my beer! Is that too much to ask? Just get me a lousy twelve pack every other day. That's it." With that, he slapped her back-handed. Out by the street you could hear her teeth crack as she fell against an end table. "Heather, why do you make me hit you? I'm so good to you and look at how you treat me."

"Billy, I forgot, that's all. Sadie got sick, and I took her to the free clinic. By the time they finished, I knew you'd be home. I know how important it is to you that I'm here when you get home."

As she got back to her feet, he hit her again, 'whack!' "Don't you move until I tell you to."

"Billy, please don't hit me. I'm sorry. I really am. I'll go get your beer right now."

"I said, you don't move until I say you do."

Brad and Beasley stopped at the end of the path leading to the house and listened. He was about fifty feet away from the tree Sadie and Jake were hiding in. He couldn't see them, but he could hear them. When they ran out of the house, he thought Sadie looked to be about seven and Jake was maybe five. Up in the tree, they were holding on to each other; Jake was crying, and Sadie kept trying to quiet him down.

"Jake, you got to stop. If'n you don't, Billy's gonna hear ya and then we will get whooped just like mama. You don't want that, do ya?"

Jake sniffed and whispered, "I want him to stop hurtin' mama. If I was big enough, I'd kill him myself."

Brad heard little Jake, and it pained him. It brought back thoughts of his own childhood. He could see Beasley looking at the door and he growled, which he never did. It was really kind of funny to see the little dog so brave. Here was this little runt of a Spaniel growling, bravely ready to take on the likes of Billy Maddox, a foe he hadn't even seen and, to top it off, the poor little dog didn't have a tooth in his mouth.

Brad knelt down and pulled Beasley's leash in close. He spoke softly to the little dog, but not loud enough for the children to hear,

"Don't worry little fellow. God's in control. God's always in control. Doesn't always seem that way, but I'm sure God will find someone to help. Come on Beasie, we need to be going home before we're missed."

Inside the house, they could hear Billy yelling, "Heather, I'm the boss around here and don't you ever forget it! You ever try to cross me and I'll not only beat the tar out of you, but I'll also hurt those rug rats of yours so bad you won't recognize them. Do you understand me?"

As Brad walked away, he heard Heather whimpering. "Billy, please, please don't hurt Sadie or Jake. I'll do anything, anything you want. Anything. Just don't hurt them. I'm sorry Billy. I know I'm blessed you took us in. Please, I'll be better."

Brad was sad… very, very sad. He knew what he had to do. Beasley stopped and peed on another dandelion.

CHAPTER 2

*F*riday, **May 18, 1992.** Reagan Lamb sat behind his desk in the small office of Glencoe Community Church. It was 9:30. He stared out the office window with its magnificent view of the treeless cement parking lot. At least the view gave him some warning of when he was about to get interrupted.

Reagan had been the pastor at Community Church for three years. He was an unusual fit as pastors and churches go. His background wouldn't lead you to believe he'd be a small town church pastor in a dying community or that he'd want to be. He was tall, trim, and handsome. He looked like one of those TV preachers. He and Prudy had bought a home outside the town limits and let the congregation rent the parsonage next to the church. The board members weren't too happy, but they wanted Reagan Lamb so they consented. Having the pastor living in the parsonage gave them some control over him. Reagan wasn't the type you could control.

He started off most days of the week the way he had today. He drove into town about 7:30 and headed to the Greasy Spoon...that's the name, really. It was a little hole in the wall diner next to the old theater that was now a Full Gospel Church. The pastor, Wayne Miller, and Reagan often met for breakfast. Wayne was a real cowboy character from Texas, and Reagan loved his droll sense of humor. One day they were playing golf and broke after nine holes for a snack and potty break.

Wayne came out of the men's room and this guy behind him said in a loud voice, "You didn't wash your hands." Wayne turns and says, "Excuse me?" The man repeats it. Wayne looks at him and, for a moment, says nothing. Then he said, in his best Texas drawl, "Mister, I don't know where y'all are from. But I'm from Texas and in Texas we don't pee on our hands." He turned and walked toward the golf cart and they were off to the tenth hole. Neither he nor Reagan said a word but just broke out in laughter.

Well, after his meet and greet at the Greasy Spoon and his usual breakfast of scrambled eggs, grits, and bacon, he went for his morning stroll up one side of the main street and down the other and back to the church on the south end of town. The main street was actually High Street because it ran along the ridge. If he saw someone he didn't know, he'd stop and introduce himself and invite them to church. After three years, that didn't happen often.

Most mornings he'd greet people and try to notice things he hadn't noticed before. Things like the display in the shoe store that hadn't changed in the last year. He could see the dust accumulating on a pair of brown brogans. He walked further and remembered stories of how prosperous Glencoe had once been. Probably fifty percent of the storefronts were now empty, but you could see how ornate the buildings had been. There were two old movie theaters in town. One was now the Full Gospel Church, and the other was a used furniture store. The owner had dreams of turning it into an antique mall, but if he wanted to do that he'd better invest in antiques. The County Courthouse was a magnificent structure representing the best of the Roaring Twenties boom era. Even the stately granite Post Office was a vote of confidence for the future of Glencoe.

One of Reagan's senior members, Paul Slater, and his brother, used to own the combination shoe store-haberdashery. Paul said to him one day. "I haven't been out of Washington County in over fifteen years." Reagan was taken aback and said, "Why not?" Paul Slater replied, "No need to ever leave Washington County. Everything anyone would ever need is here. So, why would anyone ever want to leave Glencoe?"

Reagan had figured that if you weren't fussy, you probably could get everything you needed right there in Glencoe, at least theoretically. There were two independent supermarkets, two hardware stores, a Sears catalog store, the shoe store, The Economy Clothing Store, two drug stores, a Five and Dime, and three video stores. All three video stores thrived during the 80s, because there wasn't much to do in Glencoe. In addition, there were two doctors and a small clinic, an optometrist, and a dentist came into the clinic twice a week. Being the county seat, if you needed a lawyer, just shake a tree and one would fall out.

Today he noticed something different. He realized, after being here three years, the traffic light in the center of town was the only one in all of Washington County. On his way back to the office, he waved to old Bill Bemis and his twin brother, Bob. Every morning Bill drove through town at 10 mph in the '72 Dodge pickup. Drove people crazy...10 mph with his head swiveling back and forth all the way up High Street. Reagan guessed that maybe Bill and Bob thought a new skyscraper had gone up since yesterday. Reagan never knew where they went or what they did, but about an hour later they'd come back down High Street at 10 mph and now Bob was driving. One drove into town, and the other drove home.

Elizabeth Walsh walked into the church office at five to nine. She had been the secretary at Community Church for as long as anyone could remember. Everyone called her Becky even though Reagan thought she looked more like a Lizzie. If you want to know anything in the church, you go to Becky. She was downright proud of how many pastors she'd outlasted. She was in her late seventies, computer illiterate, and refused to even use a photocopier. She refused to have anything to do with technology. She lived a block from the church and had for the sixty plus years she was married. Reagan couldn't wait to replace her. But institutions like Becky were hard to displace. They paid her to come into the office on Monday, Wednesday, and Friday from nine to noon, but you could usually find her there on Tuesday and Thursday as well and most afternoons. Community Church was her life since her husband, Franklin, died 15 years ago. There was some conjecture that living with Becky might have killed him.

As Reagan sat musing about the upcoming Sunday, Becky knocked on the door. You could tell it was Becky because she was hard of hearing so she knocked harder. She figured if she couldn't hear you, you couldn't hear her. But this knock seemed to be more urgent. She knocked and said, "Pastor Lamb, I got a call from Bethany Memorial."

Bethany Memorial was in Upton and was the closest hospital. It was about 30 miles, but with the winding roads that followed the contours of the hills, the trip took almost an hour. Glencoe was the county seat, but Washington County had no hospital. The population of the whole county was under thirteen thousand people and dropping fast. The new medical center was open 8 a.m.-5 p.m. Monday through Friday. If you'd been a lifelong patient of Dr. Lanny Whitcomb, you could call him anytime for any emergency. But, most people thought you were better off taking your chances and calling the EMS. Lanny was getting on and probably shouldn't even be practicing medicine. The new medical center took most of his patients, but the old timers swore by him.

Becky hadn't waited for the traditional "Come in" or as Reagan said, "Enter." She knocked and barged in. "Pastor," always Pastor, her generation just couldn't bring themselves to refer to the Pastor by his first name. Members of the Ladies' Guild cringed when they heard Pastor Lamb referred to by his first name. Such disrespect for authority. "That was the trouble with the church today."

She announced, "They said they admitted Heather Delaney to the emergency room about 2:00 a.m. this morning."

"Really! What happened?"

Becky prided herself on always knowing everything. But this time she had gone to the pastor with little information. She must be slipping. She hated to admit it, but she had to answer, "I don't really know what happened. I asked, but they wouldn't tell me anything. They said they have a new policy. If I'm not family they can't tell me anything." and she stomped her foot. "Makes it hard for me to do my job if people refuse to give me the information I need."

Becky's job was to keep the whole town informed, not just Reagan. Inwardly, Reagan smiled at her comment. For three years he had delighted in watching her try to get privileged information from him with no success.

Reagan continued, "What do you know? Hear anything on the grapevine?"

Becky put on a stern, serious face, "Well, you know I don't gossip Pastor, but when I picked up the mail I heard that Billy went on a tear Thursday night about 7:30. She didn't buy him beer yesterday, so apparently he beat her real bad. Now mind you, that's what I heard, but that doesn't mean it's true." For Becky, what she heard was good enough to be Gospel.

"Billy Delaney," Reagan mused. "Nope, I don't think I've met him. Has he ever come to church?" asked Reagan.

"They aren't married. His name is Maddox, and no, it's doubtful you know him. He lives in a junkyard in the Oaks. Disgusting place. And no, I'd bet he's never stepped foot in a church in his entire life."

"Okay, that name I know. I never made the connection. How long have Heather and the kids been coming here?"

"Let me see," and then Becky paused, searching her memory bank, "I'd say about four years. Yup, she first attended just before you came. She took up with Billy about the time that mine Number Four shut down. He was okay at first. He's not the man you want your daughter to marry, but he cared for them. Then he was out of work for about a year and began turning mean. Watched everything Heather did. Wouldn't let her out of his sight. Treated her kids like slaves. About the only time they were out of his sight was to come to church. At least that's what Heather told me. And apparently, he put a stop to her attendance."

Reagan said, "Now that I think about it, I haven't seen her or the kids for quite a while."

"No, Billy stopped the kids from coming to Sunday School and it's been a few months since Heather was here. People suspect the beatings are happening more often. He probably won't let her leave the house if there's any bruising."

"How come I knew nothing about this?" Reagan wasn't really asking her. It was more rhetorical, but she answered anyway.

"Well, they live out in the Oaks, and that's a private place out there. If a man wants to beat his wife, that's his right. Those people don't think like we do," said Becky,

"The railroad tracks are the dividing line, and that is the attitude of most people on this side of the line. Heather and the kids aren't typical of our membership, so they get lost in the cracks. She's a nice girl and the kids couldn't be any cuter. She needs to get out of there. That's what she needs to do."

Reagan had to admit she and the kids definitely got lost in the cracks. If she was somebody prominent or a big giver, someone would point it out to him after she missed the second week.

"Look, I'm going over to Upton to see her. I'm not feeling real good about this whole thing. I want you to call Tinker and set up a meeting for late this afternoon. His place or here. Doesn't matter. I'll be back at about three."

Reagan left the town limits, and he down-shifted the Miata to second gear on a sharp curve, floored it up to 3500 rpm's and shifted into third. The roads in Washington County had so many curves he seldom got Molly into fifth gear. The first time he and Prudence had visited Glencoe, he decided if the church offered him a position, and he accepted a call, the first thing he'd have to do is get a sports car and name her Molly. No particular reason for the name Molly. He thought it fit a pretty little roadster. They did, and he did. Molly was a 1991 Miata MX-5 with a five-speed transmission and 140 hp. On these roads, Molly would leave a Corvette sniffing her exhaust and wondering what happened.

As Reagan headed toward Upton, he thought about seeing Heather, Sadie, and Jake and yet never really seeing them. He partially blamed himself. He knew there are people who you don't notice because they are perhaps shy, introverted, or insecure. Heather was all these things, but that was no excuse. Reagan blamed himself for not knowing more about them. How sad that someone can become invisible in a church of one hundred and thirty people. He reflected on Becky's statement that people in the Oaks "aren't like us". He should have reminded her that God sees us all the same way... sinners in need of grace. Then he thought, "What part of community in Community Church does this congregation still not understand?"

It upset Reagan as he recalled his own past, "What possesses a man to be so cowardly that he'd beat his wife? And why would a woman stay in a physically abusive relationship?" He understood none of this. He'd read that unless you were a victim of physical and verbal abuse, you couldn't understand the power the abuser held over them.

As he made his way to the ICU, he didn't know what to expect. He'd seen beaten women, and each wife beater had his own special techniques and signature marks. Most tried not to leave marks where anyone would see them. This allowed someone to see the victim in public and give the appearance of a happily married couple. This was the mark of the real pro. A real coward is what he really is.

Billy Maddox was different. He wasn't afraid of anything or anyone. He stood about six four and was an intimidating two hundred and eighty pounds of muscle. He'd practiced "mean," off and on, for about thirty five years. There were periods when he'd seem to get his life together, but those periods never seemed to last long. The first couple of years with Heather seemed to be about the best he'd ever done. When he was ten, he pulled the legs off frogs and tried to set his sister's kitten on fire. His parents didn't know what to do as his behavior got worse, so when he was thirteen they kicked him out, locked the doors, and wouldn't let him back in. His father threatened to shoot him if he showed his face around there. There was no

Department of Children's Services in rural southern Illinois, so he'd been on his own ever since. At fourteen they picked him up in Chicago, put him into the system, and he bounced from place to place. He had learned how to manipulate people to get what he wanted. For girls who loved a bad boy, he was the bad boy of their dreams. He was suave in a coarse sort of way. He learned how to tell a woman just what she wanted to hear and how to get them to submit to his demonic wiles. If they resisted, the beatings began. Gentle, almost playful to begin with. Enough so they'd know he was boss. Then ever more sadistic until he had them under his control, believing they were nothing but sluts, unworthy of someone as good as Billy Maddox.

As he walked into the room, Reagan's eyes told his brain what he was seeing couldn't be true, but it was. Heather's face was the size of a soccer ball on one side. Her right eye was totally closed, and he wasn't sure she could see out of the swollen left eye. The whole right side of her face was purple, black, and an awful blue and just below her lip were sixteen stitches. He could see her nose was still bent. She had a neck brace, and they restrained her in the bed. Even though heavily sedated, she kept screaming, "Please, Billy, stop. I'll be a good wife. I promise I will. Please." Reagan couldn't look at her any longer and Heather was so sedated she didn't know he was there. He gently took her hand, offered a prayer, looked up, shook his head, turned and walked out.

When Reagan walked back into the church office, Becky informed him that Tinker couldn't meet with him until Saturday morning. Disappointed, Reagan called it a day.

CHAPTER 3

Saturday, May 19, 1992. When Reagan arrived the next morning, Tinker was sitting in the outer office area talking with Becky. Becky never came in on Saturday, but there was no way she would miss this information gathering session. Undoubtedly, she had already been trying to pump information out of the Sheriff that she could use on BNN, the Becky News Network. But Tink was too smart to be taken in by an old gossip. He had known Becky for fifty years.

"Tinker, thanks for coming over. Let's go to my office. Becky, thanks for opening, but you can leave now." Of course, Becky didn't leave and Reagan smiled. He knew that would never happen. They went into the study and closed the door. Becky decided it was time to clean the mimeograph machine outside Reagan's office door. Nobody had used it for over twenty years, but you didn't take things out of "Becky's office" without her consent. So there it sat. They stepped into the office and Reagan put a cassette of Earth, Wind, and Fire in the tape player and turned it up a little.

Tinker Reynolds had been the Sheriff in Washington County for almost fifty years. The last time someone ran against him was in the 1960s. In a small county like Washington, you didn't have to be great at your job to get elected, you had to be likable; and there wasn't anyone more likable than Tinker Reynolds. Tinker did a good job. Most of his calls in the early years were mine-related incidents and being a silver-tongued devil and a lifelong resident made his job easy. Even drunks thanked him for throwing them in the lock-up on Saturday night because on Sunday, Tinker's wife made breakfast at the jail. Tinker had broken up a few stills in his life, but nobody was ever sure where the "product" went. Nobody asked and Tinker wasn't telling. Tinker was now about seventy and had a Santa belly, but with that smile of his, you never noticed. He was a walking, breathing history book of the last fifty years of Washington County.

Reagan asked Tinker, "What happened at the Maddox place last night? I went to see her, and he beat her up badly."

Tinker replied, "Well, I don't rightly know all the details yet. Trying to get anything out of Billy is like talking to a fence post. I got the call about 12:30 a.m, and my deputy got there about the same time the EMS did. But I'll tell you what probably happened... according to the gospel of Billy. It's the same thing that happened last month and the same thing that'll happen next month. Heather was drunk and fell down. Thing is, each month her fall is worse than the last one, and no one's ever smelled liquor on her."

"Heather was drunk and fell down? You can't do all that damage in a fall, unless it's into the Haines Quarry and you land on the rocks. Tink are you serious? Is that really the story?"

"Reagan, the story never changes and there's nothing I can do. He says she fell, and she always swears it's the truth. She won't press charges, and if she won't press charges, my hands are tied. I can arrest him and hold him for twenty four hours, but that's it, so why bother? He says she fell, and she says she fell. If she won't testify against him, there is no domestic abuse. It's just an accident."

"So you're telling me this will keep going until he finally kills her and we can't stop it."

Tinker shook his head, "I'm afraid so, Reagan. There's nothing anyone can do for now."

"I don't believe that for a minute. The man has to be stopped. This is going to take a lot of prayer. Will you pray with me?" Well, if you knew Tinker, what he heard Reagan say was, will you listen while I pray? Tinker was a good ole boy and believed in God and all, but pray out loud? Not going to happen. That's getting a little too religious and religion is a private thing. Everyone knows that.

When he opened the door from the study, there sat Becky, close to the door, rag in hand, and still looking like she was working on the mimeograph. Now she was even polishing it. Inside he chuckled again. Maybe he'd keep her. She amused him greatly. He was sure she had heard nothing and that would probably ruin the rest of her day. He said goodbye to Tinker and thanked him again.

Tinker said, "Sorry, Reagan, I wish I could do something about it." Reagan said, "So do I."

After Tinker walked out Becky said, "He wishes he could do something about what?"

"He wishes he could get the Greasy Spoon to make a decent cup of coffee. C'mon, Becky, let's call it a day. You lock the front door on the way out and I'll lock the back." He went out, fired up the Miata, and headed for home.

Prudy was in the kitchen when he walked in about 1:00 p.m. and was already preparing the evening dinner. It was lasagna, one of Prudy's many specialties. Since they'd been married, Reagan was seldom late for her lasagna or her meatballs or her Marsala. Come to think of it, he was never late for Prudy's cooking. Prudy came from a big Italian family.

Somewhere along the line the Rozelli's became Protestants, and Reagan was glad they did. His wife's name had been Prudence Rozelli... that name has a story. Prudy's mother was a first generation Italian and the way she learned English was by watching American soap operas and because soap opera storylines are the same all over the world she watched and learned English. She was infatuated with a certain famous American soap opera actress, Prudence Parnel.

They met about three years ago while Prudy was working in the family restaurant in Hoboken, New Jersey, and Reagan was in his second year at a nearby seminary. He would go there for pizza and wait to see what section she was working and then sit there. He asked her for a date after his fifth visit. He didn't tell her he was studying to be a pastor, fearing that would drive her off, nor did he know if she was a Christian. His plan was to make her fall hopelessly in love with him, then tell her. Instead, he told her he was in Public Relations which wasn't exactly a lie. He was a part-time greeter at Walmart while going to school. One thing led to another and after three months he took her home. He gave her a good-night kiss and she said, "Reagan, I love you," and fled into the house. He stood there with a goofy grin. Two months later just before asking her to marry him, he told her he had something she needed to know before she said yes. He told her his life plan, and she still said yes.

The lasagna smelled great. He'd have to wait four hours before knowing if it tasted as good as it smelled, but he knew it would.

He sat down to watch a baseball game, but even as slow as baseball is, he couldn't concentrate on the game. He kept picturing Heather and then thinking about his conversation with Tinker.

He asked the blessing as they sat down to lasagna, homemade garlic knots, and salad. But the prayer wasn't the usual blessing. He thanked God for the food, but he prayed more for Heather and her children and this evening's prayer was more for Prudy's ears than God's. He asked God for a way to help them, which was his way of telling her he had something he needed to talk about. After the amen, he then told Prudy the events of the day and although it shocked her, she learned early on that you don't ask your minister husband a lot of questions. He will tell you what you need to know. Pastors' wives learn to live with only what their husbands share and know that's to protect them. Often she'd say to one of the ladies, "Tell me more, I didn't know about that," and she didn't. Prudy and Reagan agreed that the less she knew about some things the better.

He cleaned the plate down to the white finish when the phone rang. He answered and said, "Oops, I thought it was 7:30. Okay, I'll be there in about ten minutes." Looking at Prudy, he said, " I'm sorry, I guess I missed it on my calendar. Apparently, I scheduled a premarital counseling session. I've got to go. I'll try not to be late."

"You scheduled a premarital session on Saturday night?"

"I'm sorry, hon. It's the only time they could make it."

Brad sat in his car outside Billy Maddox's house knowing he wouldn't have to wait long. Heather's kids were in the custody of Washington County Family Services right now and Heather was lying in a hospital bed thirty miles away. He knew Billy would go on the prowl. Billy exited the house at 8 p.m., dressed in his finest bar hopping clothes. A clean sleeveless T-shirt, appropriately referred to as a wife beater shirt, and khakis with the leg length two inches too short. He headed down to the Dew Drop Inn and Pizzeria. The pizza was good if you had enough to drink. Billy turned right and Brad knew exactly where he was headed, so he drove on ahead and waited. Billy took the shortcut through the alley behind the old Ford dealership that went out of business in 1988. Billy rounded the corner, opened the door of the Dew Drop and Brad got out of his car. Beasley came over to the driver's door and Brad said, "Sorry buddy, you've got to wait here while I take care of an itch." The music in the parking lot was so loud the building seemed to shake. The Dew Drop was located in the old railroad area, so a seedy joint like this didn't really bother the towns-people. Lots of fights here, most were never called in and usually over before one of Tinker's deputies could get there. There were even accusations they drove to the Dew Drop slowly in hopes it would be over—no paperwork.

Billy walked into the Dew Drop like he owned the place. Tonight Billy was feeling cocky. He walked in and announced, "A drink for everyone. I'm buying." Brad peered through a scraped off spot in the blacked-out window on the south side of the building. He watched Billy prance about as if he owned the place. Billy proceeded to make the rounds like an entertainer working the crowd before show time. He showed no remorse for what he'd done and it was obvious. By now everyone knew what happened, but no one spoke a word. In fact, some nightly patrons admired his chutzpah even though they did not understand what chutzpah was or how to spell it. Billy was a man's man for those who are cowardly men who like to slap women around.

After the third Old Milwaukee draft, it was time to make room for some New Milwaukee. He slapped the back of each person at the bar on the way by, walked around the corner, and down a thirty-foot hall to the filthy bathroom next to the back door. He stepped in and slid the deadbolt. There were only two screws holding it on. No problem...honor among drunks. You gave a gentle push on the door and if it didn't open, you waited or went outside the back door.

Billy entered the filthy little room and stood at the rust stained urinal with his back to the door. He heard the door jiggle and said, "Just hold on buddy, you're next after me."

Before he finished the sentence, the door crashed in. Billy felt his face crushed against the wall, the urinal handle and water pipe crushed his chest and he felt pee running down his pants leg. In a second swift move, Brad grabbed Billy's right arm, pulled it up behind him and Billy peed on his other leg.

Brad spoke without emotion and with great authority, "Don't move a muscle. The last thing you want to do is see my face. Seeing me would be a huge mistake on your part. Because it might be the last thing you ever see."

While Billy stood there shaking, Brad propped a chair under the door handle to secure it against an unwanted and ill-timed intruder.

Nobody ever messed with or challenged Billy Maddox. This was a surprise Billy never expected. Who did this guy think he was? Billy got his composure back. He'd have to teach him a little lesson. *"Nobody messes with Billy Maddox—nobody."* Billy made his move and felt his arm go in a direction God never intended.

Brad whispered, "Billy, what part of 'don't move' don't you understand? Now listen carefully, because with one quick twist you will never use this arm again. Now, do I have your attention? Billy, just nod your head." Billy nodded.

"Billy, I think you're the worst form of human there is. I know you're a wife beater. I don't like wife beaters. You're a child abuser, and

I really don't like child abusers. And most of all, you're a coward and a bully. I grew up with a father just like you. I wanted him to stop beating my momma, but he wouldn't do it. When I tried to protect her, he'd kick me and backhand me until I couldn't move. Billy, you know what he really liked to do? He'd grab me by the belt and hang me on a nail on the wall and make me watch the horrible things he'd do to my momma. Billy, do you have any idea what it's like for a child to live through that? You're watching your momma get beaten and you want to kill him, but you're too small to hurt him. Do you know the rage I feel when a man beats a defenseless woman whose only sin is that she's guilty of trying to love and please this miserable piece of filth?"

A knock came on the door and Brad whispered to Billy, "Tell them you have issues and you'll be awhile." Brad turned Billy's arm a little more and Billy repeated the words with the authentic sound of being in distress.

Brad had Billy's attention and Billy no longer tried to struggle, mostly because of the pain. But Billy was ever defiant and demanded, "Who are you? What do you want?"

Brad said, "Billy, I'm the one person you hoped you'd never meet. More importantly, I may be the only person in this town who is not afraid of you. I'm not going to hurt you now unless you force me to do it. With the feelings I have for you, it sure would be easy to hurt you badly. And to tell the truth, I might even enjoy it.

"Who am I? Some call me the Angel of Justice from the Book of Revelation. I help defenseless people get rid of their bullies. And since I'm an angel, I will give you a chance. Let's call it a social experiment dealing with change.

"I'll be watching you every day. I'll be there continuously, but you'll never see me. Billy, what I want is for you to become the father I wanted my father to be. I was too little to affect a change in him, but I'm not little anymore. Here's what I want. I want you to learn to love Heather and take care of her. I want you to be a step-dad that Sadie and Jake can look up to and be proud of. I want to look at you, Heather, Sadie, and Jake and see the family I never had. That's who I am, and that's what I want. Pretty simple, huh? What do you think, Billy, up for the challenge?"

Billy found his present situation very disturbing. He had never encountered anyone like Brad. He thought, "This guy knows too much about me." Billy couldn't believe his ears. He wants Billy Maddox to become a loving husband and a caring daddy.

Billy demanded, "Do you know who I am?" Billy could never keep his mouth shut. "Man, what kind of stuff have you been smoking?"

Brad said, seriously, "I don't smoke. I believe a man can change. I've seen it. All he needs is a little motivation. Billy, I'm your motivation. Now, I want you to begin by going to see Heather and telling her about the 'vision' you had tonight. Tell her how God's already changed your life through a dramatic encounter and that from today on you will love her and protect her and never hurt her again. And most importantly, you better believe it yourself."

Billy is Billy. "Why would I go do that?"

This last comment was too much. Brad said, "Because you'll already be at the hospital getting your broken arm fixed." Crack! Brad reached back, pulled the chair away, opened the door, and threw Billy to the floor where he ended up covered in urine. He sucker punched a guy waiting at the door who went down without ever seeing his face. He went out the back and disappeared. He approached the car and saw two little eyes staring from the driver's seat. He opened the door and petted the little Spaniel and said, "See, God has ways of reaching the lost. Okay, Beasie, move over. Time to go home."

CHAPTER 4

*M*onday, **May 21, 1992.** Tinker arrived at the Washington County Courthouse at 9:00 a.m. for the arraignment of Micah Barnes on a charge of aggravated assault.

While the rest of the United States seemed to have an economy that was rebounding, it left behind Washington County. Micah was another of those left behind. Micah was a fairly good student and an even better football player. These were the two best options for breaking the poverty cycle in Washington County, but few opted to get out. You could get a job at the Aluminum plant on the river. It was unionized and paid well; but it was hot, back-breaking work. A few mines were still open, but they were old and dangerous, but again the pay wasn't bad. And the logging industry in the area was going strong and paying well. All were hard, labor-intensive jobs that left you tired at the end of your shift and not for the lazy.

The major industry in Washington County was welfare. It was easy money and the only labor involved was going to the welfare office to sign for the check. Micah was a part of a fourth generation welfare family. The third largest employer in the county was the Welfare Department headed by a retired Army officer named Mike Pembly. Mike, like most of the more prominent people in Glencoe, belonged to the Community Church. Together, Mike and Reagan had tried to begin a ministry for members of the welfare community, but most just wanted their checks and nothing more. One year the employees and church members planted a huge garden behind the Welfare Office. They tended it, weeded it, and even watered it in the dry season. In August the harvest came in. When the welfare recipients came in, they told them about the garden, gave them a bag, and said they could pick all they wanted... they wouldn't even bother to take the bag. The only way they got rid of all those vegetables was for the employees to pick them, bring them in the foyer to the office, and then give it away. They even had to bag the food.

Family members taught the next generation how to work the welfare system. There was seldom any encouragement to go on to higher education. No prodding to get out of the system. A family consisting of three generations living under one roof could make more tax-free money on welfare than a husband and wife working a forty-hour week. Such was the reality of Glencoe and Washington County. The only population growth in the county in the last six years came from Lincoln County to the north where they had made it a lot harder to receive welfare, so their recipients loaded their old pickup trucks and moved to Washington County.

Micah might have been able to get out of the system if he hadn't messed up his knee early in his senior year. He was big and quick, but a low chop block from the back put an end to any dreams he might have had for a college football scholarship...if he ever really had a chance. Who knows? Dreams die fast and easy in that part of town. Micah was a fairly good student, but without football, his grades weren't good enough for a scholarship. And right out of high school Micah couldn't get on welfare unless he got a girl pregnant, and he was smart enough not to do that. Several families in town had encouraged their teenage daughters to get pregnant, but warned, don't you even think about getting married. There was good money in babies. Grandma and Grandpa on welfare. Mom and Dad with four kids on welfare. Three of the daughters with two kids each...all under one roof. Fourteen sources of welfare money. You do the math.

Micah got a laborer job with the sawmill that paid $7.90 an hour. If he could work his way up to be a blade operator, he could make $10.50 an hour. That would be more than any member of his family ever earned before they figured out how to work the system. He got off early one day and thought he'd stop by the Lazy Daisy soft ice cream drive in. It was a small seasonal place only open May through August. And it might be closed any day if the owner didn't want to work. Micah drove in and saw Katie with another guy and she was sitting a little too close to him.

Katie's father ran the hardware store and had forbidden Katie to see Micah. You know what a forbidden teenage girl and a bad boy equals, don't you? They'd seen each other on the sly for about six months. Micah thought it was a lot more serious than Katie did. For him, it was a chance to have the girl every guy in town wanted. Who knows, maybe even get married and get a good job working for his father-in-law. For Katie, it was nothing more than a chance to defy her father. If only Micah had known this before he stopped at the Lazy Daisy.

When Micah saw them together he was furious. He thought Katie was his girl, and she was cheating on him. He felt betrayed and wondered if he was the laughingstock of Glencoe. Did everyone know about Katie and Bobby Lee, but Micah? He put his old pickup into low gear and hit the accelerator from about twenty feet behind the Mustang convertible. He pushed in the trunk and the car moved within three feet of the building. He saw Katie's ice cream get pushed right up her nose. Bobby Lee was furious. He jumped up, over, and out of the car without opening the door. He got to the pickup. Micah opened the door which slammed Bobby Lee to the ground. He jumped out, kicked him in the head, then ran to the passenger side of the Mustang. "Katie, get out. You're coming with me." Katie looked at him in disbelief that he could ever have taken their relationship seriously. He grabbed her by the hair and pulled.

She yelled, "Let go of me! You are such a loser. I'm not going anywhere with you. Get out of here. I never want to see you again." He lost it, slapped her hard, and the sirens got louder. It seemed like Tinker came out of nowhere and got out of the car.

~

Tinker sat behind the District Attorney and Katie and looked over at Micah sitting with the Public Defender. Tinker had seen hundreds of these cases over the years. It broke his heart, but he had a job to do. They filled their lives with "if onlys." If only Micah's parents hadn't tried to beat the system. If only Micah hadn't broken his knee. If only Micah had just studied harder. If only someone had been there to encourage him and mentor him. If only a week ago Micah had just walked away.

Tinker knew from years of experience that for the incarcerated, life was a matter of "if onlys" and "what ifs." What if I'd only done this instead of this? Unfortunately, most of the kids in the foster system, welfare system, and in the grip of poverty never learned the difference between good choices and bad choices. They had no one to teach them how to make good decisions. All they ever saw were their parents making the same decisions they always had made and yet expecting a different result. It never happened. And here sat one more example of poor decision making.

Reagan Lamb walked in and sat down near the back. He had a vested interest in the Barnes family. He was helping Micah's sister, Charlotte, get her life on the right track. She wasn't off welfare yet, but she wanted to be. When the system wraps its tentacles around you, it squeezes the life out of you. It's hard to break the cycle without a support system. Reagan was her only support system. She had made the first step. She attended worship regularly, but most of the members weren't excited about any Okie at Community Church. Each Sunday she heard Reagan share more about Jesus and it created a hunger within her. She learned of God's forgiveness, about his grace, and second chances. She was determined to get herself and her baby, Sara, out of the stranglehold of the system.

Charlotte worried about her "little" brother and asked Reagan to look in on him. He couldn't refuse, but it was one of those pastoral dilemmas. He had led Charlotte to Christ, and he knew she had a lot of influence on him. He believed he had a good chance of reaching Micah. On the other side of the room, Katie sat with her parents two rows behind her. They were prominent members of Community Church going back three generations.

Reagan was sitting in the middle near the back. He looked over to Micah. The only one seated behind Micah was Charlotte. Noticeably absent was his father, who was about as useful as a wooden frying pan. What a contrast. Behind Katie was her family. Friends. Bobby Lee and his family. And there was Micah with only his sister.

The bailiff yelled, "All rise." The judge, Lloyd Chadwick, who was another member of Community Church, entered and said, "Be seated." The lawyers made their motions, the judge banged his gavel, and they set the bail at twenty thousand. Reagan couldn't figure this one out. That meant he had to post two thousand dollars to get out. This kid had never seen two thousand dollars. And yet, if he didn't raise bail he could sit in jail for two months awaiting trial, while someone like Billy Maddox walked the streets. Micah was led away and everyone filed out.

Reagan waited in the hall for Tinker to come out. He reflected on how unjust it was for a kid to sit in a cell because he made a stupid decision while Billy Maddox was free and hell-bent on more destruction.

Funny thing about life. God created us with a free will. We can make any choice we want. Yet some people seem to make one bad decision after another. Reagan knew well that a bad decision will lead to consequences you don't want. He had made a few bad decisions, and he'd paid. Then there were the Billy Maddoxs of the world who seem to get away with everything. And here was Micah. Micah had made some bad decisions as had Charlotte, but that didn't make them bad people. They were people who could definitely be redeemed. But Billy? He needed something that seemed to go beyond redemption. Something convinced Reagan even God's grace couldn't reach Billy.

Reagan knew about bad decisions. He'd made a lot growing up. Thing is, God apparently was watching over his life so he got away with a lot of things. His life didn't really change until seminary when he met Prudy. Not that Reagan was ever out of control. He had grown up with no father. Since his mother worked, there was no one to guide him or be a role model. When he was in the eighth grade he and a friend had stolen cedar lumber to build a magnificent tree house. It was beautiful. They even stole windows and shingles for the roof. The contractor noticed material missing and put two and two together and it added up to Reagan. When the police knocked on the door, Reagan knew what it was about. They took him in for questioning to scare him. He worked as a gofer for the contractor until the debt was paid. He got off easy.

Reagan didn't learn his lesson. He got into fights, sat in the principal's office for hours, spent time in detention for bullying. The next year he tried to blow up an aerosol can, which seemed harmless enough except the wind came up and he burned down fifteen acres and threatened about ten homes. Fifteen volunteer firefighters had to be paid to put out the fire.

Most of the time he made the right decision before it was too late. His freshman year in high school he ran with a bad crowd. The plan was to break into the local tannery and bust open the vending machines. About a block away Reagan had a bad feeling. They tried to talk him into it, called him names, and one even threatened him, but he walked away. The others got caught on-site, with the money. All three did six months in juvenile detention. There was a guiding force in Reagan's life that he had yet to recognize. He would intentionally, or unintentionally, make bad choices, but something always changed the course of his life. Reagan liked to think of himself as a bad boy. Reagan was complicated. He was running away from something and he was running toward something. He didn't know what he was running from or toward. He knew his life could go either way and when his mother looked at the final report card of his junior year; she said the words that helped to turn his life around. "Reagan, I give up. It's your life, do what you want..." She dropped the report card on the floor and walked away. He knew he needed discipline. With no role model in his life, Reagan joined the Army after graduation.

As Tinker exited the courtroom, Reagan moved toward him when Billy Maddox appeared, also moving toward Tinker. Billy's arm was in a cast, he was limping and there were several stitches on his forehead along with several bodily bruises. Reagan waited this one out and took a seat with his back to Tinker and Billy but he could hear every word.

Tinker had a grin on his face as Billy walked up to him and he said, "There is a God in heaven who metes out justice." He looked Billy up and down, "My, my, my. What did you run into Billy? Whatever it was, it looks like you lost."

"Sheriff, you got to do something. I was minding my business at the Dew Drop Inn and some guy attacked me in the john. Banged my head into the wall and broke my arm in three places."

"Well, Billy, I'm the Sheriff and it's my job to protect all the citizens of Washington County. So let's see how I can help. What did the guy look like?"

Billy said, "I don't know Sheriff, I didn't see him."

Tinker said, "Okay, so what was he wearing?"

Billy was getting exasperated, "I told you I didn't see him."

Tinker smiled, "Oh yeah, you said that. Okay, then just give me a list of witnesses who saw this guy attack you."

Billy was really ripped by now and said, "Nobody saw anything!"

Tinker is grinning from ear to ear. "Billy, you don't know what he looked like. You don't know what he wore. And there aren't any witnesses. I guess I'll just have to assume you were drunk and fell down the steps. Best be careful you don't fall again. It could be a lot worse next time." Tinker laughed out loud and walked away.

Reagan followed Tinker out of the building and caught up with him halfway down the forty three granite steps leading to the sidewalk. "Listen, Tinker, I want to post Micah's bond, but I want no one except you to know I put up the bond."

"Why would you do that? You know he's guilty, and he will go to jail. What's in it for you? If he skips town you're out two grand."

"Everything you say is right, but he won't skip. I'm caught in the middle between the Pierces and Micah's sister. Adam Pierce could go really hard on Micah and as a father, I wouldn't blame him. This could start him down the same road as Billy Maddox or his father. Hopefully not that bad, but in the same direction. I've spent a lot of time with Charlotte and I think I've got pretty good insight into Micah. Tinker, he is not a bad kid. He handled the situation the only way he has ever known. He had a choice, and he made the wrong one. But I can't allow one bad choice to turn him into a Billy Maddox. Tinker, I've got to do it. Can you make it happen for me?"

Tinker said, "I understand exactly what you're saying. Been dealing with this in Washington County for 50 years and it never seems to change."

They released Micah to his sister the next day.

Reagan headed toward home and felt a definite hesitation in the car engine. The Miata stumbled while speeding up in third gear. And it happened again and again. "Nope. Molly, we can't put up with that. I'll take care of that after dinner."

Reagan drove home and thought of all the Micahs, Sadies, and Jakes waiting for a chance at life. Wouldn't adoption really be the right thing to do? All these helpless, unwanted children living in homes with parents who don't want them. He thought, "Yes. Prudy and I need to look at adoption." He pulled into the drive and he smelled it immediately. The aroma took him to another dimension. Tonight was chicken parmigiana. It was good to be married to an Italian!

Prudy and Reagan had been trying to get pregnant for two years, but somehow nothing worked. At age thirty-six time was running out. There was nothing wrong with either of them medically. It seemed the eggs and sperm refused to cooperate. Her family wasn't much help with each of her siblings having four or five children bang, bang,

bang. And Mama Maria put in her two cents every chance she had, "So when do I get my grandchild?" A lot of pressure.

After supper, he went out to the garage to work on Molly and see if he could find that miss fire. Molly wasn't Prudy, but she was something special. When he finished taking the car for a quick spin, he decided he would talk with Prudy about adopting.

Brad was on a mission tonight. He left Beasley home because he didn't know where he might end up. Billy was just too predictable. He left the Dew Drop Inn and headed down the alley. When he was behind the old Ford dealership he had the urge. He didn't really care for the men's room at the Dew Drop anymore. At least not until they fixed that lock. He moved into the corner where the garage met a cinderblock wall.

Brad waited until he heard a good solid stream and moved up silently behind Billy. Good training was like riding a bike, you never forget how to do it. Billy never saw him or heard him. This time he grabbed Billy's left arm and twisted it up. Again, Billy peed all over himself.

Brad spoke just as softly and calmly as before, "Billy, didn't I tell you I'd be watching you? Right now I don't like what I'm seeing. Here you are still drinking and wearing that cast like a badge of honor. Betcha didn't bother to tell anyone at the Dew Drop how you got it or why. You're acting like you don't really believe me.

"Billy, I'm your only hope. You may not want to change, but you are my personal project now. You will change. Do you hear me? I want you to go see Heather tomorrow and I will know if you don't go. I also have sources, so I know she will come home soon. You better make all the plans a loving and attentive husband would make.

"Just a reminder. You've got one good arm left. Be a shame to fall and break it. And, Billy, you peed yourself again. That's becoming a bad habit. You've got to stop doing that...especially in public." Billy turned and Brad was gone.

~

Zoom, Zoom. "Molly, that sounds better." All she needed was a number 3 spark plug. Reagan put the car away and went to the den where Prudy snuggled up with a good book by R. Marshall Wright. She'd read everything he'd written. Reagan sat down and said, "Prudy, I've been thinking about our baby."

She looked over at him, "How did you find out?"

He said, "Honey, how did I find out what?"

"How did you find out about the baby?"

"But, Prudy, I'm not sure what you're talking about. What baby?"

She replied, "You said you've been thinking about our baby."

"I have and since we can't seem to get pregnant, I think we should adopt."

Prudy looked at him and smiled, "I agree, we could adopt the second one, but first let's have this one." She patted her stomach as Reagan fell into his chair. "Thank you, Jesus! God is Good!"

CHAPTER 5

*T*uesday, May 22, 1992. The next day Reagan drove Molly to Upton. Today he was driving much more cautiously... he would be a daddy. Reagan wondered what it would be like to have a close, loving family. He'd never had the experience of a father's love.

His dad left them when Reagan was only four and his mother was glad to see him go. He couldn't remember much about him or a time his father ever hugged him or showed him any emotion a father should feel for his child. Reagan would seek attention, but all it ever got him was further rejection. Birthday and Christmas presents were from Mom and Dad, but Dad was never there. It was years before his mother told him the truth.

Since meeting Prudy, he'd spent lots of holidays with the Rozelli family. No question they loved each other, and they'd fight to the death to protect each other. But there was no warmth there. He felt like they loved each other, but didn't care about each other. Then he thought about the Barnes family and how dysfunctional they were. Was there ever any real love there? Charlotte loved Micah, and he'd seen her cry over him. But what about their parents? Did they ever have any feelings at all?

Then he thought of Sadie and Jake in the foster system while their mother fought for her life in Upton. He still kept asking himself, what kind of man could beat a woman?

The abuser says, "She deserved it!" No! No woman has ever deserved a beating. *"Oh, Billy, can God ever get his hands on you?"*

Reagan entered Heather's room. She looked better than she had two days ago. She had both eyes open, but they were a deep purple. Good thing Heather couldn't see herself. There were no mirrors in this room, intentionally. Her ear was wrapped, and it appeared she might live. She put down the Gideon Bible she'd been reading. He noticed it was opened to Ephesians 5 and he assumed Paul's instructions to husbands and wives but said nothing to Heather. She could dream all she wanted, but if Billy wouldn't listen to these teachings, they meant nothing. He didn't see that happening anytime soon. Heather put the Bible down, "Billy came to see me last night. He told me he wanted me to come home."

"Heather, Billy always wants you to come home. You go and you know it will happen all over. Why do you stay with him? He treats you and the kids like pond scum. You know I can help you escape this abuse. There's a shelter right here in Upton. They'll take you and the kids."

"Pastor, this time there really was something different about him. Somehow it seemed like he had the fear of God put in him. He came in this morning with his head down and kinda shuffling. He wasn't the cocky 'I'm the boss' Billy. He brought those flowers." Reagan looked over at a beautiful bouquet of a dozen long stem roses. "Billy has never given me flowers, ever! And he gave me a package of Reese's Cups. May not seem like much to you, but he remembered they are my favorite candy. He had his arm in a sling. Said he fell off the porch trying to fix it and broke his arm. I think he probably got in a fight at the Dew Drop and someone probably broke it for him, but no matter, it seems to have humbled him. He told me God appeared to him in a vision and told him it was time to change his ways. He said it was so real it was like God was standing right behind him speaking into his ear. He said he loved me and would never lay another hand on me or the kids. Pastor, he really promised. I know he's said it before, but never like this."

"Heather, do you really believe what you're saying or do you just want to believe it? He can change, but will he ever change?"

"Pastor Lamb, I got nowhere else to go. I've got no family. And if I do, I don't know where they are. I ran away at thirteen and had Sadie at fourteen. Don't know who the father was, could have been half the guys in the town. Had Jake at sixteen and I know who his daddy is, but he took off as soon as he found out I was pregnant. Billy took me in when no one else would. He was good to me, he really was. We were happy and then the mine closed. Billy tried to find a job, but no one in the county was hiring. Or maybe they wouldn't hire Billy. I could see Billy getting real sad, depressed like, but there was nothing I could do. Everything I tried to do just seemed to make it worse. I got a part-time job, but he made me quit. Said it made him feel like less of a man if I worked. So we went on welfare for a year. I don't know why he thought that was better than me working. I can tell you, being on welfare helped none. Then about a year ago, he got a job out at the airport cutting grass and emptying trash and stuff. We got off welfare and had enough to pay the bills, but by then he was drinking a six pack every night.

"This is the first time since the mine closed that he's been nice. First time he's ever apologized for doing what he done. He always said before that since he provided for me, he had a right to do anything he wanted to do. He always said it was my fault he hit me. Never said he loved me before. This is the first time. Pastor, I want him to change. Do you think a man like Billy can change?"

"Honestly, if I were you, I'd run and never look back. But you have to decide what to do and do what you think God wants you to do. And, yes, a lot of bad men in the Bible changed. So yes, Billy can change. My question is still, will he? Does he really want to? He can change, but he has to have a heart God can use. Remember, I'm one phone call away. And no matter what you choose, I will support you."

He prayed with Heather and left. As he walked down the hall he said, "Well, God, you got your work cut out for you this time. Hope you've got something in mind."

So far, this had been a long week, and it wasn't looking any better. Ordinarily, by now, Reagan knew what Sunday's message would be, but as of yet, he didn't have a clue. There was a lot going on in this town right now and somehow it all seemed to connect back to Community Church. Reagan was used to tension and stress in life. He could handle it, but it didn't mean he liked it. Maybe he'd preach about God's grace. That was always a needed subject that bore repeating. Lord knows they needed a little grace. And he settled in on Ephesians 2:8-10. "For you are saved by grace through faith. Not of good works should anyone boast. But, you have been saved by God to do good works." Yes, everyone knows Ephesians 2:8-9, but they always forget verse 10… the reason God saved you.

Adam was in the hardware store office when Maddie came barging in. No knock. No greeting. Just barged in, in a full rage. "Adam, do you realize that worthless Barnes kid got out on bail? How could that have happened? You assured me it was all taken care of. You said he'd never be able to hurt Katie again…"

"Maddie, I did what you asked. I met with Lloyd for breakfast over in Upton on Wednesday. We talked about it. He understands that people like them need to be taught a little respect for law and…"

Maddie cut him off mid-sentence, "Welfare frauds and bums, every one. Micah's what? Third or fourth generation? And that sister of his comes to church every week proudly carrying that illegitimate baby of hers. Those kinds of people need to be stopped or people like Katie will never be safe."

Adam tried to continue, "Lloyd said he'd set the bond high enough he couldn't make bail. Said if we set it too high it would look like the verdict was in without due process. Seemed like twenty thousand was plenty high. We both agreed there was no way he could come up with twenty thousand. His old man wouldn't help him, that's for sure. Nobody else in this town would help him. So I don't have a clue, Maddie, I don't know how he got out. Nobody knows who posted the bail. And Tinker says he can't reveal any information like that."

"Well, as long as he's out there, then Katie's at risk."

"Look, Maddie, I seriously doubt that. We are angry and Katie could have been badly hurt, but she wasn't. He slapped her and her nose hurt, but he didn't break it and he sure could have. He pulled her hair, yes. People saw it. It was an assault, but not premeditated. It wasn't planned. I don't believe he really meant to hurt her. And I don't think he's dangerous."

"Hold on a minute. Where is this going? A few minutes ago you were ready to put him away for years and now, listen to yourself. This is our daughter we're talking about."

"First, I've never said I wanted to put him away for years. Do you remember when we first dated, and you thought I was in Upton for the night? You went out with 'Moonpie' Moon."

"His name was Ronnie Moon, and he was a nice kid. He helped me with a science project and I owed him. So I let him take me to Brother's Soda Fountain. It wasn't even a date."

Adam jumped in, "Exactly my point. It wasn't a date. But Moonpie didn't know that, and I didn't know that. Do you remember what I did the next day in school?"

"Yes, you embarrassed me, that's what you did. You pushed him up against a locker and said if he ever came near me again, you'd break his face."

"Bingo, and I did that after I had all night to think about it. What if I had accidentally come upon the two of you outside Brother's Soda Fountain?"

"I don't think you'd have made a public scene or slapped me. I don't think you would have beat up Moonpie, I mean Ronnie."

"You don't think I would, but we'll never know for sure. I was angry, furious, but our parents brought Micah and I up differently. I had good parents. We went to church, Sunday School, and Youth Group. They gave me responsibility, and I learned how to make good decisions. But I'm not sure Micah knows decisions have consequences. It's something you're taught. Do we want to ruin his life forever or just teach him a good lesson? Bobby Lee's family didn't even press charges against him. Micah had insurance to repair the Mustang. They saw it as two guys fighting over a girl."

Outside the door stood a now angry, vengeful and ever defiant Katie Pierce listening to every word. She felt that her father didn't understand or even care about her. It was like he believed Micah more than her. She had been there for almost the whole conversation and heard it all. She could see her father having a conscience. Katie had been lying to herself and her parents for so long she didn't know the truth anymore. One thing she knew for sure, she wasn't about to let the likes of Micah Barnes get away with hurting her and embarrassing her the way he did at the Lazy Daisy. He literally ruined her life. She liked him okay, but no one was ever supposed to find out she went out with him. He ruined everything that day and now she'd never be Homecoming Queen. But what if there was a way to get everyone in town on her side? What if she was the victim? She knocked on the door and said in her sweetest adorable teen voice, "I've been thinking and praying about this hard. I have to tell someone. I didn't tell you before, because I was afraid and ashamed. For a long time, I thought it was my fault. But now I know it wasn't. Micah Barnes raped me." Maddie flew into a rage, picked up the phone and said, "Adam, you call Tinker right this minute."

Tinker had been taking a little snooze in cell number one. Emma had forced him to buy a new mattress for the cot. The new mattress put ideas in the aging sheriff's mind. Save cell number one and use it only when necessary. Today it was necessary. The phone rang and the deputy on duty woke him up.

Maddie grabbed the phone, "Tinker, you get over here to the hardware store right now! Use the back entrance." She hung up. Tinker scratched his head, but could tell by her tone it was important. After he got Maddie calmed down, he asked her to leave the office. He asked Katie a lot of questions and Katie lied through her teeth... every word out of her mouth was a lie. She even told Sheriff Reynolds there was a witness, but that she was out of town right now. Now, she'd have to get to her when she returned before the Sheriff did. Three hours later, Tinker placed Micah back behind bars with his bail revoked. He wasn't sure of the validity of Katie's statement, but he had little choice in the matter right now. The new charge pending...statutory rape of a minor. Mandatory twenty five years in prison if convicted. The witness was the key. It was so long ago, there was no evidence of rape. Otherwise, it was a he said she said case and with a jury, that could go either way.

Reagan focused, trying to get his thoughts on paper, "Grace means God doesn't give you what you earn or even deserve..." Bang, bang, bang! He was so deep in thought it sounded like gunshots. He jumped out of his seat and automatically hit the floor behind his desk. Loud noises still bothered him. It had been about ten years since he led secret military missions that never officially took place. It was a period of his life he tried to forget. The military had taught him the discipline he had needed, but backfires, gunshots, fireworks, and other loud noises brought back memories and triggered fears. His training taught him if you wanted to survive you dove for cover, and if you heard the second shot, you were still alive. Reagan still fought survivors' guilt almost every day. Ten years ago he heard a shot and took cover, but four of his squad didn't make it. Reagan didn't hear the second shot. He woke up in a hospital in Germany with no memory of what had happened. Four of his friends would never come home and he couldn't remember much of anything. Sergeant Lamb asked the Army Doc how bad it was. The Doc said, "Son, your SEAL days are over." Over a long period of time, that day came back in bits and pieces and it was always the same. It should have been a routine mission to take out a radical Muslim leader. But they had bad intel. The enemy used a decoy. Reagan thought his sniper had the Taliban leader in his sight, but it wasn't him. It was a mannequin. Before they could fall back, the Taliban ambushed from three sides.

Prudy had noticed nothing unusual until they went to a 4th of July celebration. She could see him wince every time a shell went off. She said nothing at the time, but noticed it again weeks later when a car backfired and Reagan ducked. It continued until one evening when they cuddled in front of a roaring fire she confronted him.

She lay her head on his shoulder, "Tell me what happened over there."

Reagan went still and quiet. He'd only ever told the VA Psychiatrist and really thought he was over it. "What are you talking about? I enlisted, served my time, and came home. That's pretty much it."

"Stop trying to protect me or hide or whatever you're doing. I've seen the terrible scars on your back and leg and I've watched you when loud noises go off. There is a lot more there than you're willing to talk about. I love you. If we will be together the rest of our lives, then you've got to let me in."

Silence followed. Reagan stared into the flames and through them until he again saw the firefight. He closed his eyes and cried for the first time in ten years. He held her tight and told her everything that happened. Every bloody detail. She and VA psychiatrists were the only ones who knew all about his past and the inner battles he fought daily. The church didn't know about his past. He never talked about the military and never put it on his resume. They were the lost years of his life, but they kept finding him.

He recovered just as the office door flung open with Tinker and Charlotte both trying to squeeze through the doorway at the same time. Tinker spoke first. Charlotte was fighting tears and holding her daughter. "Micah's back in jail. I had no choice. I had to pick him up. Katie has filed new charges of rape. Gave a whole statement of what happened that night...date, time, place, and a witness. Her parents are livid. Seems Adam was ready to back off the original charges and then Katie dropped this bombshell."

Charlotte said, "Pastor Reagan, he couldn't have done it. He was with me. That's my birthday, and we have always spent our birthdays together ever since we were kids."

Reagan said, "Looks like he will need a good lawyer now. Even if he was with you, and I believe you, she'll just say she got the date wrong. Micah's got a fight on his hands with no real alibi and with the testimony and tears from a sixteen-year-old girl, it will be who the jury believes. She tells the story and Micah will say it's not true. With what the D. A. might have, there is no attorney in town good enough to go up against her."

Tinker said, "Reagan, it makes no sense. Why didn't she come forward a year ago when the incident took place? Why would she wait until her father wanted to lessen the charges? Seems the whole thing could be bogus, but I don't have a way to prove it. Yet."

Charlotte asked, "But we've still got three weeks right?"

Tinker sat in the chair, "Actually, we've got a lot longer now and that may or may not be good. His arraignment will be on the new charges in a few days and if the D.A. thinks she's got a winnable case, I doubt Judge Chadwick will give him bail. That means he could sit there for five or six months or more before trial." Charlotte couldn't hold it back any longer and broke down. Reagan knew now that Sunday's sermon on grace was on target, and it better be the most powerful he ever preached.

It was Tuesday night, and Reagan had a lot of pondering to do. How often does a pastor find himself the stuffing in the middle of a congregational sandwich? The Judge was a church Elder. Maybe good, maybe bad. Too soon to tell. The plaintiff's father was the head of one of the church's leading families that went back three generations. And he was one of the top givers in the church. He could be a tough nut to crack, but there were at least four months before a trial. He'd had the plaintiff, Katie, in Confirmation, and she had been in the youth group. The defendant's sister was a baby Christian looking to him for spiritual guidance. And the defendant was a young kid, who maybe just made a bad choice and a false accusation could ruin his life. Oh yes, and don't forget the county sheriff who was a sixty year member of Community Church. "Eney, meanie, minie, moe, now decide which way to go."

CHAPTER 6

*W*ednesday, May 23, 1992. Late in the day, they released Heather from Bethany Memorial. The staff didn't want her returning home with Billy. Heather might have believed all the words that came out of Billy's mouth and the nice things he had done, but the staff wasn't buying it. Billy was showing all the classic signs of an abuser's regret. The kind gestures and the promises, it will never happen again. They had all seen it over and over. And then they'd see a woman return and the same cycle would begin once more. So the staff of doctors, followed by a meeting with the director of the Upton Women's Shelter, conducted a formal exit interview. Nothing would persuade her. They all shook their heads as they watched the wheelchair being pushed out the front door. Nobody, including Reagan Lamb, thought this was the sane thing to do. Heather was just one push and a sharp table corner away from dying. Next time could be the one. But nothing would change her mind. She kept insisting something really happened with Billy. She said she could already see he was different. It was as if something was at work in his life.

Billy's '66 GTO convertible rumbled up to the front door. The engine had the deep blub, blub, blub sound that only comes from the old V8's, but the rest of the car sadly needed restoration. Billy's comment was always the same, "It's a classic muscle car. It's worth a lot of money." Well, it had been at one time, and might be again… someday, but not now. It was about $40,000 away from a full restoration, which he insisted he was getting ready to start. Heather wasn't anywhere near old enough to appreciate a "muscle car" in any condition. She thought it was a piece of junk, and she was ashamed to ride in it. Not words she dared to verbalize to Billy.

He jumped out and ran around to assist the aide, but with only one good arm, he wasn't of much use. Brad watched from behind a lilac bush on the edge of the visitors' parking lot and wondered if this was the new Billy or the one who knows how to play the right card at the right time. Was Billy now on stage and giving the performance of a lifetime? Brad would keep a vigilant eye on him.

Heather got into the car slowly and gingerly, but at least it was a car big enough to get in and out of easily. The aide pulled the wheelchair back, and Billy slammed the door shut. Again. One more time. On the third slam, it finally closed. He got behind the wheel and put the GTO in gear. It rumbled loudly, but he drove off as quietly as the GTO could. Brad thought, "Time will tell and I'm not giving you much time. I'm gonna be watching you closely. Very closely."

Heather was hoping for the best and praying her instincts were right. She had been around abusive men most of her life. She knew the pattern of behavior they showed, but this was the first time Billy had ever apologized. This was the first time he'd ever been contrite. They drove the winding roads and Billy seemed aware of her discomfort and drove cautiously. He seemed to be in a good mood and just talked and talked. This wasn't like Billy, but she liked it. She decided she'd have to take baby steps to find out if Billy meant what he'd said at the hospital. No big demands. In the past, she'd never dare ask anything of Billy. She'd just drop little hints now and see if he picked up. As they neared town, she decided there was no point in waiting to see if her intuition was off and if she'd made a mistake. This first "test" took every nerve she could muster. The Burger Barn came into view.

She said, "I can't remember the last time I had a cheeseburger and shake." Wait. Wait. Wait...here it comes.

"Sure, I guess we can stop. I have planned nothing for supper."

"You have planned nothing for supper? Okay, who are you and what have you done with Billy? You didn't plan anything for supper. When did you ever plan anything for supper?" Oops. She looked over at Billy and hoped these thoughts were in her head. No reaction from Billy; so they must be.

They pulled into the near-empty gravel parking lot, and Heather reached for the door handle but Billy was there to open the door. They entered, and the waitress looked at Heather's face and then at Billy, but never said a word. People in Glencoe knew you didn't converse with Billy Maddox unless he started the conversation. The meal came, and she inhaled the wonderful smell of fried food and tried to remember the last time Billy took her out to eat. Did he ever? She couldn't recall. She still hurt a lot and chewing wasn't easy, but it tasted so good. Billy was nice. He was polite to the waitress, who was expecting trouble that never came. After paying the check, Billy said on the way out, "See y'all again soon." Heather gave her a hopeful little smile.

When they got home, Billy pulled the car right up to the steps of the house. You can do that in the Oaks if you can get your car between the old stove and the mold-covered boat lying in the front yard. There is no such thing as a real driveway. There might be two bare stretches with no grass, but it wasn't really a designated driveway; it was a habit. The whole yard is a driveway and most of the yards were full of cars that hadn't run in years. You don't have them towed off. You park them and get another. Never know when you might need a part. He got out and again went around to open the door. Heather couldn't help but notice the lumber over by the corner of the porch but said nothing. Was he really going to fix it? Well, it would wait awhile now with that broken arm. On the porch, the old coon dog just lay there. It was like he never moved. He opened an eye, tilted a floppy ear, thumped his tail one time, but otherwise never budged. "Welcome home, I'm so excited to see you."

As they walked in, Heather thought they were in the wrong house. It was clean. Really clean. He did all the dishes and put them away. She searched her mind trying to think what to say. For four years she'd been so careful with every word she uttered. She just said, "It looks nice Billy." She was tired and went into the bedroom to lie down and closed her eyes. Was it a dream? If so, she didn't want to wake up.

You might call him a peeping Tom, but I'm guessing not to his face. Brad turned away from the window and returned to his car. He opened the door, and Beasley wagged a cheerful greeting. "Okay, Beasie, let's go home. I've prepared your favorite meal... Blue Buffalo mush." Beasley had no teeth.

CHAPTER 7

Thursday, May 24, 1992. That afternoon, Reagan stopped by the Washington County Jail to visit Micah, who was the only guest. Tinker's deputy led him back to the three cells. It was kind of like the Mayberry jail. For nearly fifty years Tinker's wife had been the honorary matron, by default. She couldn't stand a sterile environment for any human.

She said, "Tink, they're innocent until proven guilty and they need to be treated with dignity." Tinker Reynolds might be the elected Sheriff of Washington County, but he wasn't about to argue with Emma.

Glencoe is a strange little town. So each cell had a comfortable chair, one even had an old Lazyboy recliner. The faded chair was in really good shape. There were bedspreads and matching curtains on the barred windows. Each wall had a large picture of a scenic view. Emma mounted the pictures in old window frames so the guests, not prisoners... guests, could have a view from their room, not cell... room. And each room had a bookcase full of old paperbacks.

There was the Gideon Bible which Emma placed prominently on the pillow. All this stuff came from local garage sales and every couple of years Emma would make the garage sale rounds. When they saw

Emma coming, they knew she was redecorating the jail. Taking good care of the guests was Emma's witness and ministry. The Washington County jail was her B&B.

Micah was sitting in the chair with the Bible open in his lap, but his mind was elsewhere. He didn't even hear Reagan approaching. Reagan noticed and wondered if Charlotte could get him to look at the Bible. Didn't matter, either way, Micah was looking at it, hopefully reading it. He badly needed Jesus in his life and probably still didn't know that. Micah looked up with just a faint smile and closed the Bible. It didn't seem to him that he'd ever have a reason to smile again. Charlotte was his only visitor each day, so he was glad for the company, but today he was despondent.

"Thanks for coming, Pastor." After a quick pause, he began imme- diately, "I didn't do it. I'd never do that to Katie. I loved her. I really did. Still do. Yeah, like a dang fool, I lost it at the Lazy Daisy and I'm willing to pay for what I did. But, rape her...never. I never touched her except kissing and stuff. I wanted to take it slow with Katie because I really thought she cared and that I had a chance with her. I thought she cared about me, maybe even falling in love with me. I wanted to spend the rest of my life with her. I guess I was just dreaming, but I thought we might get married and I could work at the hardware store. But apparently, I was a joke, someone to string along and then laugh at. I'm a Barnes and I guess that's all I'll ever be."

Reagan was speechless. He hated hearing someone say "that's all I'll ever be" as if life had no other option. Nineteen and ready to give up on living. Ready to give up his dreams and let the Oaks swallow up yet another young life. He didn't know Micah real well, but he could see the despair in his eyes of a soul that was slowly slipping away. Charlotte was determined she'd break the welfare cycle, and he believed Micah could too. Micah was giving up on himself, but Char- lotte would never allow it to happen. Reagan was determined he'd help her even at the expense of some prominent church members snubbing her and his efforts. "After all, she isn't like us." Reagan thought to himself, "No she isn't, but it would be nice if you people were more like her."

He believed Micah was telling the truth, but proving it would be a lot harder. If Katie were from the Oaks, Micah would stand a better chance, but she's not and he is. He wasn't sure Micah had all the right motives, but he was making the only choices he knew how to make. Micah didn't see himself being able to "work" his way out, so he dreamed of marrying his way out. But Reagan realized it didn't really matter because Micah's heart was in the right place. He was a good boy and his initial instinct was right. But how do you make a vengeful teenage girl see the light? Sunday's coming.

As Reagan emerged from the cell block, excuse me, the guest accommodations, Tinker was sitting at his desk with his feet up. Coffee cup in one hand and a newspaper crossword puzzle in the other. The sheriff's department used to be much bigger than it was now. The population of the county had once hit about sixteen thousand and on Saturday night, Glencoe was the place to be. Everything stayed open until 9 p.m. on both Friday and Saturday and both movie theaters were thriving. Back then a young Tinker Reynolds was kept pretty busy. Now he had four deputies rotating shifts. Tinker worked banker's hours now at the insistence of Emma. Glencoe had its own police department with a one-room office in city hall and a ten-year-old cruiser. Chief Larry Hodges worked days and his deputy worked four to eleven. The sheriff's office covered eleven to seven.

"Hey, pastor. What's a six letter word for a religious cleric?"

Reagan said, "Tink, you are kidding right? Uhh… pastor." You could see Tinker's embarrassment as he quickly changed the subject.

"Dang, I hate to see that kid locked up in there. I talked to Katie and I think there are real holes in the story. I'm sure something happened to her at some point. But my fifty years of experience says it isn't Micah that did it. But my opinion doesn't count for much. I've got to hold him until the bail hearing."

"Yeah, I guess bail will be a lot higher than $2000 now. I'm guessing the D.A. will push for no bail this time. That will just ruin both of them. Charlotte and Micah really only have each other. With Micah in jail, she and Sara have to deal with Paul by themselves." Paul Barnes was a wretched man who had driven his wife to run off in the night and then alienated his two kids and practically everyone in town.

Reagan and Tinker said their farewells and Reagan headed for home wondering what tonight's menu might be. It was good to be married to an Italian who loved to cook.

CHAPTER 8

*S*unday, May 27, 1992. Pastor Reagan Lamb sat in the pulpit chair to the side of the lectern and waited for the organist to finish up the prelude. Music was the one thing he'd change at Community Church, if he could. Maybe it was just him, but every piece of music the 80-year-old organist played sounded exactly the same as the last one. Were people really listening to this, or like him, just enduring it? He tuned out the music and looked out at the congregation. The sanctuary was Akron style which meant the seating was curved and each row slightly elevated. No steps, just a slight elevation from front to rear giving each worshiper an unobstructed view. In the front and center was this massive old pipe organ that was the congregation's pride and joy. The pipes covered about twenty five running feet. Who came up with the bright idea to make the organ pipes the center focal point of the sanctuary? There was a five foot wall that almost hid the organist and in front of it stood the dark oak communion table. The choir loft was to the Pastor's right and the pulpit to his far left. The green carpet needed to be replaced.

Pastor Lamb began his mental check of who was there and if they were in their correct seats. It always amused him that people had certain places to sit and some people would get upset if someone took their seat. When they had visitors, invariably the visitor would sit in someone's seat. Now the amusing part was that the next week the offended member would arrive 20 minutes early to reclaim the family pew just in case the visitor came back and wanted to claim it as their own in their "new church." One Sunday Mrs. Higgins had come in and someone was in her seat...fourth row down aisle seat. Now mind you, there are six fourth row down aisle seats in an Akron style. Mrs. Higgins turned around and walked out.

This morning things seemed to be in the right order. In the back, off to the side was Charlotte sitting all by herself. More often than not she sat by herself. He loved Charlotte's gutsiness. No way they would drive her away from Jesus and he sensed that God was ringing her with a hedge of protection. There were those who looked at her as if she was the accused rapist since she was a Barnes. Reagan smiled at her and then Prudy entered the row and sat next to Charlotte. Prudy sat all over the sanctuary while most church members expected the pastor's wife to be in the choir. Prudy was God blessed as a great cook, but couldn't sing a note.

Emma Reynolds was there, but there was no sign of Tinker. Tinker came to church on Christmas and Easter and faithfully every Sunday for the two months before elections. When Tinker walked into church, someone would invariably say, "Must be election time." Tinker would laugh and so would everyone else. He continued his scan. Judge and Mrs. Chadwick were near the front in their usual place. Adam and Maddie Pierce were there, but there was no sign of Katie. She was the one that needed to hear about grace. He continued to scan and his eyes passed a couple in the middle. His eyes came to a dead stop, refocused, and went back. There sat Billy and with his left arm around Heather and his right arm in the sling. Reagan wondered what Billy had up his sleeve? He didn't know this was Heather's second test and act of bravery.

They were sitting there the night before watching an old rerun of SNL. Dana Carvey was doing his skit of the church lady, one of the all-time great skits. That was back when SNL was still funny. Heather looked over at Billy and said, "Will you take me to church tomorrow?" Billy was aghast. It was about the last thing he expected she'd ask.

"That doesn't seem like a good idea. You've got all those bruises? I don't want everyone seein' what I done to you. Maybe next week." Billy hoped that was the end of the conversation. Billy thought of Brad. Yeah, if the guy was watching him he'd change his ways a little, but going to church... not going to happen.

Heather charged ahead, "Makeup will hide most of the bruises. The swelling has gone. And I think I need to be there to pray for Sadie and Jake."

"Heather, you can pray for them anywhere. You don't need a church."

"Maybe, but I know God will hear me if I'm in church. Please?" Billy was feeling the abuser's regret, so he caved.

Billy had met his match when he'd come up against Brad. He didn't want to admit it, but for the first time since his dad whooped him, he was afraid of someone. Billy sat looking around. He hadn't spotted him, but then again he didn't know what he looked like so he wouldn't know him if he was sitting next to him. He knew he didn't want to do anything that would get him angrier. Billy didn't know if he'd change, could change, or even if he wanted to change, but he would put on a show and see where it would take him. So going to church really ought to impress this guy.

Reagan stood up as the organist finally finished. He turned and nodded toward her and thanked her for the fine selection. He wondered, "Is there an all organ, all the time radio station?" He sure hoped not. He proceeded with the morning announcements for the week's coming events and morning worship began. They came to prayers and concerns which Reagan wanted to do away with as well. When he asked for prayers and concerns, he never knew where it was going. The first prayer request was from Edith Abbott and he knew where this was going. This had to be the tenth week praying for Aunt Rosie's skin ulcer on her right foot that refused to heal. But to Edith it was important. They gave two or three other prayer requests and a couple of praises like "I want to praise God for the biggest tomato harvest I've ever had." Never mind that Fred had bought all the Miracle-Gro in town. So, the question was which one performed the miracle, God or the chemical company? Then when Charlotte stood up, you could hear a pin drop. Dead silence.

Charlotte said, "Most of you know me and you know of my family. I'm so grateful for this church and this pastor. I wandered in here one day looking for a handout. I wanted diapers for my baby. It was three days to the end of the month. Pastor Reagan didn't shame me or turn me away. Instead, he did something that changed my life. He said he'd give me a voucher if I wanted to work for it. I asked what he had in mind. Figuring he was a man, and I thought I knew what he wanted."

There were a few gasps in the congregation. You don't talk like that in Sunday worship.

Pastor Reagan pointed at a flower bed outside and said, "If you pull weeds for half an hour I'll give you the voucher."

I said, "I can't. I've got the baby."

He said, "You pull the weeds and I'll hold the baby."

"Since Sara was born I haven't worked for anything. Most months I get by, but that month I hadn't. I pulled the weeds for thirty minutes while he entertained Sara and he gave me the voucher."

He handed it to me and said, "Don't you feel better? You worked and earned the money to buy the diapers for your child."

"I walked away, and I did feel better. I had worked to provide for my baby for the first time.

'I'm rambling, I know. I asked if I could come back and talk with him. I've been meeting with him every week for about a year, and three months ago I accepted Christ as my Savior."

There was no reaction from members of the congregation, which didn't surprise Reagan.

"I've accepted Jesus and I want to be baptized and I'm dedicating my little girl to God. I tell you all this because I need your prayers. Not for me, but for my brother Micah. Most of you know he's in jail accused of rape. I know he didn't do it. But he's a Barnes, and that means he's automatically guilty."

As she sat down and cried Prudy put her arm around her. Would this be a mistake? You could see the smoke coming off Maddie Pierce's head. Actually, they sat in the second-row center so only Reagan saw her disdain and anger.

After an intense and carefully worded time of prayer, Reagan moved to the pulpit. He stood silently with his eyes moving around the room.

"I stand before you this morning, as a sinner saved by grace. I've done a lot of things in my life I'm not proud of. Things that probably would have kept you from hiring me if you knew. But I found Jesus Christ about four years ago, or better stated, He found me. Ephesians 2:8-10 teaches that we are saved by faith in Jesus Christ. We can't save ourselves and the truth is we don't deserve to be saved at all. Well, at least I know I didn't deserve to be saved.

Paul says it's not by good works either. In other words, there is absolutely nothing I could do to earn God's favor. The truth is, we don't deserve God's grace. The sin I carried around for ten years consumed me and was like a pallet of bricks sitting on my chest. I was being crushed by my sin.

After I found Christ, I understood what God did for me on the cross. I discovered that God so loved Reagan Lamb that he sent his only Son so that if Reagan Lamb would believe in him he would not perish, but live forever. That load of bricks on my chest? His blood and that cross took every brick away.

The problem is that I'm still Reagan Lamb and I fight every day to be Christ-like, but it's hard. Like Paul says in Romans 7, 'The things I want to do, the right things, those are the things I don't do. And those things I don't want to do, those things that cause me to not be like Christ, those are the things I do.'

For ten years I needed to forgive the people responsible for taking the lives of four of my best friends. For ten years I wanted to find them and kill them. Watch them suffer... slowly. Four years ago I met Christ who forgave me of everything I ever did to him. And yet, I could not forgive those people for taking my friend's lives.

Today I realize they don't deserve my forgiveness. They will never deserve my forgiveness. But today, I decided I forgive them, because I finally realized I didn't deserve forgiveness, but God forgave me. It's called grace and you can remember it this way, God's Riches At Christ's Expense. GRACE." Reagan continued on.

Was Billy processing any of this? It was hard to tell. His expression seemed to suggest, "I'm here. What more do you want? Hey guy, whoever you are, do you see me? I'm in church. See, I'm changing."

Reagan moved to the door to greet the parishioners. He already knew that anyone who said, "Great sermon, Pastor," hadn't heard a word he said.

Judge Chadwick and his wife came out, and he commented, "Reagan, you've given me a lot to think about that's for sure."

Reagan replied, "Judge, you've got a tough job and a lot of responsibility. Lives literally hang on your decisions. Better you than me."

As Charlotte passed, she held her baby in her arms. "Thank you, Pastor, I know everything will be alright."

Shirley Comstock came out and looked at him with some disdain. Shirley had been another tough nut to crack, and she hadn't cracked yet. She was an old mainline Protestant who still believed that works and being a good person would get her to heaven. She was into Social Justice Issues based on God is love. Judge not that you are not judged. And most committed to the second commandment 'Love thy neighbor,' with no mention of the first, 'Love the Lord your God with heart, soul, strength, and mind.'

She said, "Reagan." She was one of a few older ladies who called him by his first name. "All you ever talk about is Jesus. When are you going to talk about something else?"

Reagan knew he shouldn't say it, he couldn't resist. "Shirley, you might be happier at St. Mark's, they never talk about Jesus over there." She huffed out with more disdain for this Bible-thumping preacher.

He noticed that Adam and Maddie Pierce went out the other door, or at least he assumed they did. Receiving grace is a lot easier to handle than giving grace to those who have hurt us and need it. Few realize how much they hurt themselves when they refuse to forgive those who they think have wronged them. The perceived wrongdoer sleeps at night while they let hate and anger fester and tear them apart inside. They continue with their life while those who refuse to grant grace to them destroy their relationship with the God who poured out his grace on them. He was sure this is where Maddie was and he would have to visit them. He didn't look forward to that visit. It didn't surprise him that Billy and Heather went out quickly and quietly. It did, however, surprise and perhaps even shock him to see them. He needed to go visit them too. He didn't really look forward to that.

Brad and his wife went out the side door and got in the car. Beasley was in the back seat wagging his tail and jumped on the console as soon as Brad unlocked the doors. Beasley didn't mind waiting in the car for his humans. If he was in the car, it meant they were coming back. Brad asked his wife where she wanted to go for lunch. She thought the Chicken Coop north of the Interstate sounded good and off they went for Sunday dinner.

Sadie and Jake were somewhere in the county with a foster family and since Heather and Billy didn't get home until after the Courthouse closed on Friday, they did not know where they were and wouldn't be able to find out until 9:30 on Monday. That was the earliest they'd give her an appointment and nobody would answer her questions over the phone.

She wept and said, "I miss my kids. When do you think I can see them?"

He said, "I don't know. I tried to find out where they were, but I figured they wouldn't tell me anything. Said it was because I'm not related to them, so they can't talk. But we both know the truth. We'll go first thing tomorrow and you can check. Best if I probably wait outside."

When Adam and Maddie arrived home, they saw Katie sprawled out on the sectional couch still wearing her Hello Kitty lounging flannels, a tee, and earbuds growing out of the side of her head. She ignored them when they came into the house. With Katie, they'd seen this a lot in the last two years. One day she was a sweet thirteen-year-old who thought she was twenty. She started really caring about her appearance and knew she was pretty. She noticed boys and they noticed her. Then, she suddenly stopped communicating. She'd come in and go right to her room. Come out for supper and back into her room. Get up for breakfast, go to school and repeat...day after day. They'd talk to the school counselor who just said, "She's a normal fourteen-year-old, she'll grow out of it."

When she turned fifteen, things got a little better and then a lot worse. At sixteen she communicated with Maddie, but she still shut Adam out most of the time. She quickly learned how to manipulate them and use them against each other. Maddie was so happy Katiee was talking to her that she tried to be her buddy instead of her mom. That had the expected results. Maddie was so blinded by the manipulation she couldn't see it. Katie took advantage of her mother every chance she could. More than once there had been calls from school about Katie playing hooky or violations of the dress code. Adam received none of these calls. He really did not understand what was going on between Maddie and Katie. He thought everything was fine, and she had snapped out of the mood swings. He didn't know she had turned into a spoiled, manipulative, sneaky, defiant little witch. He made an appointment with the school counselor who shocked him with the size of the file she pulled from the cabinet. When he saw the thickness of the file, he knew this would be a long session. There was everything in there from skipping algebra classes, to smoking in the bathroom, to getting caught under the bleachers with Bobby Lee. He asked, "How did all these happen without my knowledge?"

The counselor replied, "We notified you every time there was an issue."

"Well, I received no calls from anyone. What number did you call?"

She read off the number in the file.

"That explains everything. That's my wife's personal phone. We need to change that number." He changed the contact number, thanked her for her time, and left for the store furious with Maddie. They were about to have it out.

Maddie didn't come to the store that day, and that was probably the best thing that could have happened. It gave him time to cool down. He thought about some things Katie had said and done over the last few months. He remembered that when he asked Maddie questions, she gave him some strange, evasive, but plausible answers. He should have pressed for more information.

So here was Adam, caught between his Christian faith and the love for his daughter. He was now getting a picture of how Katie had been acting for quite a while and how Maddie had been abetting and covering for her. He realized how close he was to convincing Maddie to drop the charges against Micah. Before they finished the conversation, Katie pops in out of the blue with this story about being raped by Micah. Adam fell for it as would any father and would have beaten him to a pulp if he had the chance. Maddie now thought of herself as Katie's friend and would stand behind her, defend her and do anything else it took to hold on to her daughter, even if it was wrong. He thought about Reagan's message. He couldn't believe how vulnerable and open Reagan had been this morning. It was like through his confession he hoped others would examine their own lives. One person who needed to hear it wasn't there. But another who needed to hear it was there. Adam understood how important God's grace was to his salvation, but he also knew that if God ever withheld his forgiveness, he'd get what he deserved.

Adam came from one of the privileged families in Glencoe. They weren't wealthy, but the hardware store did well and he never wanted for anything growing up. Adam was privileged, but not spoiled. He learned the principles of hard work early. While other kids in seventh grade were out playing and riding bikes, Adam was stocking shelves in the family store. In high school his friends were playing sports while Adam was taking inventory, ordering paints and sundries, and manning the checkout. He always understood he would take over the family business. But after graduating, Adam wanted to spread his wings. He said nothing to his dad, but running a hardware store seemed boring.

Adam saw a business opportunity in the logging industry. The problem was he didn't know the first thing about logging. Over in the Oaks was a classmate, Charlie Bowen. His family had been in logging until his father lost his license for drunk driving. The problem was he was drunk driving in a fully loaded 60,000-pound logging truck. He lost not only his license, but every logging company blacklisted him in the eastern part of the state. Charlie's father had taken him with him ever since he was about five. Mama wasn't healthy so Charlie went with his dad on Saturdays, school breaks, and pretty much all summer, except the week he went to visit cousins in Cleveland. When Charlie was about sixteen he got hired on too. Charlie's family would never get out of the Oaks, but they were among the most well to do, until right after Charlie's 17th birthday. That's when his father's employment ended. His father drank heavily after that and then came welfare. This was something Charlie could not accept. Never. Not him. He saw what it did to families.

So here was Adam who had the business experience he gained in the hardware business and a friend with years of logging experience and no job. They sat and talked. It seemed like a dream made in heaven. Two young guys ready to conquer the world, well, maybe Washington County. The dream started for Adam when he saw the abandoned sawmill on River Road. He knew who it had belonged to and why the business folded. Two brothers, who are hard-headed twins, probably don't make the best business partners. So the mill was for sale and the price was right. Charlie's dad still had the tractor cab to pull the logging trailers, and the mill had a front-end loader. The basics were there. They could do their own logging and supplement the rest of the business through contractors who independently logged, but had no mill. After they put the business plan together, which amounted to a single typewritten page, they went to Adam's dad for a loan to buy the mill.

It took a little convincing, but Adam's father remembered it took three years before his father could get him interested in the hardware business. His father co-signed and they were in business. Charlie proved to be a hard worker, diligent, and Adam knew he'd made a good choice in a partner. No conflicts. He was essentially the brains and the money man and Charlie was the brawn in charge of hiring, training, and supervision.

Business was good and things went well until Adam saw himself as the success behind Pierce and Bowen Milling Operations. Little things came up and Adam overreacted. He saw himself being better than Charlie.

About a year and a half earlier, Adam had fallen in love with Maddie Whitcomb who was Doc Whitcomb's only daughter. They had been schoolmates since kindergarten, dated a few times in high school, but there was never any real attraction. Maddie was a nerd who just studied and sat and watched other kids take risks while she played it safe. Adam had worked in the store. Neither of them ever went to dances, not even the prom. Maddie came home from college after her freshman year. Adam was walking by the Sears Catalog Store one day as Maddie came out. He took one look at her and said, "That's who I'm going to marry."

Well, now we have the son of a successful business owner, who also runs a successful business, engaged to the daughter of the town's doctor. Now you've got a young power couple and Charlie Bowen from the Oaks.

The partnership got very strained. Each little thing seemed to annoy Adam and the little things mounted up. There were no real big problems, but Adam saw all the little things together as a big thing. Plus, Maddie didn't like Charlie and that hurt matters. Things went on festering between Adam and Charlie for another year and a half. The problem was Charlie didn't know there was a problem. Maddie graduated from college, they announced the engagement, and set the wedding date. It was the wedding plans that brought everything to a boil. Poor Charlie was blindsided. Seemed Adam would let these little things just grate at him and never mention them to Charlie. He was a passive-aggressive guy leaning toward the passive. He couldn't really deal with confrontation.

Charlie, on the other hand, was living the dream. He had found a way out of the Oaks which is more of an expression than fact. If you lived in the Oaks, there was a stereotype and you were automatically stereotyped. Charlie still lived in the Oaks, but not with his parents or even near them. He found a nice place close to the main center of Glencoe, but not Glencoe proper. He was doing well enough he could have purchased one of the lesser Victorians on the side streets, but he knew he didn't fit. Charlie never tried to be who he wasn't. He never tried to put on airs and he never looked down on anyone. If a man tried to make an honest living, he would always get the benefit of the doubt from Charlie Bowen.

It was not quite the same for Adam and the future Mrs. Pierce. A little pride goes a long way and Adam was becoming proud. He was engaged to one of the best catches in Glencoe where pickings weren't that good. He came from a successful family. They were church and civic leaders. He owned his own company and conveniently forgot that the loan came from his dad. And he was only twenty two years old. Not bad.

Maddie and her mother were preparing the wedding plans. The church would be Community Church. The Moose Hall or Masonic Lodge were not suitable for the reception. There was a lovely park setting they could reserve but the weather in May was too iffy. There was only one place suitable, and that was the Country Club in Bentley. It was across the river in the next state, but it was on the river and worth the drive. The guest list wasn't that tricky, they ran in the same circles and both were prominent families. For Maddie and her mother, there was just one problem. Charlie Bowen. They both agreed this uncouth man had no place at Glencoe's wedding of the decade.

Maddie showed Adam the guest list for his approval. He wasn't interested. Any time Maddie had said, "What do you think..." he'd say, "Whatever you want is fine." At first, he did the same thing with the guest list, but then he looked at the list again. Charlie's name wasn't on the list. Well, the discussion went forward as you might well imagine. Maddie gave him a dozen reasons why Charlie shouldn't be in attendance. Who could we possibly seat him with? What if he brought a guest? Can you imagine? And the one that made the most sense was the way Adam was now seeing their relationship. "You aren't inviting any of your other employees, so why would you invite Charlie?" Maddie continued, "Come on. It's your company. It wouldn't exist without you. He's really nothing but your foreman."

"Maddie we started out as partners…" Cut off.

"Partners? How much money did he put up? Where are the partnership papers?" Passive aggressive people always lose to aggressive people. They didn't invite Charlie. Two weeks after the wedding Charlie got an offer from a competitor and walked away. Four months later Pierce and Bowen Lumber Operations was no more.

Adam went to work in the hardware store and he and Maddie never spoke of Charlie again.

But after this morning's sermon, he couldn't stop thinking of Charlie. He never showed Charlie the grace God had shown to him. And now he had another chance to show grace. Not toward Charlie, that ship sailed years ago. But maybe to another of God's children instead. Maybe the charges against Micah were true, and if so, letting Micah go free would surely haunt him. But not nearly as much as if Micah was innocent and they put him away for twenty-five years. But what if this was Katie acting out just to get revenge? What if there was no rape? And why could she have this much hatred for Micah? There was no question he would serve time. He already told the judge he took full responsibility for what happened. Even if neither family pressed charges he was going away for a while. So why try to send him away for twenty-five years...especially if he never raped her? The battle continued to rage over his love for Katie versus the grace of God.

≈

Viola Newton was a grandmotherly fifty-four-year-old woman who everyone liked. She became a foster parent several months after her husband had been killed in a mine collapse at the Big Trace mine or as the company called it, Number Nine. It hadn't shut down the mine, but the one tunnel had been closed off and sealed. No rescue attempt was ever made. The shoring was so bad they were afraid the whole hill would come down if they tried to get the bodies out. Outside the mine, as a constant safety reminder, was a plaque with the names of the seven miners of team four who were never brought out. Glencoe was used to mine accidents and deaths, but seven deaths at one time would be long remembered. Viola often recalled the day that four hundred people, including the Governor, had crowded into the area in front of the mine opening for a memorial service. They read the list of names and she realized she was a fifty-four-year-old widow, with no miner's pension, and a small $5000 insurance policy. Vance had worked hard his whole life to take care of his family and he pushed both kids, V.J. and Beth, hard enough in school to get them into a state school on a miners scholarship. Both had moved away from Glencoe. There weren't many opportunities in Glencoe and even if there were, you could make a lot more money elsewhere doing the same thing. V.J., Vance Jr., had to leave the day after the service, but Beth could stay for another week to help Mom. For most of the week, everything was a blur to Viola. Lots of friends visited and representatives from the mine came by and then as quickly as the attention started, it stopped. Now she was just the Widow Newton.

She tried to get involved in things to keep her busy, but they were all volunteer things that didn't pay the bills. Her savings and insurance money was getting worrisomely low. One day she picked up a copy of the Washington County weekly called the Lighthouse and browsed it from back to front. She figured after she read the front page every-thing was anticlimactic, so she'd save the first for last. In a place like Glencoe, everyone already knew what had happened before the paper came out each week, but you wouldn't be much of a gossiper if you couldn't honestly say, "Did you see in the Lighthouse…?" See, if you see it in the Lighthouse then it's not gossip.

Viola started in the help-wanted section, but never held out much hope. Her only qualifications were she'd been a great mom, a good cook, and a loving wife. "Let's see who's hiring for what. Used car sales, nope. Hair Stylist, nope. Part-time assistant librarian, nope. Courthouse stenographer, definitely no." And so it went, same as last week and the week before. She turned the page and saw an article placed by the Department of Family Services. It was right to the point: Foster Families Needed. Now, this was something Viola could do. She loved children, and they were attracted to her. Then she saw it paid! It paid nine hundred a month per child. She dropped the paper, grabbed her purse, and headed for the Courthouse.

This week she had two very special children. Sadie and Jake had been a pleasure and perhaps the best behaved and most appreciative children she'd had. She knew about their situation. Family Services had briefed her, but in this town, it was unnecessary. Everyone knew who Billy Maddox was and what had happened to Heather. It broke her heart every time Jake would ask her, "When can I see my mommy?" She'd hold him close and promise him it would be soon, but the truth was she didn't know. She had heard Heather was home so maybe it wouldn't be too long. She guessed it would depend on what Heather did.

Jake and Sadie got ready for bed on Sunday evening knowing they'd return to school tomorrow. Viola wanted to keep them together, so she put them in the room with twin beds. Jake finished getting ready first and Viola tucked him into bed. Sadie made it clear she was big enough to tuck herself in. When she was ready, she went downstairs and hugged Mrs. Newton and went back up. She walked into the room, but Jake wasn't in bed.

All she could see was his legs sticking out from under the bed. Sadie whispered, "Jake, what in the world are you doing?"

Jake whispered back, "I'm looking for God. I think he may be under here. I already checked the closet, and he wasn't there."

"So, why do you think he'd be under the bed?"

Jake said, "My Sunday School teacher said God is everywhere. I've checked everywhere except under the bed. Sadie, I think maybe this is where he lives."

"But why are you even trying to find him?"

"Cause I need to talk to him real bad right now."

Sadie tried to explain he didn't need to be under the bed to talk to God, but Jake wasn't buying it. So Sadie got on the floor and crawled under the bed with her little brother. "Okay Jake, you go ahead and pray."

"Now I'm here, I don't know what to say. All I've ever prayed is now I lay me down to sleep."

Sadie encouraged him, "All you need to do is just talk to him. Tell him how you feel and what you want."

Jake sniffled a little, "I want mommy."

"Then tell him that."

"God, it's Jake. You probably don't remember me with all the people you talk to. I'm mommy's little boy. You know mommy. Billy Maddox hit her and she got hurt real bad. She's been in the hospital and I miss her. God, can you please fix her and send my mommy back to me? Sadie and me like Mrs. Newton and she makes the best peanut butter and jelly sandwich ever, but she's not mommy."

Outside the door, Viola smiled and tears flowed down her face. How sad.

Inside. "Sadie, you want to say anything?"

"Yes, Jake, yes I do. God, you need to listen to my little brother. He's just a child. I remember the Sunday School teacher saying Jesus told the big people to let the little children come to him. She said, little kids believe things adults don't believe and that their trust in you is powerful. God, you got to bring momma to us." She waited until she heard the children climb into bed and the bed springs squeaked. What she didn't know was it was the sound of only one bed. Sadie put her arm over Jake, spooning him, as they went to sleep.

CHAPTER 9

*M*onday, May 28, 1992. Monday morning arrived in Glencoe with a beautiful sunrise that started at the river and climbed the hills to town. Reagan arrived in town and headed for the Greasy Spoon. He didn't care for the tone of the conversation this morning. After ordering he had thoughts about leaving, but that would be a waste of food and in two hours he'd be starving. There was always the old man gossip going on here, but this morning it was like they were the judge and jury for Micah Barnes and the verdict was already in. If lynching was allowed, they would have him swinging from the nearest oak. Most of them didn't even know Micah, but they knew Adam Pierce and that's all that mattered. "Adam's a good guy. Fair prices. Order what you need, no extra charge. His Pappy was a real pillar in this town," and they went on and on. So, if his daughter said the Barnes boy raped her then it must be true. Reagan thought no matter who makes up the jury, he heard the verdict already. After they ran that subject into the ground there was silence for about thirty seconds until someone said, "I saw Billy Maddox and Heather at the Burger Barn on Friday night. You should have seen her face." Off they went again. Most noticed that Reagan sat in the corner eating and never said a word. When he finished he got up, went to the cash register, paid, and walked out. Never said a word out of fear of what he might say. But it was Glencoe, so the next time he went in there'd be a new discussion and Micah would be history.

He took his usual morning stroll up High Street, but this morning it wasn't to greet people or notice things he had never noticed. He needed to clear his head. While he loved the provincialism of Glencoe and it was one of the things that attracted him, it also frustrated him that no one could keep an open mind about anything. Not that they saw black and white. It was they saw their own white that might have really been black anywhere else. The town was divided and the railroad tracks ran down the center. He walked along and Reagan noticed that somebody bought the old hotel. There was a sign in the window: Coming soon, Oriental Luck Chinese Restaurant. That brought a curious smile to his face. He wondered how many in Glencoe had ever eaten Chinese. He continued toward the Courthouse and the '72 Dodge pickup drove by at 10 mph and Bill and Bob waved at Reagan. Even though they'd never met, they were friends. Bill just kept going, ten miles per hour, with eight vehicles creeping along behind him.

It was 8:30 and parts of the Courthouse were open for business. He passed by Kennedy and Kennedy Law Partners. He knew them, but only from civic events. They were fairly new to town. Husband and wife team. She handled many things, including, divorce, wills, and real estate, but he handled only criminal cases. Reagan wondered which one was really more successful. Criminal cases were plentiful in Washington County, but not very lucrative since most cases went to the Public Defender from clients who couldn't afford an attorney.

He continued on one more block to the Courthouse. He saw Billy sitting by himself in the old GTO listening to the radio and keeping beat to the song on the steering wheel. He guessed that Heather must be inside and was waiting outside the office door when they opened. Reagan couldn't ignore Billy no matter how uncomfortable the encounter might be. This might be just the break he needed. That Billy and Heather were at church at all was amazing. Reagan thought, "Maybe even a God thing." He walked over to the passenger's side and leaned down toward the open window which he didn't know was always open. It hadn't worked for three years. "Hi, couldn't help but notice you and Heather left by the side door yesterday, so I didn't have time to say hello and officially welcome you to Community Church. Hope we will see you again." He let the conversation hang. Billy, your move.

And Billy, who we know is never at a loss for words, responded. "Well, to be honest with you preacher, I was there because Heather said she wanted to go, so I took her to church." He made it quite clear he was a reluctant attendee only there as a favor to Heather. "I'm trying to change my ways a little, but religion is not for me."

The "trying to change my ways a little" got Reagan's attention. "I'm curious, what would cause you to want to change? You don't strike me as a guy who thought he needed to change anything. No offense intended."

"None taken, preacher. While Heather was in the hospital I had a kind of vision so to speak. I mean I didn't see God or nothin' like that. But it was real. It was like he was standing right behind me encouraging me to be a better man."

Reagan said, "Heather deserves a lot better than what she's had for a couple of years. Again, no offense, just telling you like it is."

That was enough for now, time to change the subject. "Where is she?"

"She's in with Family Services trying to find out where they put Sadie and Jake. She's worried real bad."

Reagan said, "I got a few minutes before court. I'll go see if I can help."

~

Reagan started up the 43 steps to the Courthouse entrance. "Lord, I could use a little help and guidance." What did Jesus say, "You have not because you ask not."

As he approached the revolving door, Guy, (pronounced Gee with a hard G,) Kennedy emerged. Obviously an Irish father and a French mother. Reagan said, "Good morning, Counselor," and Guy replied,

"And good morning to you, Pastor Lamb and what brings you here on this fine day?"

Reagan told him about Billy and Heather and how it involved him. "Don't know what will happen. Seems Billy is trying right now, but it's only been five days so who knows. With Billy, you never know if it's all a big con game. And you never know what or who could set him off. But Heather really loves those kids and they are good kids despite what they've been through with Billy."

"Pastor, my wife, has dealt with a lot of cases like Heather's. She believes strongly in women's rights so she usually takes those cases as gratis. We knew when we came to Glencoe we would not get rich. We didn't want to be in the city anymore so we looked for a place where we could help the people whose lives seem to have stomped on. Sounds like Heather's been stomped on."

Reagan told him, "There is a good chance Heather might need all the help she can get. Everyone in the county knows Billy just a little too well, but Heather is a real good mother especially considering all she's been through. But the main reason I'm here is they have accused Micah Barnes of rape."

Guy put on his lawyer smile and said, "Pastor, now you've got my attention. Accused of rape you say. Did he do it?"

Taking a shot in the dark, Reagan said, "No, I don't think he did. They're about to start the arraignment, you got a few minutes? If so, you can decide."

Guy surprised him by saying, "Sure. Can't hurt to see what's going on. And right now my caseload is light." That was better than saying he had no clients.

"You don't know how much I appreciate this. We have about 15 minutes and I need to check on Heather. I'll see you in the courtroom."

He took the stairs down to the lower level, better known as the basement. He followed the red line painted on the floor to the door that read Family Services and wondered why you needed a red line on the floor to go to the first door on the right that had a big sign hanging from the ceiling that said Family Services. He opened the door and walked up to the information desk. The nameplate on her desk read, Betsy Palmer. He knew of some Palmers out in the Minster area, but Betsy didn't ring a bell. So he introduced himself to her and asked if she was related to Cyrus Palmer. She told him he was her uncle. Now Reagan knew one more person and then invited her to church. He asked about Heather Delaney and found out Heather was in with a Child Advocate counselor, so he asked her to check and see if he might join them.

The office was pretty much what you'd expect in a basement. One cellar type window that was too high to see out. Mismatched oak furniture, three green four-drawer filing cabinets and two old office armchairs with sagging blue padded seats. Not a very inspiring atmosphere to be at your best. He was thankful for his view of the parking lot. He waited and thought about who might work here for the small amount they're paid. It was either someone who truly loves what they do or someone who punched in at nine and watched the clock all day. Which one was the woman talking to Heather?

Reagan said, "Thanks for letting me sit in. I'm Reagan Lamb, the pastor of Glencoe Community Church and I'm also Heather's pastor." That made Heather feel good... she had a pastor. She never thought of it that way. Community Church was a place she sent the kids until Billy had forbidden it. She had been a Christmas/Easter member at best. And yet, she felt like Reagan really cared about her, Sadie and Jake. It was a good feeling.

Glancing at the nameplate it read Patricia Garcia. Funny, her husband must be Hispanic, because she was so pale you couldn't see her if she was lying on a white sheet. "May I call you Patricia?"

"Please call me Pat. I asked for Pat on the nameplate, but they say it was too informal for clients."

"Okay, Pat it is. Pat, can you quickly bring me up to date on what's happening?"

"Honestly, Billy complicates everything. Even though there are no charges against him, everyone knows what happened. Heather says she loves him and that he's already changed. Thing is, there's nothing to prove it. He could start in on her tomorrow for all we know. I know she loves the kids, but her feelings for Billy really screw up her chances of getting custody for at least six months. And that's where we're at."

Reagan knew the state-run office of the Department of Family Services is like the EPA. They seem to do what they want and answer to no one. In some situations, all that power and authority was a good thing, but other times not so much.

Heather didn't know where to go or the questions to ask and Reagan could tell how upset she was. She would not get her kids. The business of Family Services was to protect the children, not help the parents find the loopholes in the system for exceptions and there were plenty. Yes, they wanted to reunite families, but some families shouldn't be reunited. That's where getting a lawyer would help, but most of those who lost custody of their children couldn't afford a lawyer. The Child Advocates knew of Ginny Kennedy's presence in town, but nobody knew yet if she'd be a thorn in the agency's side.

So Reagan tried coming to the rescue. No mother should go without at least seeing her children. He brought up the subject of weekly visitation. Patricia said, "Excuse me," as the phone rang. When she finished she said, "That was the foster mom for Sadie and Jake. She's asked if Sadie and Jake could have visitations. So maybe that's your answer from above. But, I still have a security concern. A supervised visit would have to include me or one of my associates, who are all women. And Billy is a huge concern."

After a pause, Reagan said, "I think I have a solution. How about the church? A secured room and I'm there at the time? Everyone knows it's not unusual for me to lock the doors when I don't want to be disturbed."

"That's possible. I suppose it could work."

"We can work out the details later. I need to get upstairs."

As he climbed the two flights of stairs from the basement to the second floor he thought, "one down, one to go." He quietly slipped into Room 204 and sat down behind Guy. The only spoken words by the plaintiff or defendant were when Micah said, "Not Guilty." But that's what you're supposed to say to get a trial by a jury of your peers. Probably the only people in the room who believed him were, Reagan, Charlotte, Tinker, and Katie... who knew the truth but was willing to perjure herself for revenge. And actually, the revenge now was not just Micah, it was also against her father and that grace and forgiveness crap he was spouting.

It wouldn't matter if Guy believed him. As a lawyer, his job would be to get him free any way he legally could. Guy could see that if Micah went to trial with his court appointed Public Defender he was going away for a long time. The District Attorney was sharp. She was re-elected twice on her promise to clean up the county and her record proved she kept her word. The two lawyers went back and forth. Actually, the Public Defender, Adrian Atwater, went back while the District Attorney went forth. Not a pretty sight as she ate him up. Micah would get his day in court, but he wouldn't see daylight until then. Reagan and Guy cringed as they set bail at $200,000 cash. Charlotte cried and screamed and the bailiff escorted her from the room. What cash bail meant was that he needed the whole $200,000 to get out. They removed Micah from the courtroom and Tinker escorted him back to the jail a block away. The judge left the bench and everyone filed out except Reagan and Guy who sat there for a few minutes.

Guy, who had been intently staring at the floor, lifted his head and looked at Reagan, "I'll take the case."

"You'll what? You don't even know anything about it, nothing, nada, zip."

Guy replied, "I know a lot more than you think I know. While you were watching Micah and Charlotte, I never took my eyes off the girl. Reagan, she's lying. They may have had sex, but he never raped her."

Reagan said, "I believe him, but how can you make that judgment without even talking to him?"

"Reagan, let me tell you a little about me and Ginny. You're a pastor, so this is confidential, just like attorney-client. Have you ever heard of Fidelity Associates out of Chicago?"

Reagan said, "Yeah, I'm sure everyone has after the T-Bone trial"— T-Bone was a rapper from the South Side who was accused of murder and everyone thought would end up in jail for life—he didn't.

Guy continued, "Ginny and I are the founding partners of Fidelity Associates and I was the lead on that case. I'm not proud of what I did Reagan, but getting him freed was my job and I did my job and I'm good at what I do.

We spent years helping rich criminals and mob families, that we knew were guilty, go free. It made us rich, but it didn't make us happy. We were famous outcasts. Everywhere we went important people knew who we were, but they wanted nothing to do with us. And those who accepted us, we wanted nothing to do with them. A real Catch 22. The firm got bigger, richer, and we wanted out."

Reagan, looking a little confused, said, "I thought the owner of the firm was named Lawson or something like that. I know it wasn't Kennedy."

Guy smiled, "You're close. Larson. My name was Guy Kennedy Larson, and I went by G. K. Larson and Ginny used her full name, Virginia. We resigned from the firm and legally changed our last name to my middle name and go by Guy and Ginny. As I said earlier, we wanted to go someplace we could make a difference. We don't need the money and never will. And we use most of our money to help people who can't help themselves. We want to be humble country lawyers doing good deeds. Once we're established here, we plan to let the partners buy us out. Now you know and you're sworn to secrecy."

Reagan said, "It's a secret I can keep. Now if you really want to look like legitimate, humble, country lawyers you need a church."

Guy smiled and said, "Preacher we do a lot of good things now and God sees that. We don't need a church to be good Christians."

Reagan thought, "I used to think that way too, but one thing at a time. We'll get to that later." So instead of rebutting, he asked, "So this will be your first case in Washington County?"

"Yes, Pastor, and it could be a good one. One that doesn't win us a lot of friends among many of the townspeople. I may have to break Katie down on the stand and I'm not looking forward to that. Maybe you can pray it doesn't come to that. One thing I want you to know. Ginny and I may not be in church, but something has changed our lives. We have two criteria for a client: one is we have to both believe you are innocent and two, you pay us a one hundred dollar fee. We never want to be accused of working for nothing. Lunch?"

CHAPTER 10

*T*uesday, May 29, 1992 Brad parked his car, opened the door, and Beasley immediately jumped out. Going to get the latest copy of the Lighthouse every Tuesday got Beasley excited. Brad said, "Not so fast. Get your leash." Beasley jumped back up on the driver's seat, grabbed his leash, and jumped back down. He sat with it in his mouth holding it up to Brad. They made their way up a small alley between the old theater and the NAPA auto parts store. Beasley trotted along...nothing to sniff and no weeds to pee on. Besides, he was on a weekly mission far greater than sniffing weeds. They waited for the light to change and crossed the street. The sign over the door said, "Continuously Published Since 1904." Over the door a bell tinkled and everyone said hi. To Beasley, not Brad. He strained to get to where a treat awaited. This was the weekly ritual.

He took the copy outside and sat down on the bench across from the town square and perused the paper. He usually knew most things going on in town, but the Lighthouse was his insurance policy. He would read it hoping to find something of interest that needed his specialized services. He never wanted recognition for anything he did. It was between him and God although he thought Tinker might have an inkling. All he wanted to do was protect those who couldn't protect themselves. He remembered the times in his life when those he loved were hurt and he couldn't do anything but watch. All that had changed. He might hurt someone as he had with Billy. Sometimes it took pain to get and hold their attention, but Brad never killed anyone. He was an avenging angel, not a murderer. He sought justice. Sometimes he would take a situation as far as he could, causing his enemies to fear for their lives and then turn it over to the law and quickly disappear. Generally, the people Brad dealt with didn't want anyone to know he existed either. Those he turned over to the law often tried to tell the sheriff and even the courts about Brad, but they never listened. Take Billy, for example. Tinker knew what happened and probably figured it was Brad. If he knew it was Brad, he didn't say or didn't care. Brad only did what Tinker's department wished they could do.

He sat there reading with Beasley sitting on the bench beside him. There was nothing of interest on the front page to catch his interest. He turned to page two, and it immediately caught his eye. Not page two, the car parked across the street. There was an imperceptible movement to most eyes, but to a trained eye, it was there. He watched the signage stenciled on the storefront and lined it up with the trunk. He was positive. There was a definite movement in the trunk.

He folded the paper and put it under his arm. He and Beasley crossed the street. He moved closer and processed what he was seeing. Whatever was in there was alive and moving. But with the nearly imperceptible movement who or what was in the trunk was being tightly restrained. No one ties up an animal and puts it in the trunk of a Mercedes. Brad knew who the car belonged to and there could be a reason for a person to be in his car trunk, but not a good one. Brad's gut feeling said something evil had come to Glencoe.

His instincts served him well over the years. If he turned this over to Tinker now and his hunch was right, they would arrest Adrian Atwater. Whoever was in the trunk would be immediately freed. But how deep did this go? What was needed here was civil justice or the wrath of God to come upon these monsters. He moved quickly toward his car and Beasley's little legs scrambled to keep up. He drove up the alley and waited. There was no way human trafficking was ever going to happen in Brad's backyard.

He followed the car as it headed out of town toward the area of Blessed Hills in the western part of the county where few people lived. Land out here was never good for farming although settlers had tried for years. The soil was good, there just wasn't enough. There was an abundance of hollows running back into the hills. They had cut the road through the valley and you could do some tobacco or corn farming where the valley opened, but the creek was prone to flooding. Few people lived out here, but those who did liked privacy, and lived up in those hollows.

He followed at a safe distance. They drove through the valley past a barn with "Chew Mail Pouch Tobacco" painted on the side. When he saw the car turn left he slowed down. He reached the spot and watched a faint trail of white dust floating up into the air. He couldn't see the car which also meant the other driver couldn't see him. He risked driving in aways. It was a single lane path with grass growing up in the middle and then the road suddenly climbed. There was dust in the air so the car ahead was still moving. He continued, and the road narrowed to almost a path and no more dust. He was next to an opening in a crumbling stone wall. He turned around and backed out of sight. He turned off the ignition and said, "Beasie, Daddy has to go to work and you need to wait here." Beasley knew what he said and laid down on the seat with the expression of "I'll do it, but I'm not happy."

Rather than go up the path and risk being seen, he moved up the hill through the woods. Brad moved in such a way you couldn't hear him or see him. He was like an apparition that appeared and then was gone. He approached the clearing, and he saw the car. The trunk was open and empty. No sign of the driver or anyone else. In front of the car was a shack. It might have been a suitable cabin at one time. Now it leaned to the right and poles were holding it up. Oh, the stories that old cabin could probably tell. The front door was open and he could hear voices. Sounded like three voices, but muffled enough that he couldn't hear what they were saying, so he waited. About fifty feet from the cabin were two shipping containers used for cargo. There appeared to be air vents on the roof and he could hear a fan motor. He didn't have a real good feeling right now.

It was a human trafficking operation. But why in Washington County? Then he thought about it a little more. What better place! It was a large county in an area with a low population density. Small law enforcement department. People like their privacy and keep their mouths shut. It was perfect! He wondered how long it had been going on. He figured it was about three years ago when Adrian Atwater set up his law practice. It made sense that that was why he came here.

Brad settled down and waited. He didn't have to wait long. Five people came out. First, the driver followed by two big, dumb looking rednecks literally dragging two young girls. One had long hair and the first buffoon had it wrapped around his hand and was dragging her backward. She was gagged and tried to scream as her butt bounced on the stones. The other one grasped the waistband of the second girls' skin tight short shorts and was lifting and dragging her along. Adrian went ahead of them and opened the door of one of the cargo containers.

Brad brought the binoculars up to his eyes for a better look in the dark container. It helped that it was about four o'clock and the sun angled enough to put a better light into the darkened area. The door opened and Brad was taken back by what he saw. He could feel adrenaline rushing as he filled with outrage and anger. He wanted to stop this, but he had been well trained. Patience and opportunity were key. Inside were five other young girls chained to the cargo tie downs. They were soaked with sweat, dehydrated and looked like they had no fight left. They were too frightened to even speak. The two new girls were dragged in, chained up and they slammed the door shut. The driver said, "The transfer takes place at two tomorrow. White cargo van. You think you can handle that?"

One that seemed the brighter of the two replied, "We ain't stupid. This ain't our first rodeo, ya know. You gonna be here, boss?"

"You idiot. Am I ever there for a transfer? So why would I be there this time?"

Brad listened and concluded that these two were too stupid to figure out how to peel a banana. He could once again do what they trained him to. These three would wish they had never heard of Washington County.

Two o'clock tomorrow gave him lots of time. Divide and conquer, great odds. White van, easy to find. Deliver a neatly tied, if somewhat ruffled package to the Sheriff's door! Time to put the plan into motion. He sneaked away without a sound.

That afternoon Guy stopped by the jail with papers in hand; he needed to talk to Micah. Micah was finishing lunch and also his fourth day in jail. The deputy checked Guy's briefcase and patted him down before letting him back into the holding area. Guy thought the pat down and search might be necessary for the Cook County jail in Chicago, but a little overkill for here. He entered the cell area for the first time since moving to Glencoe and burst out laughing. He took one look, and he said aloud, "Mayberry lives."

The deputy chuckled and said, "If not for the bars, it would almost be home." And then added, "For most of the ones we get in here it's nicer than home and the food's better too. Here, the third cell. Just call when you're done."

Guy went into the cell and introduced himself, "I'm Guy Kennedy and I want to be your attorney."

Micah said, "Well, that would be nice, mister, but I can't afford a lawyer."

"I didn't ask if you could afford an attorney, I told you I wanted to be your attorney. So the first question you need to answer is do you want me as your attorney?" and he took a seat on the bed.

Micah said, "Yeah. Today in the courtroom was the first time I saw the court-appointed lawyer, and he never spoke a word to me. So yeah, I'd like an attorney. Are you any good?"

Guy said, "I've heard people say I'm not bad."

"Well, do you think you can get me out of this?"

Guy smiled at Micah. "That depends. Are you guilty? I don't take on clients that are guilty. I only defend the innocent. Are you innocent Micah?"

"Sir, I love Katie. I would never touch her unless she let me. I don't understand what's happened and I don't understand why she wants me in jail. No sir, I'm innocent."

Guy stood and put his hand on Micah's shoulder. "I believe you. I'll be your lawyer and here's your get out of jail free card." Guy handed him a brown business envelope with his name on it. Micah opened it and took out papers that said he was free on a $200,000 cash bond. His jaw dropped and so did the envelope as Micah sat down and cried. "But how? Who would do this?"

"Somebody in Washington County must think you're innocent. Bondsman handed me the papers to give to you." Guy did not mention why the bondsman had given him the papers. "You got a place to go when you get out?"

"I guess. I know my dad don't care much about me, but I think he'll let me stay there."

Guy said, "If there's a problem you need to see me immediately. The law says you have to have a place of residence. You wait here and I'll turn the papers over to the Sheriff to process. When he's done, he'll call me and I'll go to your father's house with you."

Tonight was Chicken Marsala, it was good to be married to an Italian who loved to cook. Now, if only she was rich she'd be perfect. No. Reagan knew from the day he enlisted in the army and saw the pay scale he'd never be rich. The fact was, he never had much as a kid, but he had a mother who loved him. She kept making excuses for the father who deserted him even though she was glad he was gone. About age eleven he realized his father was never coming back and wasn't a nice man. His mom worked hard, and he reared himself up. When he was older, he was smart enough to know the military would give him what he needed. He also knew the GI Bill was the only way he'd get an education.

He walked into the kitchen and over to the stove where Prudy was stirring the Marsala sauce. He took a sniff of the sauce and Prudy... both smelled great. He nuzzled her neck and put his hands on her belly, as a gesture, because she wasn't that far along. Reagan kissed her neck and said, "Just practicing," as he continued to rub. Then he added, "How did I ever get so blessed?"

Prudy turned her head, "You liked good pizza."

They sat down and said the blessing. He took a bite, Mmmm-mmm. He told her about his day. He often came home for lunch or picked her up and went back to Angie's across from the old railroad station. Angie was a guy. He didn't live in Glencoe which at first made people suspicious of him. But his subs and salads were so good he won the town over. His tuna sub was the best. Prudy liked him because, as you might expect, with the name Angie he was definitely Italian. In fact, he was so Italian he still had a slight accent. Today Reagan had lunch with Guy so he hadn't been home all day. He told her about his chance meeting with Guy on the Courthouse steps and how he'd mentioned Micah to him. "After the arraignment, it seemed like he might be interested in defending him."

Prudy said, "That would be great. I talked to Charlotte today. She couldn't reach you and needed an ear to listen. She's really scared for him. Said the Public Defender is a real jerk. She said it seems like he's filling up a chair while his mind is elsewhere."

"I got the same impression. It seems the judge doesn't like his attitude one bit. Maybe he'll take him off the case. Hopefully, Guy will take the case and we won't have to worry about him."

Prudy asked, "Can Micah afford an attorney? We can't afford to help and someone would probably find out if we could help."

"That's the great thing about Kennedy and Kennedy. They came here intent on helping people. They have a sliding fee scale which he and Charlotte can probably afford." He didn't mention that most of their clients would pay only one hundred dollars.

Changing the subject, he asked about her day mostly to be polite.

He cared and was interested, but already knew she probably had done nothing out of the ordinary. Prudy had always been a homebody and was happy. She was a great support to him, willingly fulfilling her church role, but she preferred to stay home and tend her garden, cook, and read. Reagan just figured it had to do with her traditional Italian upbringing. Prudy showed no desire to work outside the home after she quit waiting tables. They didn't need to have her work, and he already knew she'd be a great mom. So a stay at home mom would be even better.

She mentioned again that she talked to Charlotte and talked about the book she was reading. Then she slipped in a "by the way" my parents are coming to visit. Reagan knew they were in for a lot of free and unsolicited advice on how to do everything, especially child rearing. The nice thing about going to visit them was they could only give advice on something Reagan or Prudy might say. Thus, if they were careful about the subject, and didn't let it get personal, it was a safe and pleasant visit. Now the advice was coming to them. "Prudy, did you follow my recipe? Seems like it needs a little more garlic. You know, after you were born this is what we did. You know, I think that lamp might look better over there. Prudy, do you think that color really looks good on you?" It would be a long visit. Reagan knew he'd have to be there to support his wife during the advice bombardment, but inside he wished there was a convocation somewhere he could attend.

He again changed the subject to another less than desirable situation. He told her he had dropped by the Department of Family Services before the arraignment to check on Heather. "They aren't really going to be cooperative in that office. They wouldn't have offered her visitation if I hadn't brought it up." Prudy was excited that Heather would get to see her kids, but like everyone else wondered what Billy would do to mess it up. They hashed that around a while and it was time for the evening news. They were so far from any city there was no such thing as local news. Well, yes, there was if you counted Becky Walsh. After the network news, he left for the final task of the day. Go to visit the Pierces.

~

It was 7:30 in the evening when Reagan Lamb knocked on the door of the Pierce's home on the north end of High Street. It was a big three-story Victorian built in 1883 and had been in the family for three generations. Adam and Maddie moved in when Katie was four, to help take care of Adam's mom after her third stroke. The house had lots of gingerbread and a big wrap-around porch and was a maintenance nightmare, but it was a beautiful period home. It was good that the Pierces owned a paint and hardware store.

Reagan had a lump in his throat and didn't know how he'd be received. He hoped that Sunday's message had helped pave the way, but you never know. It was obvious after Charlotte stood up in church and indicated that she had a strong relationship with Reagan, it might not go smoothly. Prudy sitting with her probably didn't help either. Even in the church where the pastor should be able to love all members equally, it rarely happens. You were supposed to side with the "important" members of the church which usually were relatives of the founders, big givers, and people in high places. Reagan was not someone to play those games. Religious politics had no place in the church. It didn't make you popular, but it made for a clear conscience.

Adam answered the door. Reagan said, "Good evening Adam. Didn't get to talk with you after church so I thought I'd stop by."

Adam went on defense, "You didn't speak in the courtroom either. And you had the opportunity."

Reagan responded, "Touché, except I didn't speak to anyone in court. If you recall, I sat all by myself in the back. I was there as an observer with an interest in both parties. In many court cases, I would never root for one side over the other. I don't think our system is necessarily the way God would do it. Sometimes it works the way it should, and that's great. Other times it does not serve justice. In court, there are no winners. Everyone loses to some extent. So, Adam, you need to understand I'm there to listen and see if there's anything I can do for either side. Yesterday I visited Micah and tonight I'm visiting your family. And tomorrow I'll probably see Charlotte because she always stops in on Wednesday for counseling with her home situation. So I'd like to sit down and chat with you and Maddie."

"Pastor, I don't think you want to sit down with Maddie right now. She heard Micah Barnes posted bail about 4:30 this afternoon and she's as mad as a wet hen."

It surprised Reagan. He hadn't heard. "How in the world did he post $200,000 cash?"

"We have no idea. There isn't even anyone in this town that could raise that amount in just four hours. Let alone anyone who'd raise it for a Barnes. And she's outraged. She thinks somehow you had something to do with it." Adam said, "Let's step into my office and close the door."

Reagan had enough information that he was sure he knew where the bail came from, but fortunately, no one could really tie him to it. People saw him with Guy Kennedy and he wouldn't deny that. But nobody knew Guy was anything more than a country lawyer and his secret was safe now. He knew Guy would offer Micah legal counsel, but he didn't know it had already happened. So Reagan asked Adam, "What about you? What do you think? You think I'm in on it? You think I've got $200,000?"

"I don't know what to think about anything anymore. I love my daughter. I know my wife can be a handful and acts like we are the village elite even though we just own a hardware store we inherited. We've had real behavioral issues with Katie for about three years. Maddie tried to keep it from me. I found out from the school counselor how bad things were. When Katie communicated again, it was with her mom, not me. Maddie became her friend instead of her mother. She gives in to her every whim. I was the one to forbid her to see Micah Barnes or anyone else from the Oaks. I guess that was all it took for her to sneak out behind my back. Maddie might have known what was going on. Reagan, I'm telling you things I want no one else to know." Reagan nodded.

"Before they rearrested Barnes, I was thinking of dropping the charges or trying to talk to Judge Chadwick and get them lessened. Then Katie barged into the office and dropped the rape bomb on us.

We both were furious, and had him arrested on the new charges. Then Sunday you preached a great message I've needed to hear for a long time. We went home and Maddie and I had a discussion. I had done the same thing to a guy I thought she dated. Your message also reminded me of something else I've been carrying for twenty years."

He told Reagan the whole story of his partnership with Charlie, how he came to see himself as better than Charlie, the wedding snub, and the break of the partnership.

He wept a little. "Pastor, she's my daughter, but what if she's lying? Maddie will never believe that is a possibility. But I don't know. I think she may be capable of just about anything. I can't say anything without pitting both of them against me. And I'm guessing neither Maddie nor Katie will have too much to do with you or the church for a while."

CHAPTER 11

*W*ednesday, May 30, 1992. Brad tossed and turned as he lay awake going over and over the plan. He woke up when the alarm went off. It was 5:00 a.m. and Beasley thought, *"Why are we getting up in the middle of the night? Oh well, since we're up, I might as well go to the door and whine."*

Brad got ready and headed out. He drove out the Airport Road in the industrial area comprising four buildings and the city garage. A few months ago someone had started the funniest rumor ever. An international airport was coming to Glencoe. The story was so good people believed it. In fact, families were so upset about the potential noise and traffic they sold their nearly new homes and moved to the other side of the county.

He turned into D&D Radiator Repair and parked the car. One of the D's was a close friend, Don Danardo. So was the D for Don or for Danardo? Or was it both?... D&D. He'd never asked, but Don would know it was his car. He walked over to the city garage. Since there was no fenced area for the pickups and vans, someone could have their pick. Right now he needed a white van, and he counted on the rednecks being so dumb they wouldn't even notice the van said City of Glencoe on the door. It hit him...City of Glencoe. Since when was a town of fewer than 2000 people a city? Strange little town. He used a jimmy stick on the lock and reached under the dash for the wires. He touched the wires together; the van fired up, and he was off. He was hoping for a little luck today. They assigned the truck to the County Building and Code Department which was open Tuesday and Thursday. Monday, Wednesday, and Friday those two employees worked in the office for another department so they could get a full 40 hours. So, he hoped nobody would miss it. Yes, I keep trying to tell you, Glencoe was a strange little town.

It was still dark and not quite six by the time he pulled into the yard of Adrian Atwater. Atwater was a sleazy little lawyer who had been in Glencoe for about three years. He dressed like an ambulance chaser and nobody could figure out why he was here and how he made a living. Seemed that the only time he had a client was when his number came up in the public defender rotation. He had a one-room office located over the pharmacy and you had to use the outside stairs in the alley. There wasn't even a sign. He said his business was by word of mouth. Apparently, every mouth in Glencoe was zipped shut. He kept to himself and had no friends. He bought an old farmhouse three miles outside of town and just kept to himself. Grandma also said you need to keep an eye on the quiet ones. All this was now making sense.

He went in through the side door into the kitchen. Easiest lock he'd ever picked. He went into the living room and picked the most comfortable looking chair and sat down. He knew he was early, so there was no need to hurry. He'd just wait until he heard a noise upstairs. About a half hour later, he heard the water running...perfect. He went up the stairs, not concerned about being quiet. Brad was thorough, and smirked as he thought to himself, *"This isn't my first rodeo, either."*

There was no spouse, no significant other, and no pets. At the top of the stairs, the door to the bathroom was wide open. Even better, no squeaky door. He pulled the hood out of his pocket and stepped toward the translucent shower curtain. He watched, awaiting the right moment and then he pulled the curtain from its rod.

Atwater jumped and screamed, but before he could turn the hood was over his head and he never saw a thing. Brad pulled the strings tight and Atwater fought the hood. Big mistake. The strings went tight, and he went down as Brad pulled him from the tub. Brad said, "Well, Mr. Atwater, aren't you a sight to behold."

Adrian Atwater, voice muffled by the hood, yelled, "What is the meaning of this? I'll have you thrown in jail for this. Assaulting an officer of the court. Breaking and entering. You'll do a lot of time, mister."

Brad said nothing. He rolled Atwater's skinny, five foot eight body over. He took his arm and held it up behind his back. He reached for the other arm and Atwater struggled. That was his second mistake. Brad gave Atwater's arm the same upward twist he'd given Billy Maddox—crunch.

He said, "Oops, I'm sorry. Did that hurt? Let me adjust it a little."

He knew any movement at this angle would send more pain through Atwater's body...it did and Adrian Atwater screamed out a blood-curdling yell.

"I'm sorry. Apparently, having pain inflicted upon you hurts. But inflicting pain on young girls doesn't. Is that the way it goes Adrian? Does it hurt as much as being tied, thrown in a trunk and bounced around? Does it hurt as much as being dragged by the hair and chained up in a cargo container? Does it hurt as much as the sorrow of a mother whose child was stolen?"

He grabbed his other arm and bent it back as he pulled out an 18" zip tie. He pulled it as tight as he could without cutting off the circulation although he didn't care if it did. He grabbed Adrian by his broken arm and dragged him into the hallway kicking and screaming all the way.

Brad said, "Stand up. Time to go downstairs."

Atwater reached the fourth step from the bottom and he stumbled. Brad reached out instinctively and then stopped as Atwater fell.

"Oops. My bad. My reflexes aren't as good as they used to be. There was a time when I would have been able to break your fall and catch you, oh well."

Adrian landed on the broken arm and he was writhing in pain and rolling on the floor.

Brad said, "Do you suppose the four girls in the cargo container are writhing in pain from what your thugs have done to them? Mr. Attorney, I know everything."

Brad moved over to Atwater's home office and opened his IBM 386 desktop computer. He entered a few clicks and looked at Atwater and shook his head, "You really should have come up with a better password than Attorney123."

Brad took his time searching files, scribbling notes on things, and taping them in various locations. Then he put another zip tie on Adrian's arms and two more on his legs and took a rope and secured him, buck naked, to a column between the living room and dining room.

"Adrian, after the sheriff sees what I've found on your computer, I think he might be very interested in you. And best of all, you don't have to do anything at all but wait right here. The sheriff will be here about thirty minutes after I leave. What am I going to do while you're tied up, you ask? I'm going out to take care of your goons, rescue seven innocent girls, and put you and goons away for the rest of your lives. You have a nice day Counselor."

He walked out and left the door wide open.

Brad climbed into the van and reached for his cell phone to call the sheriff's office. The phone was in a bag on the seat. The bag held a huge rechargeable battery and could also be plugged into the cigarette lighter. Brad rarely took it from his car, but this adventure called for it. It rang several times. A voice answered, "Washington County Sheriff's Office, Sheriff Reynolds here. How may I help you?"

The voice said, "Sheriff, I've got a present for you at the home of Adrian Atwater. In fact, he is the present. He's a little worse for wear, but he's alive and alert and awaiting your arrival. Although you could say he's a little tied up right now. You'll find notes and his computer. I wrote his password next to his computer. Later this afternoon I'll have two more for you. Contact the FBI. You'll understand later, but the Feds will have jurisdiction on this one. Your office will look good breaking a smuggling ring."

Brad hit the call end button and backed out of the yard. On to phase two.

Tinker Reynolds scratched his head, "Smuggling ring? In Washington County? Confound it, what would anyone smuggle in Washington County? He didn't know who the caller was, but knew if he called it usually meant something big. His office would look good. It made sense to him, to just leave well enough alone. Even if the opportunity arose to discover the identity of the mysterious stranger, he wouldn't do it. He sometimes broke a few laws, but he always got bad people off the street and that was worth looking the other way. And the only person who ever got hurt was the bad guy. And when they screamed about what he did to them, Tinker always promised to investigate. But just like Billy, nobody ever saw his face. There were never any witnesses and his investigation always came to a dead end. If nobody had ever seen the man to identify him, then how do you arrest a ghost?

It was about 1:30 and Brad was on his way out to Blessed Hills. He pulled into the dirt lane and as he neared the shack; he caught a glimpse of a white van. This wasn't part of the plan. Time for last-minute improvisation. He thought, "Gravity. What goes up must come down. And maybe instead of two vile humans, I can get three or four." He backed the van down the hill until he found a spot where no one could get around the van and parked it. In one hand he had a taser and in the other a big rock. Timing would be critical. He sat down behind the stone wall on the driver's side and waited. He didn't have to wait long. The driver of the white van saw the van blocking the path and slowed down. He came to a full stop about fifty feet away.

Brad thought, "Come on. I need you closer than that. Give me another twenty-five feet." Either the driver read his mind and complied, or he got lucky. Either way, the van moved up to within about fifteen feet of the van blocking the road. The passenger got out, weapon drawn, and moved cautiously toward the driver's side of the truck. The driver was focused on what was going on in front of him and Brad counted on that. He moved within three feet of the driver's door and took out the taser. He hit the guy moving to his van squarely in the back. He dropped the gun, writhed and wiggled and hit the ground. Simultaneously, he yelled "Hey!" The driver turned and caught the rock full force in the face. Definitely broke his nose and knocked him out. His head hung out the window as his blood ran down the door. He moved to the guy with the wires hanging off his back, took a hood, put it over his head and pulled the strings tight. He then grabbed two zip ties, zip, zip, and he lay there looking like a rodeo calf. The guy was coming to and cursed loudly. Brad knew he had to quiet him down before the two up the hill heard him. A swift kick to his lower jaw seemed to do the trick. Never risk hurting your hands if you don't have to. He then went around to the driver's side, opened the door and the driver fell out and landed on his already badly disfigured face. A hood, two zip ties and he was finished.

He had heard no noise from the back of the van and that concerned him. When he opened the rear door, his heart went up into his throat. There were seven girls in there, but none were moving. He felt a pulse and then relaxed. They were all bound tightly and drugged. Probably enough to keep them out for hours as they crossed state lines to wherever the destination was. That also explained why they didn't have a third person in the back or a cage separating the front from the back. Actually, it was a good thing there wasn't a third person. He hadn't planned for that. Maybe he was slipping, getting too old for this.

He knew the girls needed attention quickly. He moved his van out of the way and then moved the other van down to the road about a quarter mile closer to Upton and ran back cutting across a field. He climbed into the van; he called 911 and told the county dispatcher he had found the van. Said it seemed like someone had drugged them or something. He quickly hung up and placed his new friends "gently" in the back of the city's cargo van. Actually, it was more like a big old farm boy throwing bales of hay up on the wagon. Didn't matter how they got there as long as they landed on the wagon. He then waited until he heard the siren and continued on up to the shack.

~

The town was fluttering with the news. The Benson mansion on Broad Street might be sold. It hadn't been lived in for five or six years. Old Doc Dyson had inherited it from an uncle who hit it big in oil in the 1890s. The uncle only had one living relative, his sister, and she'd been in a nursing home for about twelve years. Her only child was Dennis, and he was a dentist in Pittsburgh. The only condition of the will was Dennis had to live in the house for ten years or until his death. Well, it was the most beautiful home in Glencoe at one time. While everything else in town was a Victorian, the Benson mansion was a big Greek Revival with six columns across the front. It wasn't exactly a mansion, but it was about ten thousand square feet with six bedrooms and eight baths. It had a big ballroom on the second floor. You entered the home through the sixteen-foot oak double doors into the huge marble foyer. On each side of the foyer was a winding stair-case with both meeting in the middle with the ballroom entrance straight ahead. It was the only house in Glencoe with a pool and well kept English gardens. Doc Dyson decided it was an offer he couldn't refuse. In addition, there was enough money in the estate to maintain it for about forty years. Dyson doubted he'd live any longer than that. So he moved his practice to Glencoe and lived in the house all by himself. Never married. When he died there were no heirs. The house went into probate and the state got everything. It ended up selling for way below the market value because the maintenance, taxes, and utilities were more than most people earned.

The only thing the residents knew was the potential buyer would arrive on Friday or Saturday. Somebody said he was coming into the airport by private charter. Nobody could remember the last time a private charter flew into town. He was from the west coast and made his money in something called a microchip. Almost no one in Glencoe had the faintest idea what a microchip was, to them a microchip was a tiny potato chip. Since nothing had been officially signed, try as they might, no one could find out his name. For the last two weeks, there had been a lot of activity at the Benson mansion, painting, new landscaping and it was looking on the outside the way the older town residents remembered.

Protecting his identity was of the utmost importance. If Brad was ever exposed, he could no longer assist helpless victims. He could even possibly go to jail for some things he'd done. It seemed to him the bad guy had more rights than the victim, so he sought to even the odds. Through him, they could get their revenge. Sure, everyone has a right to their day in court, innocent until proven guilty and all that stuff. But, hearing a jury say "guilty," isn't always enough! Your wife and the mother of your three young children are struck by a drunk driver. She's paralyzed and will never walk again. He prances into court with a smile on his face and hears guilty, five years, but you know he'll be out in two. For your kids, is this enough? For the drunk driver there is no remorse, no feelings of guilt, no suffering and in two years he'll be out to do it again. Brad couldn't stop the system from letting people off, but he could make sure they never forgot what they did.

Brad took a mask, two hoods, rope, baseball bat, and a gas canister and headed toward the shack. The baseball bat was his favorite weapon. He could control the amount of persuasion needed. He approached the side and listened. It had been less than an hour since the exchange. So the men and the money would be in the shack. Brad assumed their instructions were to wait for Atwater. He heard movement, so it was time to move on to phase two. He moved around front and placed a looped end of the rope over the doorknob. He left it loose as it would tighten when someone tried to open the door. He tied the other end of the rope to the bumper of a rusted out '51 Chevy pickup that was sitting on blocks. He went back around to the side of the shack. He took the canister of tear gas and pulled the pin. Then he hit the pane of glass with the bat and lobbed the canister in. He heard a voice yell, "Gas!" and Brad calmly walked around the front and waited for the rope to go taut. He pulled the knife out of his boot as the coughing got louder and he heard someone yell, "Where's the door, I can't see!"

"Over here, I've got it." Brad felt the rope tighten and with the sharp knife in hand, he cut the rope. The door flew back, the guy lost his balance and landed on the floor. The other one crawled toward the light as Brad grabbed the bat and went into a baseball stance just outside the door. The first one crawled through the door and his right shoulder cracked. His arm went out from under him as he hit the porch floor in great pain. Brad grabbed his ponytail and yanked as he screamed in pain. He dragged him off the porch by the hair, put the hood over his head and pulled the strings tight. "If you want to live, don't move."

Brad moved back into position and waited for the second trafficker to find the door. When he came through the door. Brad wound up and took a swing at a knee-high pitch. Crack!! The pain had to be intense. Brad felt it was nothing compared to what they did to young teen girls regularly. He fell forward and Brad broke his fall by grabbing his left arm. But he didn't intend to break the fall. He brought the arm back, and he heard another crack. The guy screamed out a blood-curdling yell of pain.

"Oops. Did I hurt you? Big brave men like you who like to hurt little girls should be able to handle a little pain. Didn't expect retribution, did you? Sorry, you probably don't know what retribution is."

He grabbed a hood and put it over his head. "Maybe you understand payback."

He went back to the first and zip tied his hands and stood him on his feet.

The trafficker asked, "Who are you?"

Brad didn't answer right away. He pulled off his mask and stuck it in his pocket. He didn't need it anymore. He grabbed the first one by the shirt and lifted him off the ground. He wanted to quote the corny words from Dirty Harry, "I'm your worst nightmare." Instead, he said nothing. He grabbed him by the scruff and said, "Walk."

They got to the container, and the hinges screeched as Brad opened the door and threw him into the container. Head first. He hit his head and was out cold.

He walked back to the second felon who couldn't decide whether to hold his knee or his shoulder as he lay on the ground fifty feet from the storage container rolling from side to side.

Brad said, "People who prey on other people make me sick. And people who prey on children are the lowest form of life. Yesterday I watched you drag and physically abuse those girls. But, you know what? Just arresting you at that time wouldn't have been enough. I know you don't feel any guilt about what you do and I doubt you'll ever feel any remorse. You need a conscience for that. But I want you to feel the pain and suffering of all the girls and their families. Some who will never see their daughters again because you sentenced them to death. But you will have something to remind you of today. I'm methodical and if I do this right, you'll never forget today." He grabbed him by his ponytail and literally dragged him fifty feet to the container. He put zip ties on both of them, locked the door, turned off the exhaust fan and went to get the van holding his other two new friends.

He opened the barn doors on the side of the van to check on them. The one he had tasered was now trying unsuccessfully to move, and the recipient of the rock was still out cold. He backed the van up to the container, unlocked it, and threw his precious cargo into the back like two more bales of hay. He went into the shack and retrieved the money and threw that in the back. Not a bad day's work.

He drove around the block of the Sheriff's office three times looking for a parking space to leave the van. The third time's a charm and there was a spot right in front of the entrance to the jail and no one was around. He parked, got out, and walked away. He sat down on a bench over by the Courthouse where he could still see the van and took out that big phone. He dialed Sheriff Reynolds' number.

Tinker had been excited about this morning's package and the computer had all the files needed to put Atwater away for a long time. Adrian Atwater either wasn't too bright or was just too cocky. Since Brad had promised Tink more of Atwater's associates, he had paced all day waiting. Brad had said about 2 o'clock and it was now almost 5:30. Maybe something had gone wrong. He knew the girls were safe at the hospital, their parents notified, so at least that part went right. But he was becoming concerned. The phone rang.

"Washington County Sheriff's Office, Tinker Reynolds. How may I help you?"

"Sheriff, the second package is out front in the white city van... don't ask. The two near the front are a bonus. Someone sent them to pick up the girls from Atwater. They might give the Feds a lead higher up the food chain. I know this has been going on for about three years. The two in the back screaming the loudest might need a doctor at some point. They are Atwater's gofers. It's been a long day and I'm going home. You have a great day."

Tinker said, "Thank you."

Brad replied, "My pleasure as always."

He hung up and walked up High Street toward the airport. He never planned on getting involved in something as far-reaching as human trafficking, but Brad is Brad and people who hurt people need to be punished. Pain is the only thing they seem to enjoy.

Adam Pierce pulled up beside him, "Just closed up shop and am headed home, but I've got time to give you a lift. Where are you going?"

Brad replied, "Out to R&R Radiator to pick up my car."

Adam asked, "Had some trouble?"

"You could say that. Turned out to be a bigger problem than I had expected, but I caught it early enough so I think it's taken care of."

They arrived at R&R and his car was right where he left it, so that was good. The shop was closed. He got out, said thanks and headed for the car. He got in and leaned back. "Ahhh. Maybe I am getting too old for this."

~

As Reagan was leaving the church, the phone rang and he immediately recognized the voice on the other end. "Hey Wayne, what's up."

Wayne said, "I was just checking up. I haven't seen you around much this week." Reagan explained it had been one of those weeks and recapped what he could. Some were confidential things he wouldn't even share with Wayne. But the two had been a great support for each other. Their theological differences never seemed to get in the way. Wayne and Reagan clicked the way great friends do. Wayne asked, "Are we going for breakfast and prayer tomorrow morning?"

Reagan said, "I'll be honest. I'm glad you called. I think I would have forgotten. Like I said, it's been one of those weeks. I'm really in need of prayer. And I've got some exciting news to tell you. So, I'll see you at seven."

~

He smelled the Tortellini Alfredo the moment he walked in. It was waiting in the casserole dish. He looked at her and made his usual comment, but tonight he added a little, "It's good to be married to an Italian who loves to cook. And it's even better when she is carrying our baby."

Prudy said, "And it's good to be married to a man who loves the Lord and likes Italian food."

One thing they had in Glencoe was cable and he had no meetings tonight. It was Wednesday night, and the networks were already into reruns. Reagan searched for a movie they both liked and hadn't seen. The 'they both liked' part wasn't hard. They both loved fast-paced action movies with lots of bullets flying. In the end, good always triumphs over evil and that was important. They hadn't seen 'The

Avenger.' He set the VCR to record in case he had to wait for Prudy. While he waited he went into the office and turned on his new Apple MacIntosh and checked his email on Juno. He'd only had email service for about six months and most people didn't have it. He'd get one or two emails a week so he checked just in case. Nothing, as usual. He wondered if this email stuff would ever catch on.

CHAPTER 12

Thursday, May 31, 1992. Reagan got out of bed at 6:30, stretched and yawned. He thought, "I woke up from six hours of sleep, why am I yawning? That movie took a lot out of me." He went around the bed and kissed his sleeping wife on the cheek. Then he showered, shaved, let the dog out, and headed for town. He could always find a good parking space at this time of day, then realized you can find a good parking space any time of day in Glencoe. It would be a great weather day with a high of 78°. It was already 68°, so he took Molly, top-down, on that great winding road from his house to town. He got out and walked into the Greasy Spoon; Wayne was seated and ready to eat.

If you wanted gossip in Glencoe there were two real good sources. You could talk to Reagan's secretary, Becky Walsh, or you could just go to the Greasy Spoon for breakfast. So while Reagan and Wayne ate breakfast they chatted with polite words to those entering and leaving. You could often tell when they wanted Wayne and Reagan to get involved in the conversation or take a position, but neither would take the bait. Generally, one of them would say something like, "You boys can solve the problems of Glencoe without us. You've been here a lot longer than we have." One time they asked Reagan about welfare in

Washington County. He answered by saying, "Zeke, I'm going to be preaching on that topic Sunday. Why don't you boys bring your families and come to church?" He wasn't, but that ended the interrogation quickly...no one knew how to respond. After they finished, he and Wayne went next door to the old theater/church. The congregation had really done a good job of converting the building with the money they had. Off to the sides of the lobby were four rooms. They entered room number three. It was comfortably furnished and Wayne used it as a counseling room. They closed the door and talked about some personal struggles with ministry and life. Reagan shared the great news of their pregnancy and you would have thought they were two giddy teenage girls just invited to the prom. Then they prayed.

~

About 10:30 Guy finally received the call from the Sheriff that he had been expecting since yesterday. Guy said, "Sheriff Reynolds, What's going on? Why hasn't Micah been released?"

Tinker said, "It's a long story. The D.A. fought the bail, went to the judge, and he put a stop on the release until she talked to him. She was okay with the bail when she thought it would never be posted. Now she saw him as a flight risk. The judge disagreed, so you can come to get him."

~

Judge Lloyd Chadwick was known as a no-nonsense law and order judge. If you went before him and were found guilty, there would be no probation or reduction of sentence for the time served. You would be jailed for the maximum time allowed. He generally accepted the bail request of the D.A. or prosecutor. This time the D.A., Allison Dodge, got the bail she requested and Judge Chadwick refused to change it. But there was a little more to the story.

Lloyd Chadwick was reared in a Baptist family. Church three times a week and everybody goes—we are a family. He went to college in North Carolina to a liberal arts college that was more liberal than arts. Although he told his parents he went to church every Sunday, he never went, not even Christmas or Easter. When he went off to law school, it was all about the law. Forgiveness, mercy, and grace had no place in the courtroom and Lloyd believed it, graduated, and practiced it. When he was elected as Washington County Judge, the prosecution attorneys loved him.

He'd been in Glencoe for about twenty years and occupied the bench for six years now. He'd also been at Community Church for twenty years and he and his wife had sat third row center from day one. He arrived during the tenure of a beloved pastor who had been there over twenty years. He was a man who never made waves, never had high expectations of the congregation, and preached nothing controversial. By controversial we're talking about the Bible, not politics. He'd preach about social justice issues and the safe stuff in the Bible. People loved him because he made them feel good and convinced them they were living a Christian life. That had drawn Lloyd to Community Church. The pastor left about fifteen years after Lloyd began attending.

Community Church was an independent church but had always been quite liberal. The new pastor they called, was a little more conservative which many people resisted. He preached from the Bible and expected Christian commitment, and he didn't last long. When you follow a pastor who's loved and has been there over twenty years...you are the sacrificial lamb. And even more so if you preach the truth after a pastor, who for twenty-plus years, preached what their ears wanted to hear. He lasted about two tumultuous years. But the church had changed over those two years and the sacrificial lamb had made a theological impact in the way many people saw life.

Reagan knew what he was getting into when he accepted the call. He'd been where they were and remembered what it took for God to move him. He'd just do the same thing. During his first three years he impacted many lives. At this point, he felt confident about his ministry, the direction of the church, and souls saved.

Lloyd Chadwick faithfully attended every Sunday and because of his Baptist background, Reagan's preaching was making a difference in his life. He was still a tough judge, but now there was room in his heart for God.

Last Sunday's message had hit him like a dagger through the heart. On his way out he'd told Reagan he had given him a lot to think about. And think, he did. He'd grown up in a church that preached grace and mercy, but his seven-year absence from the church during college and law school had hardened his heart. Prior to Reagan's arrival at Community Church, Lloyd's only concern was what the law said. His only reason for being there was to make contacts. There were enough votes at Community Church to swing the election his way. Now, this pastor had reminded him of the truth he knew and restored his conscience.

All week Lloyd had thought about that message and reflected on some of his recent cases. Legally he did everything according to the letter of the law, so why did he now feel guilty about some of his decisions? When he was ten years old, the pastor gave an invitation to receive Christ as Lord and Savior. This wasn't anything unusual. The pastor did it every Sunday at exactly quarter past noon. But this Sunday was different because the Holy Spirit prodded the soul of one Lloyd Benjamin Chadwick to go forward. Lloyd recalled that it was through the grace of God and the blood of Christ he was saved. He didn't deserve to be saved. He had done nothing to make him worthy to live eternally in the presence of God. He sat in his chambers and verses from his youth filled his head.

It literally blew him away as he thought of all the grace poured out in the New Testament. Christ forgave the thief on the cross just hours away from death, facing the all-powerful judge, and just before the Savior took his dying breath. Yes, he died. He really died, but three days later he was alive. And grace abounds. Lloyd thought to himself, "Grace abounds... everywhere except in my courtroom. But my job is to mete out justice. That's what I'm paid to do. That's what the people elected me to do. And I do it. I follow the law."

As he sat there he heard a voice, "Lloyd, you know if I followed the letter of the law, as you've done you'd rot in hell for eternity. You're not good enough to get into my heaven. You're in a tough position and I understand fully what you go through every time you have to pronounce a sentence. I've been doing it for thousands of years. But, one of my attributes is that I'm just. That means I cannot change my mind once I decide. That makes it tough. I developed a system of blood sacrifice. There is no forgiveness without the shedding of blood. But that got messed up badly by priests who saw a way to profit from my plan. So I needed a new plan to show the world what I was like. When the time was right, I sent my Son into the world. I knew he'd be killed. I knew he'd die on a cross. It was part of my plan so that every person could receive forgiveness and eternal life through the blood of my Son, the final sacrifice acceptable to me. I knew the world wouldn't accept him. But to those who believed him when he said, "I am the Way, the Truth, and the Life. No man comes to the father except through me," to them I gave eternal life. So for those who are in Christ Jesus, there is no more condemnation. What I did was shed my grace upon the world, to the people I created, but didn't deserve it. I expected that they would rejoice that my grace was free and available to all. But what I wanted them to discover was justice tempered with mercy. I wanted them to realize what miserable sinners they are and yet I provided a way of redemption. If he did that for them, then I thought maybe they'd do the same for others. We need a world of justice, but it needs to be tempered with mercy, love, and compassion. I'm the only one who knows what's in a person's heart and that gives me an advantage. But, Lloyd, if you'll look to me first you will find the mercy I showed you. Do you understand that?"

Lloyd was still looking for the voice. Could the Living God take time to talk to him? Silence. But Lloyd bowed his head and said, "Heavenly Father, I think I do. I think I really do." And that's why the D.A. didn't get to keep Micah in jail. She was one day late.

~

Guy went over to the jail and parked his ten-year-old Ford in the 'Law Enforcement Only' parking space and went inside. What a change from having a new Lexus every year. Tinker was sitting at his desk talking to an FBI agent. The Feds were grateful for the capture of the traffickers but questioned their broken bones and bruises. Someone messed them up good. Excessive force by the police could damage the case. Tinker admitted he had a little help. He told them about this guy who took them down by himself. He didn't mention this wasn't the first time. Tink said, "Funny thing is nobody knows who he is. He caught these dregs and then called my office to tell me where to find them. And then he disappeared before we arrived." The FBI wanted more information about the help they received from this mystery man and any lead on how they might find him. Tinker, along with all four deputies, convinced them he couldn't tell them what they didn't know.

Guy sat down in an old armed wooden office chair to wait. The agent left and Tink turned to Guy, "Mr. Kennedy, good to see you. Wait here and I'll have Micah brought out."

As Micah came out, Guy could see the expression of mixed emotions. Facial expressions are a key a lawyer can use to tell if his client is being honest. Guy wasn't sure what he was seeing. He saw a lot of apprehension that was overriding the joy of being free, so he asked, "You okay?"

Micah said "I've got mixed feelings about going home. The cell is comfortable, the food is good, and everyone's been so nice, especially Mrs. Reynolds. Now I go home. No one but Charlotte's been to see me. There's nothing but yelling and screaming and bullying. My father will probably let me stay there, but he'll do everything he can to make my life miserable and make sure I understand what a great favor he's doing for me. And you can be sure there's something in it for him. So no, I'm not okay, and I don't want to go home."

Guy said to him, "Micah, let's go together and see what happens. You need a place to stay. If it doesn't work, then we need to find another place for you. They set the trial date for about four months from now and during that time you have to keep your nose clean or it's back to jail you go. Even a domestic disturbance with your dad could put you back in. So I'm trying to look out for your welfare."

~

After meeting Prudy for lunch at Angie's, Reagan drove over to the Oaks area to see if Heather and Billy were home.

He drove Molly through some streets in the Oaks. Most everything about this area was depressing and yet how do you change a culture that's been in the making for three or four generations? He knew someone could do something, but it had to happen one person at a time. Charlotte was transforming her life. It seemed like Micah had been succeeding before he did something stupid. Then Katie Pierce's rape accusation added to it. And although a lot of people would still laugh, Reagan now believed Billy and Heather stood a real good chance of making it. And if they did, there could be more in the Oaks who could make it if someone would give them a chance.

He saw Billy's 'classic muscle car' in the yard and pulled in under the shade of the old apple tree. He walked up to the house, and he noticed things seemed to be neat and clean. The house was sadly in need of paint, but it was clean. Over next to the failing corner post was lumber. He assumed it was to fix it.

He stepped onto the porch which squeaked, and over the hound dog who never looked up. He opened one eye and then let it drift shut. It was as if he took a quick peek at Reagan and said, "No danger here." Or maybe he was just too old and lazy to care, which probably was the right answer. He knocked on the door and Billy and Heather just sat and looked at each other. Nobody ever came to their door unless sirens preceded it or they had papers to serve. No sirens, so it must be papers. They looked at each other with that look that says, "Who could that be?" Billy got up and opened the door to the amazement of Heather. This was another first. For four years, every time the phone rang or there was a knock on the door Billy would yell, "Heather why are you still sittin' there? Get up and answer that."

Billy opened the door and said, "Well, hello there preacher. This is a surprise. Come on in and take a load off." Reagan walked to an empty chair, and it somewhat surprised him. The house was neat and clean inside and furnished nicely. You'd never know from the outside that the inside was so nice. Billy was a complex person and definitely had lived his life as a sociopath which was understandable. Reagan was really more concerned about Billy than Heather. Billy was the key to getting the kids back. He looked over, "How's the arm?" Billy looked down, lifted the arm up and twirled it in circles. "A lot better. It's only been a week. Doc says six to eight weeks. Next week I can use my hand as long as I don't use the arm muscles lifting."

Reagan said, "Again, anything you need help with, let me know. I noticed the lumber. I can help with that too. Looks like you've been trying to do some work around the place."

"Yeah, I can't go to work for a while yet. Most everything I do takes two arms. Course, maybe I don't even have a job anymore. I've been using my sick days and I've about run out, so I've got to go out to the airport and talk to my boss. Well, anyway, I've been keeping busy. Got rid of all the old engines, car parts, washers and other stuff I was gonna use or fix, but never got to. Made a little money off it too and that'll help right now. I dragged everything else out to the curb. Garbage guys were out there for about twenty minutes." He laughed. "But it's gone and yes it looks better. I can tell people it's the house without all the junk."

Reagan noted a sense of pride in what Billy said, "I drove around a bit before stopping here. You've got the neatest property in the neighborhood, looks good. Inside looks nice too."

"You know, preacher, I've always assumed everyone was like me. And the best way to keep people out of your house was to look poor. No point in breaking into a house that looks like it has nothing in it worth stealing. Right? So, I've always been a lot more concerned with the inside than the outside. One of the foster homes I was in, the guy was a carpenter. Stayed with them until I sold his power tools, took the money and ran off. Got caught and ended up in juvie. Anyway, I worked with him one whole summer and learned a lot. What you see is what I learned. Some other things you see like stonework on the fireplace, I bartered for that. I've been in this house 13 years and I had a lot of good years. Things didn't get bad for me personally until the mine closed and I couldn't take care of Heather and the kids." Reagan noticed he didn't say 'her kids.' "Then I drank and you know the rest. But, Heather still cares about me and while it don't make sense, it kinda makes me feel good and kinda bad at the same time."

Heather said, "Billy, I've always loved you. I know what you can be. I've seen it and I pray I'm seeing it again. You got sick, but maybe now you're getting better."

Reagan was watching Billy's reaction when Heather said he got sick. So he said, "Have you given any thought to attending an AA meeting?"

People who have worked with alcoholics know you ask them to attend one AA meeting, no long-term commitment.

Reagan expected Billy's immediate response, "AA is for alcoholics. I'm not an alcoholic, I can stop drinking anytime I want. I haven't had a drink since last Friday night. So that proves it." Reagan had heard that one before. The other guy's a drunk and he needs help, but I can stop if I want to.

Cautiously he asked Billy, "When you drink, have you ever done anything you regretted? Things you wish you hadn't?"

"Yeah, sure, I have."

"How often Billy? How often have you wished you hadn't done what you did?"

Billy hung his head. With Heather present, he couldn't lie, "Nearly every time."

"If that regret came after you sobered up then you need AA. No one's saying you're an alcoholic. But when you drink you lose control and you need help with that."

Reagan would let AA tell him he's an alcoholic because it would be useless for him to try to convince Billy.

"If you love Heather and don't want to ever hurt her again, you'll try one meeting. They meet in the church basement on Monday at 7:00 p.m. and I guarantee there'll be people there you know. How about it? One meeting?"

You could see the pleading look in Heather's eyes as he said, "Pastor, I'll do it for Heather. I don't think I need it, but I'll do it for her." He needed to do it for himself, but it was a start.

Reagan looked over at Heather, "We never got to talk about your visit. When's the next one?"

"Tuesday at 10:00 a.m.."

"Can we meet at 9:00 and talk? I'll have coffee and donuts and both of you can come to the office." They nodded and agreed.

As he walked out Billy said, "See you Sunday." Reagan smiled but didn't look back. He waved and got in the car. It was way better than he expected. But could he believe Billy? He wanted to, but it was Billy.

Guy drove Micah to the trailer. The yard was fenced in with a gate at the end of the drive to keep people out. Inside the fence were two Rottweilers, who roamed freely. Further back was an old single wide trailer with two additions on the sides. Over to the right side was one of the old square Winnebagos from the 1970s with four rotted flat tires. It hadn't moved in a long time. Outside the front door of the trailer were three folding chairs, none of which matched and a truck tire rim for a fire pit. Junk was piled up everywhere.

Micah opened the gate while the Rottweilers barked. He yelled at them and off they ran. After Guy drove in, Micah closed the gate and walked towards the trailer. The door opened before Guy could even get out of the car and there stood a three hundred pound man dressed in a shopping bag T-shirt, boxers, and holding a 30-06.

"Why are you back here? Thought you was in jail. Thought we was rid of you for good."

Micah was afraid of him, but he understood him and knew how to push the right buttons. Guy, on the other hand, was wondering about the choice he'd just made. He'd known lots of people just like Micah's dad, but there was always a cop there, or an officer of the court and they never had a deer rifle.

Micah said, "Just calm down Pa. I'm out on bail. Can we come in and sit down and talk? I can explain everything."

"I'm busy right now. Got this big deal I'm working on. You got thirty minutes."

Paul Barnes always had a big deal brewing, but nothing ever came. He'd come up with a get rich scheme and somehow he'd be the one to lose money. If you looked in the dictionary for a definition of a loser it would say, Paul Barnes.

Inside was what Guy expected. The place was filthy, and the furniture was not only old, but it was also worn and stained. Paul Barnes sat in the big overstuffed chair that was no longer overstuffed. The only seat left was the most disgusting couch Guy had ever seen. Micah sat down without hesitation, but then he'd been sitting on it for years. Guy sat down gingerly and made sure his hands touched nothing.

Micah started, "Pa, this is my lawyer, Guy Kennedy, and he somehow got me out on bail because he believes I did nothing to Katie Pierce."

Paul interrupted, "If you remember I tried to warn you that nothing good would come from that hoity-toity little tease. And a lawyer named Guy. You gotcha a little Frenchie, huh?"

"Guy's not French, he's an American. And, Pa, I fell for Katie, but I guess you were right. Now I'm out on bail until the trial and I need a place to stay. Somehow I'll pay rent after I find a job. Maybe I can get back my job at the sawmill...it's only been a few days."

Paul said, "I'll tell you what, and it's agin' my better judgment. You can stay in the Winnie if you don't bother me. I'll let you stay only cause you're blood kin. But I don't want no accused rapist staying under my roof. Reflects badly on me. And your darn right you'll pay rent. You ain't gonna freeload around here."

Micah said that would work out fine and thanked Paul profusely to appease him and Guy observed that it seemed to work. Paul loved having someone obligated to him.

They walked out to the old Winnie to see his new home. They used to play in there as kids. When they opened the door, the musty odor hit them in the face like a dank basement that hadn't been entered in years. Guy knew immediately it needed to be aired out big time and lots of bleach. But from Guy's perspective, it was nicer than the trailer they left. A hose to the outside spigot would give water to the RV. Someone had hooked up the sewer drain permanently. The electric was hard-wired to the house and they put a splitter on the big propane gas tank out back. Micah told Guy, "I had forgotten, but when we were little Pa rented this out to someone, but I remember little about it or who. Looks like everything will work and it doesn't look like anything leaks. This'll work. Better than staying in the trailer and I can come and go without getting the 3rd degree."

CHAPTER 13

*S*aturday, June 2, 1992. Saturday morning and all the tongues were wagging at the Greasy Spoon. Well, tongues always wag at the Greasy Spoon, but this was more than usual. In fact, you couldn't go anywhere in Glencoe without people telling you what they saw or asking questions about what you saw. Seems Chad Houston had arrived on a private jet. He came in about 4:30 Friday afternoon. If he'd been just another new resident, there would have been an interest in the new people and by noon Becky Walsh could tell you everything.

But Chad Houston was different. He wasn't just a new resident; he was buying the Benson mansion. Thing is, the residents had a lot more questions than answers. And most of the information that was spreading wouldn't hold up to Fact Checker. Rumors were flying like lightning bugs in June. Nobody knew anything about him and Google didn't yet exist. The only information they had was he flew in on a small corporate jet. They hadn't lengthened the runway for those big international jets yet. Then he got into Ruth Gordon's car and headed immediately for the only motel in town, the Cozy Up Inn. It was behind the buildings on High Street and had its own private alley entrance.

Ruth Gordon, the local listing realtor, had done nothing but smile for the last two months. She smiled because she was in line for the largest commission of her career and because she knew more about Chad Houston than anyone else, and she wasn't talking. This had been the biggest and most well-kept secret in the history of Glencoe. Ruth was well respected and had been a part of Glencoe eight years. She was a real estate broker and a real estate attorney. That meant she not only listed the Benson mansion, but she also sold it, and did all the paperwork. The beauty of this sale was that no one was privy to any information she didn't release. And at Chad Houston's request, nothing had been released.

When Chad got out of the car, he looked like he fit in with everyone else in town. He didn't look rich or act rich. He wore jeans, a polo shirt and sneakers. There was nothing to make him stand out except he was handsome. Most women would say beyond handsome. Before the weekend was over, eligible women in Glencoe would fall all over themselves, and each other, trying to score.

The Cozy Up Inn was the only option for lodging in town. There was the old hotel on High Street, but it had closed in the 1950s. They had used the downstairs, off and on, as a bar or restaurant. In fact, that's where the new Chinese Restaurant would be. But the upstairs would cost a lot more money to modernize and rehab than the hotel could ever make. There were 12 rooms at the Cozy Up Inn and each one was decorated with a different 1960s decor. Not much had been upgraded. When you're the only motel in town, you can do what you want. But the rooms were spotless, and the mattresses were new and comfortable. You didn't get much for amenities beyond cable, but you got a good night's sleep. Chad checked in and went straight to his room to rest and do some paperwork. After dusk, he took a walk up High Street and received stares from the locals, but he smiled and said "hello" and kept walking. Glencoe was as cute, quaint, and as laid back as he'd hoped. Yup, he felt he had made a good choice.

The next morning he went to the motel office for the free continental breakfast which consisted of bitter coffee and a day-old donut. He decided that they bought a box of donuts and kept serving them until they were gone and then bought a new box. He and Ruth could eat later. Right now, he wanted to see the house. He'd only seen pictures, and he was eager to get over to the house. Ruth picked him up at 9:00 a.m. and went straight to Benson mansion on Broad Street. What a difference a fresh coat of paint and new landscaping had made. Ruth entered the river pebble covered circular drive and pulled in front of the sixteen foot refinished oak doors. Chad was literally awestruck with the external beauty of the one-hundred-year-old home. Ruth explained that they would ordinarily enter through the solarium next to the four-car garage that had once been the stable when the house was constructed in 1890. They entered the huge main foyer, and he saw the marble floors and the matching staircases. That was all he needed to see. Chad said, "Okay. You've sold me the house. Now sell me on the town." Ruth's jaw dropped. One hundred thousand dollars and a six percent commission. While Ruth was doing an internal fist pump, so was Chad. For a hundred thousand dollars he was purchasing a house that would sell for two to three million dollars in southern California.

Everywhere they went Ruth was protective of Chad. She was determined not to lose this sale. She didn't give people an opportunity to do much more than say 'hi' as she showed him around. She took Chad to the much quieter Angie's for breakfast. If he ever found the Greasy Spoon, it would be on his own. No way she'd go there—ever.

After breakfast she took him out of town in four directions, stopping after reaching the city limit in each direction. Most everything was on route 80 West that leads to the interstate. There was the second of two hardware stores which had a lumber yard, the e-squad building, medical center and nursing home, the second of two supermarkets, a Pamida department store, a Dollar General, a car dealership, the Burger Barn and a fitness center. The bowling alley was on the road to the river, route 80 East. All the other businesses were on High Street including the two closed theaters. There was the main county road that leads north and south. If you took it south for forty minutes, on the windiest road you've ever encountered, you'd end up in a small college town on the river called Appleton. If you took it north you'd wind up in Upton with a few modern conveniences. The road east was ten miles downhill to the river. From there it was another fifteen miles in either direction to a town. Most people took the road west. It didn't go to a town but led to the interstate where there was a McDonalds, and from there to the rest of the world. Did we mention Glencoe had no fast-food restaurants, but it had a Domino's Pizza? Sal's Pizza wasn't too happy when Domino's bought the old donut shop. Remember, Glencoe isn't exactly in the middle of nowhere, but you could see it from there.

Reagan Lamb told people he always chuckled when he was in the office and a transient knocked on the church door and said they were just passing through Glencoe and ran out of gas. If you'd ever been to Glencoe, you would know that no one in its 100-year history ever just passed through. You couldn't pass through Glencoe, it was a destination only.

Chad liked what he was seeing in this little town. It seemed to him this was a town time had forgotten, and that was very appealing after ten years in Southern California. He was only thirty two, but the last ten years of his life had been 18 hour workdays and the only social life was business related. Someone always wanted something from him. All he wanted was a chance to live life. One day he looked at his partner and said, "Buy me out." The partner said, "How much?" Their company had a proprietary value of over fifty million. So when Chad said, "Ten million," his partner yelled, "Sold." And just like that Chad was unemployed.

They went back to Ruth's office and signed the papers. Chad had a cashier's check for the full amount and in less than an hour he owned the house. Chad said, "I'm not flying back to California until Sunday afternoon and will move in at the end of next week. I've got everything packed and in storage."

Ruth thought that was fast, but Chad told her, "It will take a while to slow down from my California pace. We do things fast out there."

Ruth said, "I can show you around more. My afternoon is free." Chad wanted to explore by himself. Just drive around and see where it took him. Plus, he had the keys, so he wanted to go back to the house and poke around a little and he couldn't really do those things with Ruth.

Chad said, "Do you know where I can rent a vehicle?"

Ruth laughed, "Not on the weekend. You can rent a car from the Chevy dealership, but they closed at noon. I've got my car and my husband has a little Ranger pickup."

Chad quickly said, "If he doesn't mind I'll take the Ranger." He didn't want to hurt Ruth's feelings, but he didn't want to be seen driving her Lincoln around town.

After exploring the house he made notes of some renovations that the house needed, but overall he thought the house was liveable considering. It was big enough he could move in and take his time renovating. He went exploring. Ruth had already shown him most of the town's amenities, which didn't take long, but as Paul Smith would say, "Why would anyone ever want to leave Washington County?" Chad's needs were few, he loved to cook, and for a while, at least, he wanted to be a homebody. The biggest decision he wanted to make was what to have for breakfast.

Ruth had taken him north on High Street pointing out the homes of the town's important people whose names he'd already forgotten. There were two newer subdivisions on the outskirts of town she'd shown him. One was a little more upscale than the other. The homes were a little bigger and newer. He wouldn't have time to explore the tiny villages that abounded throughout the county. Some had been thriving at one time, but now the only way to recognize most was by the small country church. Most of those churches closed years ago from a dwindling population and difficulty finding a preacher. He headed down toward Angie's by the railroad tracks and crossed the tracks into a whole new world. Ruth hadn't taken him into this area.

As he slowly drove through the Oaks in the little Ranger pickup, you'd have sworn it was old Bill in his Dodge driving up High Street at 8:00 a.m. in the morning. He was going about ten mph and his head just swiveled from side to side. He couldn't believe what he was seeing. He knew people lived in squalor in the city and he'd lived in a ghetto as a child, but in the country. He felt a little guilty about having a ten thousand square foot home all to himself, but he'd worked very hard for it. Sacrificed ten years of his life—ten years he could never get back. As he continued to drive, he got himself turned around and twisted inside out. The more he drove the more confused he became. Finally, he saw a young woman walking toward him and if he was ever to get back to town he'd have to ask for directions.

Chad pulled up beside her and after fiddling around trying to find the electric window button, without success, he rolled down the hand-cranked window. "Hi, this is embarrassing, but I'm lost. Can you tell me how to get back to the Cozy Up Inn?" He couldn't help but notice her. She was trim and took care of herself, but you could tell by her dress she probably lived in this area. She was beyond attractive, in fact, you might even say lovely. Chad thought she didn't need any of that makeup she wore. All it did was hide her good looks. Too bad. But there was something about her. And he had this Eliza Doolittle fantasy.

Charlotte just laughed, and he noticed her eyes light up and her teeth were naturally perfect as was her smile. "Happens all the time to people who don't know their way around the Oaks." She told him how to get back out and he thanked her and drove off. Charlotte stood there thinking, "That's the most beautiful man I've ever seen. Why couldn't I find someone like that?" She didn't know who he was, he was just some guy driving an old pickup truck who got lost.

CHAPTER 14

Sunday, June 3, 1992. At ten to ten Reagan stepped through the side door onto the platform. He placed his notes on the lectern and sat in the pastor's pulpit chair. He hated that great big thing that seemed more like a throne, but they expected him to sit in it. He surveyed the congregation as he did each week, but he noticed that Sunday, June 3rd, wasn't a typical June Sunday. The church wasn't packed, but it was probably a record attendance for June. He noticed several people he hadn't seen since Easter and didn't expect to see until Christmas and realized that couldn't be good. Realizing who they were and why they were there, it clicked. The Katie Pierce vs. Micah Barnes case, but he still couldn't understand what that had to do with him. He was guessing he'd find out soon enough. Judge Chadwick and his wife were front and center as always. Reagan noticed the peaceful expression on the judge's face this morning. Adam and Maddie were in their usual seats, but no Katie. Reagan figured that somehow Maddie was responsible for this great June turnout. If the offering was good, he'd have to thank her. Emma Reynolds sat near the Judge and his wife, but no sign of Tinker, but then it was only June and elections were five months away. Billy kept his promise. They were in the same seats as last week. Hopefully, a good sign. He paused for a quick prayer for them. All the regulars seemed to be in the right seat except Charlotte. He looked around and finally found her in the last pew nearest the door. Micah was sitting with her. He wasn't ready for this. Reagan quickly rewrote, in his mind, everything he had on paper. This fire needed to be put out before a single spark could fly. Just as the organist was finishing up a number he'd like to forget, a stranger walked in. The church had little old ladies who passed out bulletins, and occasionally greeters on 'more important' Sunday's. Nobody saw a need for ushers. They never expected new people and if you came in late, there were plenty of seats. Just pick one and sit. Chad Houston stood there for a few moments deciding what to do. He finally decided a seat near the door would be the least disruptive. He took a seat in the pew opposite Charlotte Barnes.

He sat down and noticed Charlotte. He smiled at her, but then noticed she was with another man. But that didn't stop her from smiling back at him with an I remember you look. Chad really had no idea she was trying to flirt with him as he turned towards the front of the church.

Reagan began worship with a passage on Christians caring for each other that led to prayer time. The usuals asked for prayer for the same things, but things got awkward when it was time to recognize Charlotte. Bless her heart, Charlotte was an excited baby Christian who truly believed that people in the church cared for each other. If only. She spoke, and it was an extension of last week's request. She stood and introduced Micah and asked the congregation to pray for guidance for her and her brother and that God would help Micah's lawyer to defend him because he was innocent. Reagan looked at the faces looking at him and knew that just would not happen church-wide. Transforming an old mainline church into an evangelical church is never easy. On the plus side, three years ago they'd have never let Charlotte into Community Church and if they had, she'd be gone by now. And Billy Maddox could never have entered in anything but a wooden box.

Reagan Lamb stepped down from the platform onto the main floor and stood front and center. And with that move, he symbolically gave up his position of power. His expression said it all. He knew he was about to take a huge risk, but he had to do it. He stood there and slowly gazed over the congregation. He moved his eyes around looking at each person as several minutes passed. It was getting uncomfortable for some. As he looked at some members, they averted his gaze. Others engaged him until he moved on to the next person.

When he had finished he said, "Last week I stood in the pulpit," he pointed, "and shared with you my life unworthy of ever receiving the grace of God. And yet, in his love for me, God sent his son to shed his blood and die on a cross, for me! Because he rose from the dead, I can have eternal life. It's mine for the taking. The Bible says, 'to as many as received him he gave them the right to become the children of God.' That was and still is the most exciting news I've ever heard."

Reagan knelt down and everyone could see his arm moving, but only a few could see his finger move on the carpet. He continued to act out the Parable of the Woman Caught in Adultery. Because of the slanted floor of the Akron style sanctuary as he lifted his eyes he could see everyone and everything. They watched him, some understanding what he was doing. Then he stood up and spoke. "The religious leaders brought a woman before Jesus. They said they caught her in the act of adultery. Jesus knelt and wrote something in the dirt. We don't know what he wrote, but apparently they did. He stood and said to them, as I now say to you, let anyone here who is without sin cast the first stone. This is your opportunity to speak your mind." There was dead silence. No one moved a muscle. "Then let us join our hearts in prayer." Reagan prayed all the usual requests before turning to the real business at hand.

"Father, Adam and Maddie Pierce have so much pain in their hearts and Katie, a child you love so dearly, is hurting more than we can imagine. They need your help, Father. Listen and look into their hearts as they seek your guidance. Let them feel your presence and reveal to them how much you love them and care about them."

As he continued praying, strange things happened and none of them were good. Maddie was suddenly feeling self-satisfied as were her Christmas/Easter church member friends. The pastor had finally seen the light. In the back, Charlotte wept as she felt betrayed by Reagan Lamb. And Micah thought, "What was all this pious talk about believing in me? These people only care about their own." Charlotte took Micah's hand and slid toward the aisle.

Chad noticed the movement, stood up, moved across the aisle and sat next to Charlotte. The Southern California lifestyle had tried to swallow Chad, but he had not succumbed to it. He gave God all the glory for his riches and his success. He knew that apart from Christ he could do nothing. Through his relationship with Christ, he had remained humble. He did not understand what was going on in this church; the dynamics involved or even who the players were. But, one thing he knew for sure. He knew all about taking big risks with faith in God and he could tell the pastor was taking a risk and betting on the power of God. He also sensed the pastor wouldn't turn his back on this girl and her brother.

He blocked her exit by sitting down next to her. He whispered, "Pretty lady, yesterday you helped me. It's my turn to help you. Please don't leave. Let this play out. You've got to trust the pastor. God has revealed what he's doing. He's betting his ministry on you right now." He gently took hold of her hand as she continued to weep, but she sat and listened.

Reagan was still praying, she had missed some, but her ears pricked up when she heard, "Father I lift up to your care dear, sweet, Charlotte... your baby girl in Christ. So young and trusting. Put your arms around her and hold her close. She needs to know what a powerful force you are in her life. And we lift up Micah who needs to come to you and join the kingdom as your child and a brother in Christ. Open his heart Father to receive what you have for him. And yes, Father, we pray for wisdom for his attorney to seek your will and guidance in all things.

"Now I pray for help for each one present to open their hearts and minds. Help them to see and understand why they feel the way they do right now. Force us to know in our own hearts, to admit with our minds, as a congregation, that there are only three people who know the truth and Father, you are one of them. Father, they may resolve this in a court of law and if so you already know there will be no winners. We beg you to take control of this situation, resolve it, be glorified and most of all bind all of our hearts in Christ."

Reagan finished, "If you stand with me in this prayer for love, unity, understanding, and will trust God, I invited you to join me, on your knees, at the front, before our holy God. I love each one of you equally and if you don't, that's okay. It's between you and God. He's the only one that knows our hearts and he's the only one who can judge. I will not preach today. I now dismiss you and may God be with you."

Nobody knew quite what to do. For many, their personal faith was still a private thing. But all eyes went to the front as the first person to rise and move to the front, was the least expected. Judge Lloyd Chadwick got down on his knees and took Reagan's hand as Reagan silently whispered, "Thank you, Jesus." The congregation was surprised, and Maddie was shocked, as Adam rose from his seat and went to the left of Reagan. Charlotte looked at Chad Houston, who was still a stranger, and whispered, "Should I?"

Chad answered, "Is God pulling you out of your seat?" She rose but looked like a scared, cowering puppy. Chad rose, took her hand and led her forward as she knelt next to Adam Pierce who, at first hesitated, and then took her hand and gently squeezed it. People rose. Some to leave and some to go forward.

After about 30 minutes of prayer and times of silence, Reagan said, "Amen." Everyone left to start a new week, but now about fifty people had a bond that tied them together, but there was one family being torn apart. Maddie was furious with Adam. How could he betray his own blood? Hopefully, Katie wouldn't find out.

Outside Chad said to Charlotte and Micah, "We weren't formally introduced. I'm Chad Houston and I'm new in town. Would both of you join me for lunch?" They kind of looked at each other.

Micah shrugged as Charlotte said, "Yes."

Chad said, "The only three places I know are the Burger Barn, Angie's Cafe, and the Mine Shaft. Your call." When you're from the Oaks, it's kind of understood there are places you really aren't welcome. The Mine Shaft was an expensive restaurant with linen tablecloths and napkins and only ten tables. It was a restaurant that seemed out of place in Glencoe. It was near the courthouse and only professionals went there. It was more like a private dinner club, but without the paid membership. Neither Charlotte nor Micah, nor anyone from the Oaks, had ever been there, could afford to go there, or could get past the maitre d' to the dining room. They kept the prices intentionally high to keep people from the Oaks and other riffraff out. Until today it had worked. Charlotte was glad the baby had stayed overnight at a friend's house. Otherwise the Burger Barn would be the restaurant of choice. Chad asked where they were parked and they said they had walked to church. "Well, let's pile in the Ranger and go eat lunch."

When they walked through the door, the people waiting to be seated turned and stared. It didn't bother Chad much. It was to be expected. He was a stranger and in Southern California a minor celebrity, so he was used to stares, pointing and comments. No one in the restaurant knew who he was. They had no idea that compared to Chad Houston they were peons. The best way to describe these folks was big fish in a small pond. They didn't realize a fish bigger than the one that swallowed Jonah had just walked in. But, the stares were aimed at Charlotte and Micah who didn't fit in and she felt it immediately. This was a bad choice and now the consequence... humiliation. Charlotte's dress was nice enough, but it was off the rack at the Economy Store on High Street. Some were sure it was off the rack long before it was hers. Micah held his head high even though he knew people recognized him as the rape suspect in the case of Katie Pierce. The mumbling in the dining room quieted down as the maitre d' pulled Chad aside and asked, "Sir, are you sure you and your party are in the right place? The Mine Shaft is quite exclusive."

Chad said, "Quite exclusive you say? Then, yes, I am in the right place." Chad moved in a little closer and lowered his voice. "And you, sir, are causing a scene and embarrassing my guests. You have no clue who I am, but I assure you I am someone with a lot of money and an excellent memory."

This was very unlike Chad, but this egotistical elitist and the haughty patrons had pushed him to his limit.

"Now, I would like to be seated and you will treat the lady like a princess and the young man with respect. Do I make myself perfectly clear or do I buy the restaurant next week and fire you?"

"No sir, I believe we have arrived at an understanding."

"Good. We are hungry. Put on a big smile and show us to our table."

The side stares continued as they realized Chad Houston and party were suddenly getting the royal treatment and wondered what he had said to the maitre d'.

With people staring, Charlotte was feeling uncomfortable and whispered to Chad, "This place looks really expensive. I'm sorry I had no idea. I'm sorry, we can leave. The menu doesn't even have prices on it."

His menu did, and yes, it was really expensive. Chad had known this woman for less than two hours and she was unlike anyone he'd ever met. Every woman for the last ten years wanted Chad Houston for what they could get. And here was a woman who would be just as happy with a cheeseburger at the Burger Barn as dining in an exclusive restaurant.

Chad smiled at the comment. "No problem. I asked where you wanted to go and here we are. And, it appears to be an excellent choice, so enjoy."

Charlotte turned the conversation to him. He told her he was from California but grew up outside St. Louis. He said he worked with computers and he wanted to slow down and enjoy life. So he bought a house in Glencoe. When she asked why Glencoe, he said he got a great deal and it seemed like a nice town. He then turned the conversation to her and Micah.

She said, "To be honest, many people here probably know who I am. I'm a Barnes , which means nothing to you now, but it will. Micah and I come from a poor family and all the baggage that goes with it. Up to a year ago, I worked the welfare system for every penny and free thing I could get, as I was taught. I went to Pastor Reagan for a hand out one day and my life changed. Chad, I have an eighteen-month-old baby girl and I don't know where the daddy is. I'm still stuck at home, still on welfare, but now I'm trying to give back. It's hard to get out and our Pa makes it even tougher. Micah had a chance until he hurt his knee playing football his senior year. He would have received a scholarship to college, but the knee finished everything. His grades were good enough to get into college, but not good enough for student aid and well, that was another dream crushed. He was working at the sawmill and was dating Katie Pierce which everyone said don't do, but he did. When Micah saw her with another guy at the Lazy Daisy, he lost it and assaulted both of them. Not really bad, but it was a dumb thing to do. Katie's dad owns the hardware store. He felt sorry for Micah and wanted to drop the charges. That's when out of the blue she yells rape. Now you have a summary of the Barnes family saga. Ready to get up and walk out?"

Chad said, "Nah, not yet, but I have to go back to California today and I'll be back next Friday. You can tell me more and then maybe I'll run."

They served the food. It was the usual fare for Chad, but dying and going to heaven good for Charlotte and Micah.

CHAPTER 15

*T*uesday, June 5, 1992. It was Tuesday morning and the gossip at the Greasy Spoon was still fast and furious and Chad Houston was the new subject. Into the middle of it walked Reagan Lamb for his morning breakfast. Since Chad had been in church, he was sure he'd be a subject of interest. The old men of Glencoe never disappoint.

"Mornin', Preacher. Tell us about Chad Houston who bought the old Benson place." Direct, to the point and all before he even sat down.

Reagan was determined to end this quickly. "I can tell you two things. First, he was in church, but all of you knew that. Second, he's a Christian and he will be an asset to the community and any church he attends."

He turned and bowed in each direction. "I'm sorry gents, and lady, that's all I got."

He sat down and said, "I'll have the usual, Gertie." He listened while keeping his attention on a copy of USA Today. Some conversations were amusing as usual. Poor Chad, did he realize what he was getting into?

After his walk up High Street and back, he got into Molly and headed out to the airport. He drove past three churches on the way out. One thing about Glencoe was there was no shortage of churches, seven in all. There were all the religious flavors you could want. He drove out High Street, and at some point, it turned into Airport Road. He figured it was at the big ninety-degree curve just past Shirley Comstock's house. When you got this far you no longer saw any Victorian homes. These were older but much newer than most homes on High Street. If you continued straight, you went into one of the two subdivisions. He headed toward the airport and past the Washington County Fairgrounds that for eleven months of the year looked abandoned. At the end of August, it came to life with a month of sulky horse racing, and the fair that lasted twelve days. Reagan could almost smell the carnival food as he drove by. This was the one place and the one time of year the whole county gathered at one spot. Rich and poor, young and old, they were all there.

Reagan swung into the airport parking lot and tried to envision the big new international airport, but try as he might, the vision would not come and he laughed. He saw Ron out by a sign that said, 'Runway #1' and laughed again. There was only one runway. He waved and Ron moved toward him. It was a little warm standing on the asphalt and Ron suggested they move into the terminal. The main terminal was a twenty by twenty room that was also Ron's office.

As they sat Reagan said, "Ron, I have a huge favor to ask." As soon as the name Billy Maddox came out of his mouth, Ron stiffened in his chair. Reagan continued, "Hear me out, Ron. I'd like you to keep Billy on. You can tell him he's on a week to week probation or whatever. If it doesn't work, fire him. I've been working with Billy and Heather for a week and a half and I've seen some real progress. Last night Billy went to AA and to be honest I haven't talked with him yet, but they are coming in this morning. They've been in church for the last two weeks. And there are other things I can't share. There was a time, not that long ago, that Billy was okay. You know, you hired him. Never real likable, but okay. Ron, I may eat my words, you never know, but I've got a good feeling about Billy."

Ron just shook his head before speaking, "Preacher, you're putting me in a tough position here. We all know what the guy is. We all know what he's done. You don't keep people like that."

"Look, Ron, we know what he is, but do we know what he can become?" Long pause.

"Okay, I'll keep him on day to day for a month. It's a favor to you. If I see the changes, then I'll reconsider hiring him back full time."

Reagan said, "That's all I can ask for. Thanks."

Reagan headed back to the church. He would be a few minutes late and hoped they'd wait. Hoped they'd wait? He just hoped they'd show up! He rounded the corner into the parking lot and squealed the tires. There was Billy's "classic muscle car."

Earlier that morning, Reagan brought in donuts and put them on a tray in the kitchen. He went to the coffee cabinet and removed all the coffee and put it in a place Becky would never find it. He was a few minutes late as he flew through the door. Becky had seated them in his office and was ready for some really juicy stuff to share. He paused just long enough to say, "Becky, there are donuts on a tray in the kitchen. Please make coffee and then bring everything in. Thanks." He entered the office and greeted Billy and Heather then turned and closed the door.

Becky said, "Oh. Phooey!" and walked to the kitchen. When she opened the coffee cabinet she muttered aloud, "Who was the dang fool who forgot to replace the coffee?" She was sure there was plenty the last time she'd looked, so where'd it go? She went to Reagan's office door and knocked. Reagan said, "Enter."

She said, "Pastor Lamb, there is no coffee in the kitchen."

Reagan said, "Becky be a dear, and go to the IGA and put it on the church bill." Yep, in Glencoe you could still have an open account with the grocery store. "Oh, and before you go, just bring in the donuts. I feel a cream filled craving coming on."

Becky brought the donuts, closed the door and left. Reagan

brought out the bag he'd brought in—three cups of hot coffee. "See, coffee and donuts, just as I promised." He laughed as he added, "And no Becky for about thirty minutes."

Reagan wanted to start with Billy. He wanted to know about the AA meeting, but Heather needed to talk with someone besides Billy. So he asked, "Tell me about your visit."

Heather said, "It was good, but it hurt real bad. To see my babies and not be able to take them home, really hurt. When we got home, I cried for hours. They tell me if I stay with Billy, it will be six months before I can get my kids because they got to watch Billy. I love Billy and I love my kids. They want to make me choose between them and that's not right. Jake kept saying, "Mommy I want to go home with you now." And it broke my heart to say he couldn't. Sadie's a little trooper. Don't think she fully understands why it'll be six months and that's probably good. I found out about the foster mom and she's good to them. So I know they're in good care. Patricia will call to set up another supervised visit this week. If all goes well, in three months we can have supervised outings. So, overall I'm sad, but if after six months we can be a real family like I always dreamed of, then it'll be worth it."

Regan asked Billy, "Sounds like a lot is resting on your shoulders. How does that make you feel?"

"Pastor, I think it's obvious that she's a dang fool to stay with me when she could have her kids now. I don't know if I could do that. But you know, Heather is the only person in my life that has ever loved me. And she loves me enough to think I can change. Yeah, that's a lot of pressure. I've never been good at making the right decisions, so I ask myself what Billy would do and then do the opposite. Like cleaning up the trash outside the house. I asked myself would Billy do that and the answer was no, so I did it. I asked myself, would Billy go to church? Of course, he wouldn't, so I did. Heather thinks I can change, and she's betting her children on it. Yeah, lots of pressure, but I'm gonna try not to disappoint her."

"Billy, did you go to AA last night?"

"Pastor, I said I would, and I did. It was definitely uncomfortable. You were right, I saw a couple people I know. There was one I didn't expect to see. Never dreamed he was an alcoholic. You'd never know to look at him."

Reagan saw the opening he needed, "That's the thing Billy, you can't always tell by looking. You can usually recognize a drunk, but it's not so easy to spot an alcoholic. It's a disease like diabetes. You can't see diabetes and you won't know who has it unless they tell you they have it. And like alcoholism there are degrees, but you still have it."

"What about the guys at the Dew Drop Inn? What are they?"

Reagan responded, "I suspect some are alcoholics and some are just drunks. Hard to tell. You have to decide for yourself what you are."

Billy paused, "I guess. Each guy that spoke gave his name and then said, I'm an alcoholic."

Reagan took the next cue, "That's it exactly. The first step to recovery is to admit it. I could tell you you're an alcoholic, but until you say it, you won't believe it. When's the next meeting? You going back?"

Billy said, "Yeah, there's one Wednesday night over in Upton. One guy offered to pick me up and take me."

Reagan, "Okay. Are you going or not? Simple question, yes or no."

Billy smiled, "Yeah pastor, I'm going. Heather already knows that. I don't think I've got a problem like some of them, but I'll give AA a chance."

Reagan said, "Great, then I've got some good news for you. I talked to Ron this morning. You need to go see him. He said he'd give you a second chance. If he sees the changes in thirty days, you'll get your job back with benefits."

Billy got a big smile and said, "That's a big relief. I don't know that anyone else in town would hire me."

Just then they heard the door. Reagan threw the coffee cups in the trash and opened the door. "I want to thank both of you for coming in. We'll meet in a couple weeks." He looked at Becky and said,

"Thanks, just put the coffee in the cabinet." He went back into his study and closed the door, with a big grin on his face. Everyone would have to depend on the Lighthouse for another week. Becky's News Service was temporarily closed.

CHAPTER 16

*W*ednesday, June 6, 1992. Charlotte put the baby in the carriage and walked to town. She needed a few things at the Five and Dime and maybe browse in the Economy Store for a new top to wear for Chad when he returned to town in just a few days. Outside the dime store, she met Betsy Winston who waited tables at Angie's. Betsy and she grew up together in the Oaks. They went to school together until Betsy dropped out the fall of her senior year thus guaranteeing her a life in the Oaks. Charlotte was determined to graduate even though her father kept telling her she'd never amount to anything, so she should drop out and get a job like Betsy did. Why waste that time learning stuff you'll never use, when you could make some good money. Yeah, $1.25 an hour plus tips at Angie's.

Charlotte hung in there and graduated and kept on Micah to do the same thing. She was three years older than Micah. When she graduated, she had no money, no car, and no way out. They had accepted her at the community college, but again no money and no car and a father who was dead set against her foolish notions. So, she got a cashier's job at the Pump 'N Go gas station at $3.25 an hour. That's where she met Bobby Gene Guthrie. He was home from Appalachian

State for the summer and she was infatuated that a college boy would take a liking to her. She was twenty one and even though she lived at home, she was no longer under Paul's control and came and went as she pleased. She went off to Cedar Point with Bobby Gene for a weekend and came back pregnant. Seems Bobby Gene didn't go to Appalachian State after all and he disappeared somewhere out west. Sara Anne was born nine months later and Charlotte became fourth generation welfare in Washington County.

She hadn't seen Betsy in a few weeks. Considering how close they had been for years, they didn't spend much time together anymore. Betsy was resigned to her lot in life, but Charlotte had yet to give up her dream of escaping the Oaks. They chit-chatted then Betsy brought up Chad Houston.

"It was during my shift he and Ruth Gordon came into Angie's and I waited on him. Oh, he is gorgeous," she said, "Oh you should see him. And he's loaded!" Charlotte agreed with the first part but ignored the second. To Betsy, anyone who could pay all their bills each month was loaded.

Charlotte replied a little smugly, "Yes, I met him. We sat together in church on Sunday and he took me out for lunch at the Mine Shaft. He'll be moving into his new house this week. I'll be seeing him this weekend."

Betsy knew an Oakie came from across the tracks, but apparently, Charlotte didn't remember that. "Why would you bother to have lunch with him? People like us don't stand a chance with Chad Houston. If he goes out with you it'll be for what he can get, Charlotte. You're not in his class. You have nothing in common with him. No way you're good enough for him and you should know that by now."

Charlotte couldn't believe what she heard Betsy saying. "He's a nice guy. He's down to earth. He bought a house here. He's not what you're implying."

Betsy asked, "Do you even know what house he bought?" Charlotte shook her head no. "He bought the Benson mansion on Broad Street. Still think he's just a regular guy?"

Charlotte didn't know what to think. He never said much about himself and yet she had told him almost everything about her. Maybe he wasn't lost. Maybe he was just trying to pick up a tramp from the Oaks. Wine her and dine her then take her to bed. This one should be easy. On welfare, an illegitimate baby, and needs money. How could she not see it? Why would she think he could be interested in her? She turned and walked away from Betsy and pushed the carriage toward the Oaks—the place she really belonged. No need for a new blouse. How foolish had she been to think Chad Houston could be interested in her.

Wednesday night was often a buzz of activity at the church. Choir practice, youth group for juniors, Guild meeting on the first Wednesday and Elders and Deacons both met the first Wednesday. Two of the Elders, both friends of Adam and Maddie Pierce, arrived early and said to Reagan, "We need to talk." They went into the office and Reagan took the seat of power behind the desk. Larry Pitts spoke first, "Pastor, there's been a lot of changes around here in the last three years. We've given you free rein. But a lot of us don't like the direction the church is going and that stunt you pulled last Sunday was the final straw."

Alex Dyson took over, "Preacher, this is a family church going back two and three generations and for some of us even four generations. We take care of our own and not the riff-raff you bring in from the Oaks. We're the ones that pay your salary, not them. We expect you to support Katie and her family and the upstanding people of the church. If you don't, then we will see that you are gone in a month."

Reagan looked at them and said, "Gentlemen, I can't believe the words I heard come out of your mouths. You call yourselves Elders of the Church of Jesus Christ. What kind of God do you serve? I'm in a tough situation that apparently, you can't comprehend. I can love all the people in this church and not just a few special people who are my friends. I will not play your silly childish game of 'if you like them, then you can't be my friend.' Now, if you are standing here, representing the Board of Elders of Glencoe Community Church, then bring charges against me. If you are standing here representing the friends of Maddie Pierce, then kindly leave my office now! You may have friends in high places, but I have a friend in higher places."

Reagan figured it was just a bullying effort and nothing would come of it. But if it did, he had the votes, and he had the lead Elder, Judge Lloyd Chadwick. This little confrontation didn't do much to enhance his mood after another long day. He didn't need to attend anything going on tonight and after the ambush by Larry and Alex, it might be a good idea to go home.

He was walking by the kitchen and the Ladies' Guild was doing something in the kitchen. He heard Shirley Comstock's voice, "I don't think I'll live much longer. Everyone in my family died in their sixties."

Reagan, who would really love to see Shirley change churches, stuck his head in the door, "Shirley, you aren't ever going to die," He waited for the facial response and added, "because God doesn't want you and the devil won't take you." He turned and walked away knowing he shouldn't have said that, but not caring. Then he heard laughter from the kitchen and recognized the loudest was coming from Shirley.

-~~~~~

Reagan pulled into the yard and said aloud, "Oh great, this day just gets better and better." Sitting in the drive was a minivan with Pennsylvania tags. He knew Gino and Rosa Rozelli were coming, but thought it was next Wednesday, not today. Mentally, he wasn't prepared for their visit. He sat there for a few minutes praying and trying to gather himself and mentally preparing for the next few days. Reagan had understood that when you marry an Italian girl, you marry her whole family. What he didn't understand was what that really meant. He'd been married to Prudy for about four years and saw his in-laws only twice a year. He was still an outsider and when they wanted his opinion, they'd ask for it. They never did. With his WASP background, he felt tolerated, but not included. He was glad he wasn't here when they arrived. It would have been all about Prudy, the baby, and "Oh, are *you* here?"

He entered the house, took a deep breath, and walked to the living room. No Prudy, but there sat Gino and Rosa. Before he sat or even could say hello, Rosa said, "So you're finally giving me a grandbaby. Do you think you can support a family on what you get paid?"

Rosa didn't know what his salary was or anything else about their finances and Reagan wanted to say, as the opening words, "It is none of your business what I make or whether we can afford to have a child."

Saved. Prudy entered and said, "Mama, we've already discussed that and I told you it is our business. So let's move on."

Probably not her best choice of words. To Rosa, moving on meant let me find something else you're doing wrong. It didn't take long.

Prudy put the lasagna in the oven as Rosa watched, but not for long. "You're cooking that at 350? It cooks better at 375, you know. Did you put a little oregano in the ricotta? That's my secret ingredient."

And so it began, just as Reagan knew it would. It would be a long five days and he knew Prudy needed him for support. He didn't want to, but he'd take as much time off as he could. He stood with Rosa between them... her back toward him, and held his hands up in prayer. He smiled at her. Gino sat there and never uttered a word. He was pretty much silent for five days. On the third day Reagan asked, "Papa, how do you stand not being able to express your opinion or get a word in?"

Gino said, "I snore all night. Very loud. That's how God lets me get even."

They laughed as Rosa yelled, "Gino what's so funny?"

Reagan replied, "Nothing mama. Papa just told a joke."

CHAPTER 17

*F*riday, June 15, 1992. Chad Houston had moved in on June 5th to a practically empty house. He had made arrangements with the local furniture store to deliver a king-size bed frame, mattress, and box spring. He also bought an inexpensive bureau, a nightstand and a lamp he would replace when he got into town. That was it. He figured he'd eat out for a few days...probably not at The Mine Shaft, doubtful he'd ever go back there. And with no TV, he'd catch up on some reading he'd been putting off. Definitely no phone for at least a month.

On Sunday he went to church, eager to see Charlotte and ended up disappointed when she wasn't there. Throughout the service he kept glancing to the back hoping she was just late. Reagan gave the benediction and still no Charlotte. Chad went out the back and shook hands with Reagan and asked about Charlotte. Reagan said it surprised him, said she seldom missed and suggested that maybe Sara was sick.

Chad took his rental Tahoe for a ride out to the Oaks to see if he could find Charlotte. Reagan had given him directions, and she lived only two houses from where he met her the first time. He pulled up to the gate and his better judgment kicked in.

Greeting him at the closed gate were two Rottweilers and there was seventy-five to one hundred feet between him, the Rottweilers and the trailer. He'd run track in college, but he'd never raced a Rottweiler. With all the racket they made, he knew that if Charlotte was in the trailer she'd be looking out. He stood in front of the gate for a few minutes just staring at the front door. But she never came out. He got back into the Tahoe and drove home. He wondered, all the way back into town, "What did I do wrong?"

Charlotte stood at the window, with Sara in her arms, and watched as he pulled away. She wanted so much to open the door and run to the gate, but she didn't realize how destructive pride can be. Her pride kept her from confronting him and saying, "Mr. Houston, exactly what are your intentions?" On the one hand, she'd never know what those intentions might be without asking. And on the other hand, she knew that a wealthy guy, who could afford the Benson mansion, couldn't have any interest in a girl from the Oaks on welfare with an illegitimate child. It was for the best. She held her baby close and said, "Sara, we'll be just fine. Yes, it's for the best. It would never have worked." She cried.

On Monday, Chad went to Berg Brothers Funeral Home to buy furniture. In many parts of Pennsylvania and Ohio, the funeral home also operated a furniture store. The practice went back several generations to pioneering days when farmers had plenty of food, but very little money. When a family member passed, they would pay for the funeral with furniture. They put this used furniture up for sale and as it piled up, the funeral home would open a used furniture store, usually next door to the funeral home. So, when Chad arrived at Berg Brothers he had the option of door #1 into the funeral home or door #2 into the furniture store. This would be the biggest sale in the history of Berg Brothers Funeral Home and Furniture Store. They had a great selection for a small town and Chad needed to furnish 10 rooms. He didn't worry about the furnishings being period correct. He was ready for comfort.

~

Two or three times each week, for the next two months, Chad would drive to the Oaks in search of Charlotte. It was like she'd disappeared off the face of the earth. Each time always with the same results. He'd stand by the gate, dogs would bark, and he would leave—broken-hearted. He talked to people who had seen her, but no one knew anything.

One day he saw her entering the bank. He had to drive a couple blocks to make a U-turn. When he got back, he had to wait as a semi blocked his turn into the parking lot. He parked, jumped out of the car, and ran into the bank. No Charlotte. He ran back outside and looked each way. No Charlotte.

On another occasion, he saw her enter and close the gate at the Paul Barnes compound. He got to the gate in time to see her open the door and go in. She never looked back. Chad sat there and wept. If he knew why she wouldn't see him, he could handle that. Not knowing why was tearing him apart.

He prayed. "Father, you gave your son to save me. Everything I have I owe to you. You led me to this town. Then you guided me here to this location. Of the seven churches in town, you led me to her church. I sat there in worship and I heard you speak to me. You told me she is to be my wife. Lord, I refuse to give up. I will pursue her like the hound of heaven. Oh, Lord soften her heart enough for her to see how much I love her." He started the engine and drove off.

He made two more trips and still no Charlotte. The next Friday, the front door finally opened and Chad's heart pounded wildly. Finally, she was coming out. But, again the result was not what Chad had hoped for. There he stood, at 5' 10" and 170 pounds. Emerging from the house was an angry 300 pound Paul Barnes. And if it could get any worse, he was holding his 30-6 at a downward angle as he walked toward Chad.

"Boy, how clear does it have to be for you to understand my girl don't wanna see you ever again? You come sniffin' around here again and I'll show you the way we settle things." Lifting the gun a little higher toward Chad he finished, "Am I clear?" He turned and walked back to the trailer, closed the door and again Chad was all alone. He couldn't understand what had just happened, but he would not wait around to discuss it. It had been over ten years since Chad Houston hadn't been able to have what he wanted. And he wanted Charlotte more than anything he'd ever wanted in his life.

CHAPTER 18

ABOUT TWO MONTHS LATER

riday, August 23, 1992. At 9:30, three Sheriff's cruisers came to a stop at the gate of Paul Barnes' fenced-in compound. Immediately the Rottweilers ran to the gate, teeth bared and growling. The deputies got out of their cars and one raised a bull-horn. "Paul Barnes, you are under arrest. Come out with your hands where we can see them."

They waited and nothing happened. The dogs kept barking. They called him out again and still nothing. One of the deputies returned to his car and came back with a gun, aimed it at one of the Rottweilers and pulled the trigger. The dog leaped at the fence and then went down as the tranquilizer took effect. He turned to the second one and did the same thing. They opened the gate and didn't have to wait long for a riled up Paul Barnes.

He came flying out of the trailer as fast as a three hundred pound man can and ran straight at the deputies screaming, "What did you do to my dogs? You got no right to come on my property less'en I open that gate." He charged the deputy holding the tranquilizer gun as he felt a dart go into his thigh. It took a while as Paul kept flailing away. The deputies just bobbed and weaved waiting for the tranquilizer to take effect. It finally slowed him down enough for them to cuff him and get him in the cruiser. They cautiously dragged the dogs to the makeshift kennel next to the trailer. The two cruisers left with Paul Barnes in the back of the first. They called ahead for assistance when they arrived at the jail.

The youngest deputy, Vaughan Johnson, stayed behind. He had been chasing after Charlotte since he graduated. Fact is, he chased anything wearing a skirt, or slacks, or jeans, or shorts. You get the idea. He was only twenty and had a reputation. Not as a ladies man. It was the reputation of being a very strange person. There had been accusations, but nothing ever proven. He thought the uniform and badge would make him irresistible to women. His daddy was the President of the First National Bank of Glencoe and he pulled some strings and voila, Deputy Vaughan Johnson. Charlotte never showed any interest in him and that made the chase more exciting to him. He had big ears and a beak nose and she kept picturing what Sara would look like if he was the father. He went up and knocked on the door of the trailer. When Charlotte answered she didn't invite him in, nor did he try to invite himself in. She just stood in the middle of the outward swing door and said, "Yes?"

"I'm sure you just saw that we took your daddy away. I wanted to check and make sure you and the baby were okay."

"We'll be just fine. Deputy Johnson, please close the gate on your way out and I'll take care of the dogs. I don't want or need your help because by this time tomorrow, Pa will be back home and he can always tell when I'm lying. I got no place else to go right now, plus I know Pa would never hurt me or Sara unless he thought we betrayed our family. So off you go."

"But, Charlotte, you and Sara can stay with me. I got the room."

"Vaughan, that is not going to happen even if Hell freezes over. As to my Pa, I can tell you right now Micah won't press charges. He won't because he'll be afraid of what he'll do to me or Sara. And Pa will be home by tomorrow night. You wait and see. In fact, I'm so sure that if he's still in jail tomorrow night, I'll go out with you."

Vaughan was excited, but Charlotte knew she was safe. She knew how things work with people in the Oaks, obviously, Vaughan didn't.

He left with a big grin on his face. He was sure he was going to score with Charlotte Barnes.

~

Tinker came back to the hospital about 10:30 and a deputy radioed that Paul Barnes was in custody. He grabbed all the necessary paperwork from the back seat and entered the hospital. Micah was moved out of ICU, and Tinker found him sitting in the chair staring out the third-floor window at the water tower with 'Welcome to the City of Upton' painted on the tank. Tinker could see that Micah was deep in thought as he pulled up a chair next to him.

Tinker said, "Good morning, we have your father in custody and I have the paperwork for you to sign so I can file aggravated assault charges against him. All you need to do is sign where the X's are and you won't have anything to worry about." Micah just glanced over at him and looked back to the water tower.

Then he said, just above a whisper, "I'm not going to sign. You just don't understand and I can't explain it. Just let him go."

Tinker had been facing this for fifty years and could never understand this mentality, but there wasn't any point in trying to reason with the victim. He put the papers back in his briefcase and said, "Okay, it's your call. If you change your mind, let me know."

~

It was opening night at the fair, and Billy and Heather walked along hand in hand. They stopped, and he bought her cotton candy. His arm was out of the cast now and he put it around her waist as they walked. Since June, he hadn't missed a Sunday in church and a lot of people still thought that was just a ruse on Billy's part. He'd eventually slip up and show his true colors. Billy, other than going to AA twice a week, Bible Study and church had become quite a homebody. A lot of people who hadn't seen him in a few months came up to talk to him. These were the people who spent more time at the Dew Drop Inn than they did at their home. Billy hadn't been to the Dew Drop since the second time Brad had paid him a visit. In fact, Billy was a model citizen as people waited for the second shoe to drop. He hadn't missed work and was reinstated with benefits over a month ago. And he had fixed the porch.

Billy brushed off most of these people who were treating him like they were his best and long-lost friends. Heather noticed he wanted nothing to do with them. She was pleased, but nonetheless curious.

She questioned him about it and he said, "I don't know. I don't feel comfortable talking to them. It's like they're people I don't want to be around. Most of them are just drunks and bums. Does that make sense?"

She stopped, swung around right by the tilt-a-whirl, hugged him and said, "It makes more sense than you can imagine. And I love you for saying it." Billy was a little confused. He didn't yet understand what was happening to him. Probably couldn't understand the loss of a craving for alcohol or subtle changes in his mindset. He'd never experienced God working in his life and you'd be hard pressed to convince him that he was being redeemed. Billy wasn't quite there.

Chad was enthralled by the sights and sounds, but sad at being all alone. He hadn't been to an old fashioned country fair in twenty years or more. Everything about it brought back memories—the sights brought back memories of going to his grandma's and the first time they walked through the arches to what seemed like a children's wonderland. The sounds of the carnival barkers and music being piped over the big tinny sounding speakers that was interrupted every two minutes with the announcements of events "beginning in only 10 minutes." The various smells that mixed together only at the fairgrounds. If the wind was just right you'd smell the barns mixed with the aroma of fried everything. The diversity of those attending defied description. If you sat on a bench for the evening, you would witness one of the greatest stage shows ever presented. He walked at a leisurely pace and bobbed and weaved in each direction to avoid running into people and to avoid being run into. The opening night crowd was a sight to behold.

Charlotte had a rough week. She worried about Micah in the hospital, but without a car that's all she could do. She was there when Paul beat him although she never saw it. Actually, she didn't know it had happened until she heard the ambulance siren which was very different from the police car sirens often heard in the Oaks. She ran outside to see Micah lying on the ground unconscious. She looked at her father but didn't dare to say anything. He'd never struck her, but in his present state, who knew? The ambulance driver refused to let her ride with her brother so she was stuck there. She had to wait two days before Paul was out of the house to call the hospital. But they wouldn't give her an update over the phone because she couldn't prove she was a relative. All these things weighed heavy on her mind and she needed a break. Her friend took Sara for the evening, and Charlotte walked two miles to the fair.

Chad was walking behind the grandstands when he saw Charlotte standing in the carnival ride ticket line. He moved into the line behind her and said, "Quite a crowd tonight."

Without realizing who it was or looking back she nodded and said, "Yes, it is."

Chad said, "Pretty lady, if I buy two Ferris Wheel tickets, will you join me?" Only one person had ever addressed her as pretty lady and apparently, he was right behind her. She wanted to run and never look back, but her heart wouldn't let her legs move. "Just give me the time on the ride and then if you want, you can walk away and I'll never bother you again. And you get a free Ferris Wheel ride. For you, it's a win-win. How about it?"

She replied seemingly sure of her pre-decision, "You've got one ride and I'm gone."

He said, "Okay, no pressure here." No words were spoken until the ride started moving.

She finally turned and said, "You lied to me. You said you bought a house."

"Yes, that's what I said, so what's the problem?"

"Chad, it's not a house, it's a mansion."

"Look, it's not really a mansion. It's just a really big house. But I still don't see the problem."

"The problem is we come from two different worlds. You knew that, but I didn't. You've made a fool out of me. A laughingstock. People are laughing at that girl from the Oaks who thinks she was good enough for the wealthiest man in town. Everybody, but me, knew you were rich. They told me I was just a diversion until you find the proper Mrs. Houston."

"Charlotte, I'm here on this ride right now because I have found the right Mrs. Houston, but apparently she doesn't know it yet. I knew it the moment I saw you in church. Please have lunch with me at Angie's at noon tomorrow and I'll explain everything. I promise. I will tell you everything about me and answer any questions. Nothing is off limits to you. Absolutely nothing."

The ride was slowing down and Charlotte's heart was speeding up. She had every intention of saying no, but "Yes" came from her lips. She walked away and thought, "We're going to get some answers tomorrow. I'll bring Sara with me. No way he wants a built-in family, especially an illegitimate child."

Chad walked away in the opposite direction. It wasn't the direction he wanted to go, but it seemed like the right thing to do.

CHAPTER 19

Saturday, August 25, 1992. Chad arrived at Angie's at 11:30 and flipped over the sign to read 'Closed'. At 11:45 he saw Charlotte cross the tracks pushing the carriage. He was surprised, but not alarmed. He knew she had a daughter. He couldn't remember if she knew that he knew about Sara. She headed toward the door, and he flipped the sign back over to 'Open'. He sat down at the table and waited. Angie held the door open for her and Sara and when they entered he stood. He walked over and took the carriage to the table as if he'd expected this might happen. She approached the table and Angie flipped the sign back to 'closed'.

She sat down and looked around at the empty restaurant and said, "Everybody must be at the fair?"

Chad said, "No, and I told you I'd be honest with you. I took some of my vast wealth and rented the place for two hours. I wanted to share things that you need to know, but that nobody else needs to know.

"Angie is preparing us a special lunch, and I took the liberty of ordering. Hope that's okay. I didn't know Sara was coming, but she's more than welcome and I'm sure we can find something she'll like."

Charlotte realized that she'd never mentioned Sara's name to him. That was interesting.

"If you'll allow me, I want to talk about three things and you can break in any time. First, when I saw you in church it caused feelings that I've only experienced one or two times in my life. In the last ten years I've dated more women than there are fleas on a junkyard dog. Most, if they stood here now, I couldn't tell you their name. No one aroused any feelings. Not one did I consider to be 'the proper' Mrs. Houston." Charlotte recalled using that phrase. "I sat down in church and looked over and you smiled. I started to smile back, and I saw Micah who I assumed was your husband or boyfriend, but that didn't stop the feelings. When you stated your prayer request I had really mixed emotions. I was immediately sad for you and your brother. I could tell you loved and relied on each other and that was beautiful. I've lost that sibling relationship. But I was also excited because that meant you were single. When I moved over to you and said, 'pretty lady' I saw two things. Yes, I think you are one of the most stunningly attractive women I've ever seen. But more important to me, I had already seen the beauty within and that's a combination created by God alone. When I reached out and took your hand it was to help calm your anxiety. But when I touched you I felt a warmth in my fingers that went through me. When I invited you to lunch I was making my first clumsy move to know you better. And a first date should always have a chaperone."

Charlotte saw the sincerity of his words as she looked deeply into his eyes. If he was lying, then he was one of the best. Where she came from you need to be a liar and you need to be really good. And you need to spot the liar who would also take what's theirs and yours. Just a way of life in the Oaks.

"But I had to find out about you from other people. You never told me anything about you. You took us to that fancy restaurant where we stuck out like a sore thumb. Who does that for no reason? Imagine how I felt when I found out. I assumed everyone was laughing at me for not knowing my place."

"Charlotte, I would never embarrass you intentionally. I wasn't being coy when I didn't share personal information. It's just that I'm used to everyone trying to take advantage of me. People don't like me for who I am. They like me for what I have, and what they can get. I was attracted to you immediately, but I wasn't going to reveal the 'wealthy me' until you knew the real me. I didn't want you to like me for my money, house, or car."

She said, "Car? You mean that Ford pickup. Yeah, really impressive Chad."

"Exactly my point. You didn't go to lunch with me for my car. And you picked the restaurant, not me. I noticed when Micah hesitated about going to the Mine Shaft, but you pushed ahead. I only knew where it was, not what it was. And frankly, I'll never step through that door again. I asked about you and you pretty much dumped everything," and he quickly added, "and I loved you for your honesty. I really did. I fell in love with you at that table when you felt it was too expensive and we could leave. I didn't feel I could be that honest with you. I enjoyed being treated like a regular guy out with a girl. I didn't want you liking me because you knew I was rich. So, if you want, I'll tell you everything about me. Or you and Sara can eat and leave. The ball is in your court."

"I guess the first thing I need to know is how does Sara fit in? She's my life. I live for her alone. She drives me to get out of the Oaks because I can't stand the thought of her growing up the way I did."

"When we were in that restaurant did you see me flinch when you said you had a little girl?" Charlotte remembered he hadn't. "That doesn't bother me. You had a life long before you ever met me. Sara's beginnings may not have worked out the way you hoped, but that's not her fault. If she's part of the package, then the package is twice as nice. Maybe my story will help you understand that I have fears too. You're not the only one who's scared. We're not nearly as different as you think we are."

Angie knocked then entered the dining room with a home style Italian meal. There was a bit of everything. Chad said, "Don't know you well enough to know what you like, but I'll watch and next time I'll know."

Charlotte watched the table fill with platters of food and exclaimed, "This must have cost a fortune!"

Chad smiled at her, "Yeah, I'm rich, remember? You said so."

They ate, small talked and gave Sara finger food that she promptly smeared all over her face or nibbled, shook her head and dropped on the floor. Charlotte watched as Chad kept washing her up thinking to herself, "You got a lot to learn. No point in doing that yet." But she said nothing as she realized, except for Sara's Uncle Micah, this was the first real male figure to enter Sara's young life. And besides, every time he talked to Sara she smiled and giggled and that pleased Charlotte.

After Angie cleared the table Chad said, "Ready for the story?"

"Yes, I want to find out if a guy like you really does exist, why he isn't taken, and what makes him tick."

"The key is to never forget your roots. That's where you came from and who you are. Sometimes you never want to forget your roots so you don't go back to them. I'm a little of both. I told you I grew up outside St. Louis. Not a lie. I grew up in East St. Louis. Does that mean anything to you?" She shook her head no. "Well, ever heard of Harlem?" She nodded yes. "Pretty much the same. My father left us when I was four and my brother was seven. Mom was forced onto welfare and we moved into a filthy fifth-floor walk up. There were a few whites and Hispanics in the neighborhood, but only a few. We were a white family in a black ghetto. The longer we lived there the more the crime increased. We weren't allowed to go outside except to go to school and mom walked us most days. My brother looked out for me and protected me. More than once the gas or electric was turned off because Mom couldn't pay the bill. But one thing that never changed was her love and devotion to us. Every Sunday we were in Sunday School and church faithfully. She taught us that anything is possible with God. She reminded us each time a prayer was answered or God provided for a need. When I was twelve, I became a Christian. Through the years I struggled with faith as the world and all it has to offer tried to pull me away. I never succumbed because I never forgot my roots. Most of my life I've made good deci-

sions because I took things to God in prayer before making a decision. When people don't trust Jesus they will make bad decisions. I
learned early on that when Jesus told his followers that 'apart from me
you can do nothing,' he was right.

"Mom forced us to study hard and expected a lot from us. Way
beyond anything our environment would suggest. I was accepted into
MIT in Computer Science. Never owned a computer at home. My
brother chose a military career. Mom died my senior year in college
knowing both her sons had made her proud. My brother and I stayed
close, talked once a week even when he was in Iraq. Then one week
two years ago the phone call didn't come, and I lost the only family I
had left." Charlotte saw his eyes mist as he talked about his brother.
She said nothing, but reached over and took his hand in hers and
caressed the back of his hand.

"I was good with computers and began to work on computer
processing chips that make the computer work faster. In ten years my
partner and I owned a fifty million dollar company."

Charlotte's eyes opened about as wide as they could without her
eyeballs falling out and rolling across the floor as she gasped, "Fifty—
million—dollars!"

Chad held up his hand, "I'm not worth fifty million. I sold the
company to my partner. I want a simple life. I want the life I can have
here. Maybe the life I can have with you and Sara."

"Okay, I don't really care. If you've twenty bucks in cash it's more
than I've got." He could see by her whole demeanor, she didn't care,
her life had never been about wealth or possessions. "But, I just have
to know, how much do you have?"

"I have enough to be quite comfortable," and he paused, lowered
his voice and said, "About ten million dollars give or take." And he
quickly put his finger to his lips, "shush!"

Charlotte slowly took it all in trying to comprehend how many
zeros that was and after a few seconds asked, "In that case, does that
mean I can have ice cream on my pecan pie?"

Chad replied, "Yes, you can. Two scoops if you would like and
some for Sara."

~

Late that afternoon Reagan drove into the fairgrounds with an excited expectant mother-to-be. He found a spot to park Molly in the grassy field. Prudy exclaimed loud enough for all to hear, "Elephant ears, I'm here. Where are you?" Reagan just shook his head. The Lambs came early since Prudy's cravings wouldn't wait, but tomorrow was a work day for Reagan. Prudy was now dragging him toward the smell of the concession stands where elephant ears would be her gourmet dinner.

Reagan felt that things between the factions in the church were calming down. A number of people were seeing their faith in a new light. Reagan had started out feeding them milk, moved to mush, then a little solid food. Some seemed to enjoy the new tasting food. About a dozen people had left the church, mostly Christmas/Easter Christians with an occasional Mother's Day attender thrown in, plus two Elders. Reagan saw it as more of a purification than a disgruntled exodus. He was now ready, after three long years, to take a chance and throw a chunk of meat at them and see if they'd eat.

He realized that it had been about six weeks since Charlotte had been in church and he couldn't seem to get any information. One thing was for sure, Maddie was thrilled that Charlotte wasn't there. He was betting that she had claimed a spiritual victory in that she had driven that minx out of the church of Jesus Christ she had remade into her perfect design minus, of course, that pastor.

Prudy found the first of four elephant ear stands scattered throughout the fairgrounds. Pacing herself she ordered one with extra powdered sugar. She planned ahead and wore one of Reagan's old T-shirts that was large enough to cover her now swelling belly. Since it was white the powdered sugar wouldn't show so much. Saying to no one in particular, "Mmmm...I wonder if this is what heaven is going to be like? Lord if so, take me now!" Reagan took her hand and walked on. After three years he knew a lot of people in the county, so it wasn't surprising that it was mostly step, step, step, stop. Repeat often.

A half hour later Prudy was ready for the next elephant ear and started dragging Reagan as she followed her nose. Cinnamon sugar was calling her name this time. With elephant ear in hand, they moved toward the exhibition area and the handiwork of some of the older church ladies who still practiced crafts that were becoming lost arts. They rounded a corner where a sign indicated the direction to the barns. The sign wasn't really necessary, it was easy enough just to follow your nose.

Reagan looked up and walking toward them were the Kennedy's. Reagan had tried to contact Guy earlier in the day, but it was Saturday and as they are now 'country lawyers' that didn't happen. He was actually surprised to see them here. They had struck him as being a little too sophisticated for the sights, sounds, and smells of a county fair. They drew closer and Reagan could tell they were trying to fit in, but the way they were dressed they looked more like a city couple on their way to a square dance.

After the wives were introduced Reagan said, "Guy, I was trying to reach you all morning. But apparently, country lawyers don't have an answering service." He grinned as he said it.

Guy smiled back, "You are correct preacher. Strictly 9-5 Monday through Friday. No answering machine at the office or home. And definitely no answering service. People who need to know where I am will know, and people who need my home phone will have it. Apparently, you don't have the number so let me give it to you." He took out a card and wrote it down.

Reagan took the card expecting the usual business card information on it. It was a business card alright, but all it had was his home phone number he'd just jotted down. "What, no business card either?"

"Nope."

Reagan changed the subject, "There are a couple of important things I'd like to discuss if you've got a few. Should take about twenty minutes."

Prudy was quick to take the hint.

≈

She looked at Ginny and said, "Let's go look at the bunny rabbits. They're right over there. And if the men are still talking when we come out I'll treat you to an elephant ear. Have you ever had one?"

"Had one? I don't even know what they are. But it sounds kind of gross."

"You haven't lived until you've had a county fair elephant ear! Let's go there now. All this talk of elephant ears is giving me another craving." They walked back in the food concession direction. "So, what do you think of our little Washington County Fair?"

"It's amazing. I've never been to a fair before. I grew up in the city and we had lots of carnivals in shopping center parking lots. I stayed in the city to attend the University of Chicago for undergraduate and law school. We met in law school and started our practice in Chicago, got so busy we were always too tired to do anything. It seemed if Guy wasn't working I was and vice versa. We had no life. Our stress level was out of control and I was on the verge of leaving him. He came to me with the idea of moving here and semi-retiring. The adjustment has been hard, but I have my husband back, so I'll take it. Anyway, it's fun watching people. And I love watching people show their animals. It's like judging a beauty pageant and everyone is so serious. And I didn't know anyone still baked pies, cakes, and bread or made quilts."

Reagan started in, "I assume you heard Micah was in the hospital? Beaten by his father."

"Yeah, I heard his father beat him up because he thought Micah was cheating him on the rent. Hard to believe the old man would charge him anything for that old motorhome. I met him and frankly he scared the bejeebers out of me. That guy's huge and mean. I'd rather face his Rottweilers than him. It's a wonder the kid turned out as good as he did."

"Yes, it was in spite of Paul. His sister, Charlotte, has had a lot of influence on him. She practically raised him. Their mother ran off a few years ago. They got up for school one morning and she was gone.

Paul wasn't much good before and a lot worse after she left. You want to know how to beat the system on anything and he's your man. All that man does is take up space and breathe the air other people need. Not that God couldn't get a hold of him, but it'd be pretty hard. We'd call it a miracle. That is one mean man.

"Micah refused to sign the papers and Paul's free. The sheriff thinks he's afraid his sister might get hurt. As I said, they are really close. Since he wouldn't sign the papers that means he's without a home and if he doesn't find a place to stay by the time he's released, he'll get moved back to the jail. Prudy and I can't take him in even temporarily. With the Pierces as church members, I just can't get caught in the middle. Even having this conversation could be bad if the wrong people overheard us. We figured with Paul in jail he could move in the house with Charlotte and that would satisfy the court."

"Look," said Guy, "I told you I came to this town to help people who can't help themselves. I will partition the court Monday morning to allow him to stay with us if we can't find someone. Honestly, it's not the best plan. The courts, judges, and prosecutors don't like that kind of familiarity between attorney and client. You can get too emotionally attached to the client. With our old clients, that was never an issue. You wanted to be through with them as soon as possible and get them out of your life. They were not nice people, but Micah, he's good people."

Prudy and Ginny were just returning, each with an elephant ear. Ginny said, "Guy, you've got to try these. They are the most incredibly delicious gross thing I've ever had."

Reagan said, "I think it's time to call it a night. I've got to work tomorrow and if Prudy eats any more elephant ears, I'll have to roll her home." It was definitely an Alka Seltzer night.

CHAPTER 20

*S*unday, September 2, 1992. Reagan entered by the side door and sat on his regal throne. It would not be that uncomfortable if someone would fix the broken spring in the seat. He wondered how many of his predecessors had this same broken spring poking them in the butt.

He began his weekly exploratory gaze around the sanctuary. Since Sunday, June 2nd, there had been a change at Community Church. Attendance had gone up a little and more people seemed to be acting a little more Christlike. Of course, there was Maddie Pierce and her first name seemed to describe her well. She had rejoiced when she thought she'd purified God's Church by driving off those Barnes people. Reagan wondered if she had turned around to look in the pew behind her. Sitting two rows behind just to her left were Charlotte and Chad, and Reagan thought, looking quite cozy. Well, he knew for sure if Maddie didn't know it yet, by the end of prayer requests she would.

Billy and Heather were in their usual spots and by now most people had accepted their presence at Community Church. They hadn't missed a Sunday since June and no one had ever seen Billy clean, sober and nice this long. Of course, the naysayers were just waiting for something to push his button. Heather was counting the days to get her children back and praying that everyone, including Family Services, would see what God was doing in Billy's life.

The one that astounded Reagan most was the Honorable Judge Lloyd Chadwick. Lloyd had always been a nice guy and a dedicated worker in the church. He had chaired the Board of Elders for three years now. He'd always seemed to be somewhat cold and distant, afraid to let anyone get close. One day Lloyd stopped by the office, it was the first time he'd come to see Reagan other than for church business. He told him about the impact June 2nd had had on him and Meg. He said, "Pastor, I grew up in a Christian home."

He told him the whole story. "June 2nd brought it all back. I realized how I had strayed from God and I was just playing church for years. I've never felt as drawn and as helpless as I did when I rose from my seat that day. Reagan, I didn't do that. You know me well enough to know I wouldn't. I'm a jurist. I'm reserved, I'm also an introvert."

Reagan grinned from ear to ear but never said a word.

"Pastor, God spoke to me a few days later. For years I've meted out justice by the book. God explained what would happen if he did the same to me. He revealed to me that justice has to be tempered with mercy and I had never understood that before. For three months I've been watching people in my courtroom scratch their heads. They never know how I'm going to rule and I don't either...until after I've gone to my chambers and prayed about it."

That visit by the church's head Elder had excited and revitalized Reagan's ministry. Today he was witnessing Judge Lloyd Chadwick sitting in church with an open Bible on his lap. Alex Dyson and Lanny Pitts had resigned from the Board of Elders. Lloyd was looking for the right 'men' to replace them and was determined he'd wait until God pointed out the people he wanted. He had a true man of God helping him lead the church.

Shirley actually smiled at him when he looked her way. Ever since that evening, he'd seen a change in her. He regretted saying to her what he had said but was now glad he did. At least it hadn't ended the way it could have. He wondered how things might have gone if he did it three years earlier. Probably not so well.

Adam and Maddie were sitting in the same pew, but there was a coldness to their relationship. It seemed that publicly she'd put on a show that everything was okay. Reagan suspected that at home she made his life a living hell and felt bad for Adam. Reagan silently prayed God would crack open a door to her heart. Adam was so close to the relationship with Christ he wanted, but he wanted Maddie to be a part of it too.

The organist finished her usually uninspiring rendition of whatever it was and Reagan graciously thanked her. He hoped that each week he did that it wasn't being taken as praise for a job well done. People would say, "Well, they're volunteers doing it for God." Reagan outwardly agreed, but thought, "Just because I love to sing doesn't mean I should sing special music on Sunday."

Prayer request time went pretty much as he had expected. He hadn't mentioned Charlotte's name but rather nodded in her direction. He suspected Maddie didn't know Charlotte was there. Subconsciously, or consciously, he was setting her up for what she deserved. Charlotte rose, "I ask your forgiveness for not being here for several weeks. You have been gracious and supportive of Sara and me and I appreciate it so much. I had a little setback in my faith and not trusting God, but now I know he has guided me all along." Maddie's face was turning beet red. "Anyway, I appreciate all the prayers for Micah. He should be released from the hospital this week. Now we need prayers that he can find a place to live. If not, he'll end up back in jail." Maddie, of course, was already praying that no place could be found. Chad squeezed Charlotte's hand tightly. He realized this woman never thought of herself.

When Reagan began prayer time he sincerely lifted up every request as equally important so that he could stress Micah's need. Of course, he was cheating on this one. Micah's housing was pretty much a done deal. Right in front of Reagan sat the man who would make that decision. Two months ago Micah might have ended up back in jail. But now Lloyd Chadwick tempered justice with mercy.

Reagan began his message about the Prodigal Son. It was appropriate for so many in this congregation. Most had heard the story several times, but do we ever hear God's Word until it applies to us? Because of Sunday, June 2nd, there were several sitting there who could say, "Hey, that's my story." Certainly, Judge Chadwick heard it differently as did Charlotte who knew she had run away from God. She thought she was running from Chad Houston, but now realized she was running from God's wonderful plan for her life. Then she heard Reagan say, "In Jeremiah 29:11, God declares, For I know the plans I have for you, plans to prosper you and not to harm you, plans to give you hope and a future." Wow! Her face turned as she looked up at Chad, squeezed his hand and she said to herself, "Father, I am blessed."

Reagan ended the message and felt led to do something he seldom did in what was considered a mainline church. But for some reason, God was telling him to do it and he wasn't going to disobey. He gave an altar call. He didn't stretch it out for all five verses of "Just As I Am." Reagan figured if anyone came forward it should only take one verse and the Holy Spirit would do the rest. He did. Billy Maddox stood up and came forward and knelt before the cross that sat on the communion table. You could hear the proverbial pin drop as people looked at each other. Some in delight and amazement and others in disbelief. Some like, Maddie Pierce, were disgusted that someone like Billy would have the audacity to put on a show like this. Others, like Lloyd Chadwick, silently praised God for what he was witnessing. Lloyd knew it was real and genuine. Billy had stood in front of his bench perhaps a dozen times, as an angry, defiant, unrepentant man full of hate. Every time Lloyd would give him what the law allowed. Billy wasn't a criminal, he was just a menace to society not caring about anyone or anything. Lloyd carried himself with authority and dignity and for the second time in three months he arose from his pew and went forward. He had heard the under-breath mumbling of Maddie Pierce when Billy walked up. Billy had to have heard it too. Lloyd walked past her and gave her the 'judge's eye', which is far worse than the Mom look. He went up, kneeled next to Billy, put his arm around him and began praying. Not real loud, but you could be sure everyone heard it.

Heather sat watching this unfold. She was dumbfounded that God would answer her prayers. She had prayed and prayed and prayed, but never really expected an answer. She'd been with Billy for four years and knew him better than anyone ever had. She could tell when Billy was playing an angle—this was real. She thought about getting up, but before her mind could communicate with her legs, she moved forward as fast as you can in heels on a sloping floor. She knelt on the other side of Billy, took his hand in hers, leaned up and kissed him. The sanctuary was quiet, and no one knew quite what to do. Reagan hadn't given the benediction, nor had he indicated they were dismissed. So they sat.

Lloyd Chadwick leaned in and hugged him. Billy stood up and turned toward the congregation and said, "Hi, my name is Billy and I'm an alcoholic." Some gasped in response that anyone would say something like that in a church. People know the response used in AA meetings and some responded, "Hi, Billy." Billy said, "This is the first time I've ever admitted that I'm an alcoholic. That's right. I'm an alcoholic, but now I'm an alcoholic in recovery forgiven by God and saved by grace. This is the day I accept Jesus as my Lord and Savior.

"Most of you have known of me for some time. Some of you have known me since the day I came to town to work the mines. Judge, I believe you met me about two weeks after I arrived." Some chuckling. "I'm a terribly flawed human being. There's not much of what I've done I'm proud of. A lot of what I did was because I didn't know how to do anything else. And a lot of what I did I never knew I did. I've only done one good thing in my life. Four years ago I took this lady and her children into my house. Heather has done nothing but love me, but I didn't know what love was. That was the first time in my life I had ever been loved. And I screwed that up and Heather lost her children. Three months ago I met a man named Reagan Lamb, and he cared about me even as Heather lay in the hospital. The first Sunday I came was because Heather wanted me to. It sure wasn't my idea."

Brad felt good about what he was seeing and hearing. All some-body needed to do was get Billy's attention. He was glad Billy hadn't mentioned anything about him. God indeed deserved all the glory.

"I came back June 3rd and after the Pastor told his story I began to think. Reagan Lamb was a really bad dude, but God loved him and if he loves him, then maybe he loves me. I challenged God, if He loved me and was real, to make himself known to me. And he did, week after week.

"I never want to be who I was. And I don't want to be who I am. By the grace of God, I can be more and I can be better. I can't do it alone and I can't do it with only God in my life. I need more. I need the only person who has ever loved me."

In front of hundred and forty three people, Billy Maddox dropped to one knee and said, "Heather Delaney, I've hurt you over and over again. I've tried to destroy the best thing that ever happened to me. I know God has been trying to reach me for the last four years and now he has. As God is my witness from this day forward, I'll be your protector Heather Delaney. You will never be hurt again. Will you, Sadie, and Jake marry me?"

She never answered him, but the hugging, kissing and jumping up and down pretty well said it all, as the angels of heaven danced for joy. High fives all around… "God, we did it!"

Brad smiled more than anyone.

Four other lives would be affected by what happened at Commu-nity Church on September 2, 1992... perhaps each in a different way.

CHAPTER 21

*M*onday, September 3, 1992. Guy knocked on the door of the Judge's chamber about 9:28 for a 9:30 appointment. When he entered, D.A. Allison Dodge was already seated and Guy sensed he had interrupted something as the conversation immediately ceased in mid-sentence. The good morning counselor pleasantries were exchanged. Allison had only informally met Guy and knew almost nothing about him. She had been trying to find out his background, but she kept hitting brick walls. She figured all the public information was out there somewhere and she'd find it. There were two problems. Problem number one was the D.A.'s office was a three-man operation. There was herself, her secretary, and a part-time private detective from Upton. Problem number two was Guy and Ginny had changed their identities and being lawyers they had done a good job.

Guy had made a courtesy call on Judge Chadwick two days after he and Ginny had hung out their new shingle. You never want a judge to find out things from other sources that you should have told him yourself. Guy told Judge Chadwick his story knowing that if this judge was worth his salt everything he said would remain confidential. Lloyd didn't seem particularly impressed with Guy's credentials, but it wasn't his job to be impressed.

Lloyd began, "Mr. Kennedy, it's my understanding that you wish to petition the court to allow you to provide lodging for Micah Barnes until the time of the trial. Is this correct?"

"Yes, your honor, as you are aware Micah was living in and paying rent for an old camper on Paul Barnes' property. Paul felt he was being cheated by Micah and beat him until he was unconscious. Micah is being released this week and needs a place to live until the trial or he returns to jail per your order. We wanted to have him stay with Chad Houston, but he doesn't yet meet residency requirements."

Lloyd, bringing Guy up to date, "I gave Ms. Dodge a heads up on this so she wouldn't be blindsided this morning. Ms. Dodge, what is your response to Mr. Kennedy's petition?"

"Well, your honor, this is highly irregular and I don't like it. Mr. Kennedy has been retained to defend Micah Barnes, not be a surrogate father to him. This arrangement could create a bond that even Mr. Kennedy, as an attorney, should seek to avoid and he should feel very uncomfortable about even entering this type of arrangement. I'm also concerned how it might affect public opinion and possibly even jury selection with such a small pool available."

"Your honor, if I may, being a small town is part of the problem. There is no place for him to stay. This young man claims he's innocent and I have good reason to believe he is or I wouldn't defend him. The assault charge is justified. The kid made a bad choice, granted, but the rape allegations are unfounded and I can prove it." At this point, Guy was bluffing but was hoping Allison Dodge might worry a little. "To put him back in jail would exacerbate the whole situation and wouldn't be beneficial to anyone. And yes, this is a very uncomfortable situation for my wife and I, but we also know the extenuating circumstances."

Judge Chadwick raised his hand to stop him, indicating he'd heard enough. "You both make very valid points. Mr. Kennedy, I'm giving you custody for two weeks. During that time you will find a home for him other than your own. If you don't, I may have no choice but to put him back in jail. Mr. Kennedy, please don't let me down. If there is no other discussion, and there isn't, we are dismissed."

~

Sheriff Reynolds wasn't surprised that he had to release Paul Barnes, nor was he surprised when Micah wouldn't press charges. It was a way of life in Washington County. Tinker said he felt more like the Department of Fisheries catch and release program. He went back by himself to release Paul and closed the big steel door separating the office from the cells. The door was normally left open during the day, but Tinker wanted a little privacy. Paul Barnes stood in the cell in all his glory. Unless you would be a long-term guest the Washington County Sheriff's Office didn't issue prison overalls. So he had socks, but no shoes, just as they found him. Dirty jeans held up by suspenders over a wife-beater T-shirt. The stains pretty much identified his last ten meals as did the bits of food still in his beard.

"Well, you are a free man. I've been the Sheriff for over fifty years. Paul, I want you to know you've earned a very special place in my heart. So special that I'm going to get you and put you away, and nobody will care when I do. You are a disgusting human being. You don't seem to have any redeeming qualities. You drove your wife away years ago. You've made welfare slaves of your kids. They both hate you but are scared to death of you. If you had a heart attack and fell over dead on the street not one person in this town would stop to help you. Sound about right?"

Paul ignored the last remark. "Sheriff, I doubt if you'll ever put me away. I'm too smart for you. It took four deputies and a tranquilizer gun to take me down on a false charge. Micah got beaten, but it weren't by me. He came home and collapsed and like a good father I called 911. See, Sheriff, no one will testify against me. Now, if you'll let me out I've got to go make sure my girl and grandbaby are okay. They've been all alone while you illegally locked me up. I've a mind to bring charges agin' your department. I've got important business to attend to and you keeping me here don't help. So if you don't mind I'll be going."

Tink said, "It'll be a pleasure to let you out. Cause the sooner you're out the sooner you'll be back. Paul, we both know I can't touch you unless you break a law. But as soon as I release you, you need to spend every minute looking over your shoulder. There's a man in the town who's not afraid of you, and he's coming for you because of the way you've treated your kids. You know how I know? I'm going to tell him. Stay alert Paul, cause you won't see him coming. No one ever does. You've been warned." Tink could see the apprehension in his eyes.

Paul had to walk his three hundred pound frame all the way home alone. By the time he got to the tracks, he was soaked with sweat and huffing and puffing like he might have a coronary at any moment. He had to agree with the sheriff, no one would care if he did die, even his kids wished he was gone. Not a single person spoke to him or offered him a ride. He hated the people of this town. The little compound he had created was his kingdom and kept all these two faced bottom feeders out. He arrived at the gate and the two Rottweilers ran to greet him. They were the only two living things in the world that loved him and they were just as mean as he was. He entered, played with the dogs and then walked toward his single-wide mansion. As he got close, Charlotte opened the door with a big fake smile. "Welcome back Daddy. Sara missed you." The last part was the only truth she told. At eighteen months Sara pretty much loved everyone.

Paul was glad to be home because he could always depend on Charlotte to be there for him. He had no knowledge about the renewed relationship between Charlotte and Chad. Since nobody would talk to him, he had no way of finding out his daughter wouldn't be his prisoner for much longer. He told her stories of all the horrible things that they did to him in jail. He was denied food and a lawyer. Charlotte just let him go on and on. Truth was, Tinker had tried to get him a lawyer after reading him his rights, but no attorney in town would represent him. He'd have to wait until Monday to get Paul a court-appointed attorney and Tinker knew he'd be out by then.

Charlotte had been praying continuously for her father and that

God would provide a way out of that trailer. She couldn't ask Chad for help and never complained about her situation. She wanted Chad's love, not his pity. And while she had slept around in the past, Chad was different and she'd never move into his house without the benefit of marriage. Hokey, old-fashioned, maybe, but she was now a new creation, and the old had passed away.

CHAPTER 22

*T*uesday, **September 4, 1992.** It was getting warm early this morning so Reagan decided to mix it up. He went for his morning walk up High Street first thing. The town was so quiet this time of day. He wondered if Bill Bemis and Bob Bemis would be upset that he wouldn't be there for the morning wave. Sunday had been another great day, the fair was in full swing, and with it came Prudy's new craving for Italian sausage sandwiches. He knew where he was going for supper tonight. He walked past New Life Fellowship and Wayne was just arriving. Reagan said, "On my way for breakfast. Join me. My treat." Wayne never turned down free food and you could tell. Wayne always wore cowboy boots and jeans, a well-worn cowboy hat and a plaid shirt covering the belly hanging over the big belt buckle. They entered the Greasy Spoon and took their usual table. Paul Barnes was the main topic of this morning's discussion. Needless to say, nothing good was said.

When Reagan entered his office, there was a note on the door saying Micah would be released from the hospital before noon. How sad that he was Micah's contact. He had no real family, other than Charlotte, who had no car and no access to a phone most of the time. Reagan called Guy, Guy picked him up and together they went to

Upton. Micah signed himself out, and the staff brought him out to the car. He didn't look good, and it seemed his spirit was broken. He didn't say much on the way home. He was happy not to be going to the Winnie, but not really thrilled about living with people he didn't know.

They arrived at Guy's big white Victorian with a wrap around porch and a carport by the side entrance. Reagan knew it was time for a graceful exit. He thanked Guy and asked Micah to join Chad and Charlotte for worship Sunday. Micah's only commitment was, "If I feel up to it." Right now he wasn't sure how he felt about God or anything else.

It was getting really warm, and he was a good mile from the church. Now he had no choice but to walk. He headed south on High Street. He seldom walked in this part of town so it gave him a chance to notice things he'd never noticed, and that wasn't hard. He gazed at beautiful gardens, ornate gingerbread trim, and lush lawns. Many homes were owned by members of the church and he'd visited but never observed. He approached the corner of High and Broad and saw Chad Houston standing on the corner as if waiting for a bus that would never come.

He looked at Chad and said, "You know, I see you in church every week, but we never get to talk. I don't seem to be able to separate you from Charlotte."

Chad smiled, "Pastor, I don't think I ever want to be separated from her. I'd marry her right now, but I guess she needs more time. A lot of stuff going on in her life. Like most guys, I'm a fixer, but I think right now she needs support. I'd gladly take Micah into my home, but they tell me that even though I own property, I don't meet the residency requirements yet. So that didn't work out."

"Walk with me and let me tell you a few things about Charlotte Barnes. How much did Charlotte tell you about her situation?"

"She's been very open about her past, but the present is somewhat of a mystery. It seems that she is internalizing things. I know she has feelings for me but right now I feel I'm more committed to the relationship than she is."

As they walked, Reagan shared non-confidential things. He finally got to the complete story of Micah from his sports injury to the present. "Charlotte really has two children. She's been Micah's mom for a long time. Their mother walked out in the middle of the night several years ago. Chances are without her he'd be headed toward becoming like his father. She loves him as much as she loves Sara. And, right now, if she had to choose between you and Micah, I think you're right, she'd pick Micah. Not because she doesn't love you. She loves you more than you can imagine. But she is so devoted, she'd sacrifice her happiness for his. This woman is a prize and a keeper. She just needs to get through the next four months. You walk her through this and she's yours forever."

"Pastor, God has directed my whole life. He's been a part of every decision I've ever made for as long as I can recall. He brought me to Glencoe and on my first Sunday in church he said, 'Chad, this is the woman I've chosen for you.' Everything she says and everything she does only makes me love her more. She's tried to scare me away with a baby, a horrible father, and the excuse that she wasn't good enough for me. The real question is can I ever be good enough for her?

"Hey, look. Thanks for walking with me and thanks for the talk. We'll see you Sunday." It wasn't personal. Chad wanted to walk a while by himself. He had even more to think about.

Tuesday was the next visitation day and Heather was excited. She was taking Sadie and Jake to the fair. They arrived at the gate at 2:00 pm. The chaperone told Heather she'd hang back 15-20 feet. Billy wasn't an issue to Family Services anymore since he was working full time, sober, and apparently one of those people who thought they were 'born again.' Even before any rides, Sadie and Jake insisted on cotton candy. Jake wanted blue and Sadie said it was gross because cotton candy is supposed to be pink and she added: "everybody knows that!" After a few rides, Heather suggested they go see the horses. On the way to the barns, there was a shady path through the trees with benches and Heather sat down with one on each side. The chaperone sat down three benches away, but Heather was talking softly and with the background noise knew she couldn't hear.

"Guys, I want to talk about Billy."

Jake jumped in immediately, "I don't. I hate him. I don't ever want to see him again. Mama, he hurt you real bad. I hate him, I hate him, I hate him!"

This would be tougher than she thought. "Billy was a bad man, Jake. A very bad man. He was sick, baby, and needed help. He's been getting help. Lots of people are helping him get better. He goes to work every day. He's cleaned up the yard, fixed the porch and the house. He goes to church every week and last Sunday he asked Jesus to come into his heart...in front of everybody. He takes me places and buys me things. You know he never did that. He hasn't touched me or hurt me."

Sadie said, "Mama can people really change? Maybe he's just trying to trick you."

"Baby girl, I thought of that too. I wanted him to change cause even though he did those things I still loved him. But I keep asking things of him that the old Billy wouldn't ever do, like take me to church. The pastor thinks he's changed, and his doctors (she was referring to AA) think he's changed, and even some important people in the church think he's changed. But there are only two people who can decide if he's really changed, and that's you guys. I'd like you to let him visit with the three of us a couple of times. I know he can't fool you. And if you say no, then I'll leave him and we'll go away by ourselves."

Sadie said, "I'll do it for you mama, but I won't make any promises. We miss you, but it's been nice to live without him."

"Fair enough, baby girl. What about you, little man?"

"I'll try because I've always wanted a daddy, but I don't want a mean daddy like Billy was, who yells at us and hurts you. If he's not going to be a good daddy I don't want him. I want a daddy who will take me fishing."

"Honey, I'll take you fishing."

"No you won't. You're scared of worms."

~

It had been about three months and things were not good at the Pierce household. Most of their friends weren't aware of anything wrong. Maddie was a good actress who knew her station in the community and would hold on to it at any cost. Her friends had seen Maddie moody from time to time, but there was nothing unusual about that. Adam wasn't as talkative and jovial with customers as he used to be. Some attributed it to the competing hardware store and maybe Pierce's Hardware was in a financial bind.

Tuesday afternoon, near 4:00, Maddie left for a dentist appointment and Adam had happened to come home early. He went in and found Katie in the room that had once been an extensive library in the home's early years, but now was a den. Katie was sitting on the big old leather sofa with her earbuds in, as usual. Adam closed the door, moved a chair in front of it and sat down. He knew he was in Katie's peripheral vision so he sat and waited. Eventually, she caved before he did and just stared at him and said, "What?"

Adam, who everyone considered mild mannered and soft spoken wasn't today. "Now that I have your attention, turn that thing off and take the earbuds out!"

She stared at him defiantly and didn't move, but he did. He got up quickly and grabbed the portable CD player, which also pulled the buds out of her ears and he threw it against the brick fireplace. It broke into several pieces. "Now, do I have your attention?"

She'd never seen her father this angry as she backed into the corner of the sofa and nodded. Adam saw no need to sit in the chair that now blocked the door, he'd made his point. "It's time we had a talk. I choose not to do all the talking, but if I have to I will. You have shut me out of your life for the last three years and I don't know why. It has hurt me deeply and made me angry. One day you were a happy, fun-loving teen and the next it was like having a stranger in the house. You have become Jekyll and Hyde. I went to your school counselor and she said don't worry about it, she'll grow out of it, but you didn't. Then several months ago you seemed to come back part way to being the girl we knew. Your mother was so thrilled you communicated she couldn't see you weren't really Katie. I don't know who you are, but you're not our Katie. You've figured out how to play your mother and manipulate her to get whatever you want. You are mean, you are nasty, and you are vindictive. And I don't understand it."

Katie yelled back, "Of course you don't understand, you're a man. Men are all the same...they stick together. All you've done for three years is say no. I can't do this and I can't do that. I'm old enough to make my own decisions and mom understands that. I heard you in the office. You wanted mom to change her mind and let Micah Barnes off with a light sentence. He raped me and you don't care!"

"First of all, yes, you're right. I did want her to let him off easier. He made a bad decision and a bad mistake. I did the same thing at his age when I thought your mom was cheating on me. But when you said he raped you that changed everything. It made me angry. I might have even killed him on the spot if I could. I love you and all I want to do is protect you. That's why I forbid you to see Micah in the first place. But now, I'm afraid for you Katie. Some things about your story make sense, but other things don't. Something happened that you're not telling me about. That much I know. But what really happened is what I don't know. I don't want to see you do something you'll regret. I love you, but I'm not convinced that Micah Barnes raped you. And if he didn't do it, I don't think you can live with yourself for the next 25 years. But if he did it, then yes, you have a right to demand justice, and I'll stand with you. You're my daughter and I'll never stop loving you and trying to protect you. Even from yourself."

"I can take care of myself, thank you very much." Conversation ended. Adam got up, moved the chair and before he walked out said, "Katie, I love you." He hoped he'd given her something to think about. He was more convinced than ever that she was hiding something.

∼

Chad continued his afternoon stroll, thinking about recent events. He turned onto Pine Street and decided it was a dumb name since he couldn't see a single pine anywhere, but then again, maple was lined with oaks. He walked along and noticed that most of these were nice Victorian homes. A few could use some TLC. They were not nearly as grand as the homes on High Street and Broad Street. Between two old Victorian homes stood a cute little bungalow with a big porch. The house was set back and you might not even notice it most of the time. He guessed it replaced a home that burned or was torn down and judging from the style he'd guessed it was probably built sometime in the 1930s. In the window, he noticed the small for sale sign. Those little cartoon bubbles began popping up over his head with a pling, pling, pling.

Chad kicked back into fixer mode and prayed God was guiding him. Charlotte had been struggling to get out of the Oaks for nearly two years. Paul was becoming more domineering and demanding each day; and recent events might make living under the same roof with him unbearable. One of the many things he loved about Charlotte was her fierce independence. The problem with that was she'd never ask for help. He was sure they both knew that soon they'd be married, but neither one had mentioned it. His fixer mind thought of a somewhat devious plan that just might work. That night he contacted the number in the window and two days later owned a second home.

When Katie went to the fair that evening she was in a very foul mood. There was a pavilion behind the horse arena where the hay bales were stacked and this is where her group hung out. Bobby Lee was sitting on a bale drinking a beer and she sat in his lap. They had the cooler hidden in the bales. In a town like Glencoe beer was easy to get. For five bucks anyone from the Oaks would buy beer for you, no questions asked. Once you were in high school in Washington County, there weren't many who didn't drink. It was easy to get and there was not much else to do in this town. There was the bowling alley, but that was for the nerds. The Bible thumpers hung out playing table games in each other's homes, like that was fun. They had occasional dances at the high school, but the real parties always happened later. If you had a car you could go to Upton or across the river, otherwise, there just wasn't much to do. Some parents saw Glencoe as a great, safe, place to raise kids and others had no idea where their kids were or what they were doing.

Lettie Pike and Katie had known each other since first grade. Lettie's dad owned the feed and grain store near the tracks. They looked nothing alike and on the surface seemed to have little in common, but after knowing each other for eleven years they were twinkies. They'd finish each other's sentences. Had the same taste in clothes and boys. And both pushed their parents to the limits. If one of them lied the other would swear to it.

There were eight of them laughing, talking, and drinking tonight with a ninth standing lookout on the other side of the pavilion. If someone came to get hay the lookout would pretend to be sleeping on bales of hay but would bang a piece of wooden dowel one time on the metal pole and everyone would hush until they got the okay signal with another tap on the pole. If there was an imminent threat, the lookout would bang twice, the beer was stashed, and they quieted down to a Kumbaya setting.

They were getting a little rowdy, and the lookout didn't tap. He came running around and just said, "Vaughan's on his way." Everyone scattered in every direction, taking their beer with them. Katie and Lettie stood up to run, but literally ran into each other, got their legs tangled, and both went down. Before they could completely recover, Vaughan was standing there looking down. "Well, well. What do we have here? Two young ladies, who've had a little too much to drink?" He then extended a hand to each and helped them up. He looked at Lettie and said, "You're free to go. Katie and I have a little talking to do."

Brad had been in the hardware store on Monday and overheard bits and pieces of the conversation Adam was having with a lifelong friend over his doubts about Katie's truthfulness and how he believed there was more there than what she was saying. At this point, Brad knew from what he heard in church that things weren't looking good for Micah. While Brad knew Katie could be telling the truth, he also heard her father say he wasn't sure she was. He couldn't stand by, do nothing, and see an innocent boy go to jail for twenty-five years. So Brad decided to do what Brad does.

He followed Katie from the moment she entered the fairgrounds and stayed out of sight as he reconnoitered the situation to see what might develop. He watched Deputy Johnson approach and decided to move in closer. An arrest for underage drinking could end this evening quickly. He stood behind the bales with a vantage point of having a peephole which he suspected was designed to be used from the other side. He watched Deputy Johnson help the two girls up and dismiss the one he didn't know. He needed to find out who she was and how she fit in.

Vaughan said, "Given the situation, I thought maybe you and I needed to have a little reunion." He moved closer and sat on the bale next to her. Brad watched her stiffen as he touched her face. He could almost smell the fear and he watched her shake. "What's the matter? You liked it before."

"Don't touch me or I'll scream. I swear I will."

"No. No, you won't. You remember our little deal? You say nothing about what happened and I won't make things worse for you and your family and I know you don't want that. I'm going to leave now, but remember I can always get to you. I'm the law. Everyone will believe me."

Brad looked up. "Thank you, Lord, I think you just showed me who we are looking for. If I can find out how that other girl fits in we may have Micah Barnes home free." He watched Deputy Johnson leave and decided not to follow him. He wasn't going to get anything out of him tonight.

~

He watched Katie as she sat there frozen in place, shaking as if a cold wind was blowing through. He could see the mounting fear. This girl was beyond afraid. He was sure the deputy was connected to everything and was the key. Shortly Lettie returned and sat beside her. "What was that all about?"

"Nothing really. He's been after me for three years to go out with him and I won't. Lettie, there is something about him. He's just creepy. And that nose, those ears, and the uniform just makes him creepier."

Brad could see she was lying. He was done for the night. He felt he had the answer to Adam's suspicions—there was way more to the story than what she was telling. But why go after Micah Barnes? Doesn't make sense. At least he knew her friend's name was Lettie and finding out more shouldn't be too difficult. He called it a night and returned to the car. "Hi, Beazie, ready to go home?"

CHAPTER 23

*T*hursday, September 6, 1992. Wednesday Chad went to the offices of Kennedy and Kennedy. He introduced himself to Guy and explained his relationship to Micah. Actually, what he said was, "He will soon be my brother-in-law and I want to help." He explained the new house and how Charlotte and Sara would live with Micah. From a legal standpoint, there didn't seem to be any issues that the D.A. could fault. Charlotte was of age to be Micah's legal guardian and had been serving in that capacity for several years. Both knew the judge wouldn't have issues with it.

That afternoon, Chad made plans to meet Micah and Charlotte. All he told them was that he had a surprise. At 3:30 he parked one house east of the Barnes' compound and waited for Charlotte. He told her to bring Sara. She came out carrying her and as she approached she said, "You need to drive carefully. I can't afford a car seat." Typical Charlotte. Never ask the wealthiest man in the county to get a car seat.

Chad said, "Ah, just throw her in the back. She'll be okay." He opened the back door of the Tahoe that was no longer a rental. He really liked it and decided it was a great family car and he hoped he'd soon have a family. When he moved out of the way Charlotte saw the new car seat. Chad just smiled. Charlotte hugged him. They drove over to the lumberyard, and Micah followed them in his old pickup with the bashed in front end.

They pulled up to the front of the bungalow and parked in the street. Micah pulled in behind. In Glencoe, an alley runs between each street in the older section. Originally it was to keep the horses away from the front of the house. The old stables had been converted to garages or torn down and replaced. Chad didn't want to park in the back as this garage was a converted stable from the first home and it didn't give the back of the house much curb appeal. He got out and walked onto the front lawn. "Well, are you coming?"

"Coming where?"

"To look at your new house."

"Chad you can't do this. You can't keep buying things for me. People will talk. They will say I'm getting these things for the wrong reasons. I want ours to be a love story. I don't want to be known as a kept woman."

Chad grinned sheepishly. "I knew that's exactly what you'd say, and I respect that. I bought the car seat because it's the law and I'd never forgive myself if Sara got hurt. I will continue to do the little things until you love me enough to let me do more. But, Charlotte, this house isn't yours."

She had this strange look on her face that said, 'Excuse me, I don't understand.'

He turned away from her and looked at Micah and handed him the keys. "It's his house, but I'll bet he'll let you and Sara live with him. And that old pickup of yours is okay for going to work, but there's a Grand Am in the garage you can let your sister use if she treats you right."

Turning back to Charlotte he said, "By the way, I bought a car seat for it. Hope that's all right."

She put Sara down on the grass and said, "I give up. What did I do that God should give you to me?" She put her arms around his neck and kissed him.

When she stepped back, Chad smiled and said with a gosh, shucks, ma'am, "When you think about it, I've given your brother a lot more than I've given you."

"No. You've given me what no amount of money can buy."

CHAPTER 24

*F*riday, September 7, 1992. Things had been going really well for Heather. It was over three months since Billy began his transformation and he'd never been nicer nor she happier, but there was still one thing. She missed Sadie and Jake every minute of the day. It seemed wrong that the state and county should be able to have that much power. Yes, she had been glad they were safe but wasn't she the one to decide when the danger was over? The county didn't know her heart or Billy's. All they knew was his past. They only assumed what he was and not what he'd become. She had set up a meeting with Patricia Garcia to bring Billy back into the family.

She arrived promptly at 10:30 with her whole argument carefully worked out. Betsy showed her into Pat's office. Pat came in with a stack of papers and sat down. Heather thanked her for seeing her. "We had a great time at the fair this week. It made me realize how I want to do things like that every day."

"Well, you can. Just leave Billy and you can get them back in just a few days."

Her terse comment stunned Heather. "First, it sounds like you're telling me who I can love and who I can't. You're holding my children hostage until I meet your demands. We talked at the fair and I told them how much Billy has changed and they'd like to let him join us for two supervised visits if you'll allow it. That's why I'm here."

"I'm sorry Heather, that will not happen. We consider Billy Maddox a danger to you and the children. The longest we can legally keep them without a hearing is six months, and that's what we will do. And you should know we plan to fight to put them in permanent foster care."

"But Billy has changed. He never misses work and his boss is happy with his performance and attitude. He received a raise and has more responsibility. He goes to two AA meetings a week and hasn't touched a drop in three months. He doesn't associate with any of his former friends. He's been in church every week and last week he accepted Christ into his life. Even the pastor says it's genuine."

"Heather, you can stop right there. Some of what you say may be true. We aren't a big enough agency to go out and investigate these things. Cases verify that the percentage of people who make a permanent change are less than five percent. By holding the children for six months we make the best effort to protect them. And the religion card, you'd be amazed at how many people try to play that one. Personally, I don't buy that Jesus stuff. It's just trying to use something you can't prove to get what you want. In three months I may not be able to stop you from getting custody if that bum continues to behave, but I'll try. Your weekly supervised visits will continue and I'll see you in three months."

Heather said, "But..."

"Heather, I think that ends our conversation. Good day."

Heather stood and became a woman of determination and full of the power of the Holy Spirit. "Ms. Garcia, you'll see me a lot sooner than that. We're going to court."

Pat Garcia knew she would battle with Ginny Kennedy at some point but didn't know when. The battle with Ginny Kennedy was set.

At two o'clock, four Sheriff's cars once again pulled up to the gates of the Barnes' compound and once again the Rottweilers ran to the gate growling, with teeth bared. They remembered their last encounter with these uniforms and were letting them know they were ready for them this time. Out came the bullhorn, "Paul, come out and call off the dogs. You are not, I repeat, you are not under arrest. Come out and I'll explain." They saw the curtain being pulled aside, but no movement. "Paul, you have ten seconds. And this time the gun has bullets, not tranquilizer darts." Paul watched a Deputy raise his rifle and aim at a dog. Paul came out.

"Now, chain the dogs and come back and open the gate." Paul did as directed and then asked, "What's the meaning of this? This is private property and you're trespassing."

A deputy pulled out the court order. "It's moving day and we are the escort service." With that said, Micah pulled in with his pickup truck with Guy Kennedy in the passenger's seat. This truck was undoubtedly a first for Guy, but he was the one who wanted to be a country lawyer. A truck from the lumber yard followed them with Tinker driving. He tipped his hat to Paul as he pulled in.

Paul took to mean at top speed. "Well, no great loss here. Don't want no cheating, thieving, rapist living on my property anyhow. Good riddance. Get your stuff and get out."

Tinker strolled over to Paul. "Paul, Paul, Paul, apparently you've only got half of what's happening here today. Charlotte and Sara are moving out too." The look in Paul's eyes said he was ready to explode, his teeth gritted and his fists clenched, but he pulled back as two deputies raised their weapons in his direction.

Tinker said, "I told you I would get you. Here's where it starts, Paul. The welfare check you've been stealing from Charlotte and Sara each month? Poof, gone. You're down to just your piddling little monthly check. I think that will make you desperate and stupid enough to do something that's dumb even for you. And I will have one deputy dedicated to sitting out here and following your every move. Won't that be fun?"

They loaded everything and Charlotte and Sara got in the back of a cruiser. Charlotte gave a sad, pathetic look to the man who had held her captive. The six vehicles pulled away leaving an angry Paul Barnes in their wake.

~

Heather prayed as she crossed the street to the door marked Kennedy and Kennedy Attorneys at Law and walked in. "Is Miss Ginny available?" she asked.

They ushered her back and she told Ginny the whole story. Ginny hadn't had a courtroom case since they'd moved to Glencoe. She salivated at the prospect of getting in the courtroom with what she believed was a slam dunk case. She knew the County would bring in an attorney from the state office and their only witnesses were from Family Services. But they would try to use Billy as their witness.

Ginny picked up the phone and called the courthouse to determine when they could get on the Family Court docket. After Heather left, she prepared her petition and walked across the street to the Courthouse to file it. September 14 at 9:30. Small county. Judge Lloyd Chadwick sat on the bench for all the courts and while Ginny didn't know his background Heather did. You would think Lloyd would have to recuse himself, but this is Glencoe, Washington County. A strange little town in a strange little county.

CHAPTER 25

*S*aturday, September 8, 1992. Vaughan Johnson was on the schedule for the Saturday night shift. Actually, he enjoyed this shift. This was the night the teens in town were out looking for a good time which usually meant parking in a secluded area. He enjoyed sneaking up on parked cars, watching for a while and then suddenly rousting them. The badge gave him more authority at 21 years of age than anyone else in Washington County. He ate it up, and most often overstepped his bounds. With his daddy's contacts and money, he planned on being Sheriff before too long. He showed the power of his position with every opportunity, especially if he thought he could impress a teenage girl or intimidate her. He didn't really care which. Unfortunately for him, most weren't, which only made him more determined to score. He'd caught a lot of kids in illegal activities, but rather than arresting them he chose blackmail. It was rumored that he kept a notebook with names, dates, and offenses and called in favors as he wanted. The kids talked about the book, but nobody had seen it and they weren't going to their parents. Vaughan got in the patrol car, checked the lights and siren and was ready to roll.

As he cruised the back roads, he saw lights flash on the dirt road out to the old Frost Cemetery. The cemetery was full and not used often. It wouldn't be loved ones visiting a grave this time of night. He drove up in the dark and used the cruiser to block the road. He waited about 15 minutes and went to have a peek. He scooched low behind the stones as he crept up to the car. The couple inside were in a passionate embrace and Vaughan the voyeur was immediately oblivious to his surroundings. He liked to watch. Tonight that was mistake #1.

Brad pulled his ski mask down and approached so quietly Vaughan heard nothing. But he felt his head crack against the roof of the car and his arm go into the position so many others had felt. The teens jumped, and the girl screamed. Before Vaughan could react, his holster was empty. Using his right hand Brad relieved him of his cuffs, baton, and mace.

As Vaughan recovered, he squirmed around and Brad said, "It might be best for you if you don't irritate or rile me too much. I have known people to get their arms broken. I believe you have seen a few. And I'm guessing you never thought I'd be standing behind you... Mr. Lawman. And I'm assuming that even though you don't know me, you know who I am, right?"

Deputy Johnson nodded.

"Good, that should make my work easier if you are compliant. Resisting me has never been a good idea for anyone." He lifted higher on the arm until he could tell Vaughan was in great pain and pulled him off the car. He told the driver who was shaking like a leaf to open the window and said, "You are free to go. But I have one question, what did you see out here tonight?"

"Honestly, I really don't know what we saw, but I believe the correct answer is we were never here."

"That's the correct answer. Smart kid. You were never here, and you saw nothing. This is between Deputy Johnson and me. It doesn't involve you. I suggest you go to the fair and let people see you. And I assure you, you need not fear Deputy Johnson, am I correct Vaughan?"

Vaughan said, "Yes," as he felt his arm give a little more.

As they drove away Brad walked the deputy over to a waist-high grave marker and pushed him over it. "Deputy Johnson it would be best if you don't move. I really don't want you to end your shift with a broken arm because you tripped over something and broke it. Although, I would like to see you explain it to Tinker.

"Now listen carefully. This is our first encounter, but it won't be our last. I know you are the one who raped Katie Pierce when she was about fourteen. You know it and I know it, but right now I can't prove it. But, before you're tempted to smile, I will prove it. I wouldn't be here tonight unless I was sure I could.

"And what do you think would happen if you go to Tinker and tell him what I did to you? Probably wouldn't be good for you. He knows that when I go after someone they are guilty of something. So if he finds out I'm after you he will want to get involved too. I'm sure you are aware, he doesn't know who I am, and he doesn't want to know. We have what they call an understanding. So, this was just a friendly visit to let you know I'm coming to get you. Next time I won't be so friendly." He put the keys to the handcuffs in Vaughan's mouth, pulled a hood over his head and put the handcuffs on him. "I'm sure you'll be able to get free by the end of your shift."

Now, Brad needed to pay a visit to Lettie Pike. He was sure she fit into this somewhere. And maybe Katie too. Lettie knew Vaughan Johnson raped Katie, but what or who was she protecting?

CHAPTER 26

*M*onday, September 10, 1992. Labor Day attendance at the Washington County Fair was always big. Tinker had one deputy in town and stationed the rest of the deputies around the fairgrounds at various locations. He even had six part-time deputies on duty. He wasn't expecting anything other than the usual Labor Day drunks and the occasional fight they caused. The families and children deserved a good closing day, and he was determined to give it to them.

Katie's group wandered aimlessly around the grounds, occasionally stopping to talk and often pointing out 'geeks' and making fun of them. Kids had made fun of Brad when he was young. Some things never change, kids were mean bullies then, and they were now. He knew Katie didn't used to be like that. He had seen her around church for years and he remembered her as a great kid. He wasn't a trained psychologist, but he guessed the sexual assault had a drastic impact on her personality. Someone had hurt her, she asked for no counseling and received none. She was trying to heal herself and it wasn't working. Now she lashed out at everyone around her. But he still couldn't figure it out... why Micah? How did he fit into this? If you admit to being raped, why not name the real rapist?

Brad focused on Lettie. He needed to separate her from the herd. He heard her say, "I've got to pee. I'll catch up with you." This might be the break he'd waited for. He trailed about twenty feet behind her. They passed Vaughan Johnson, and she looked the other way and didn't acknowledge him. Brad noted that. He intentionally moved a little closer to say hi. Vaughan awoke from his boredom of being assigned to this part of the fairgrounds and immediately recognized Brad and waved to him.

They rounded the corner of the poultry barns and Lettie looked for a Port-a-John with the little green open button and headed straight to it. With no one around Brad quickened his pace and followed her in before the spring-loaded door could slam behind and Lettie could slide the latch. Brad put one arm around the front of her and the other over her mouth. "Lettie don't panic, I won't hurt you. You're safe as long as you don't scream. I need to ask you a few questions concerning Katie's rape allegations against Micah. Can I let you go?" Lettie nodded. Brad let go of her, reached behind, and changed the latch from green to red. There wasn't room to move, but Brad said, "It's best if you don't turn around and see me. That wouldn't be good for you. So just listen and answer my questions. And if you hear someone enter the next John, stop talking."

"I was there the other night when you and Katie knocked each other down trying to run from Deputy Johnson. I heard everything after you left. I also know you are the witness to the night of the alleged rape. What I want to hear from you is what's in the sworn deposition you gave last week. Word for word."

"They instructed me not to say anything about it to anyone."

"I understand that. Now the question is, who are you more afraid of right now? The D.A. or me? So, keep talking."

"Well, the night of the rape I was walking the dog in front of the old abandoned Bigby house on Sycamore St. It's been abandoned for like forty years. The trees and shrubs have grown so high you can't see the house. And there's a big chain-link fence around it and a padlock on the gate. I could hear voices inside the fence and one sounded like Katie and the other was a guy. She was yelling stop, you're hurting me, get off me and things like that. I couldn't get in and it scared me, so I left. I called her an hour later, and she told me what happened. Micah raped her. I asked if she called the sheriff and she said she couldn't, didn't want her parents to find out cause they forbid her to be with him." That last statement made little sense to Brad. He knew she was lying.

"So, then you never saw Micah, did you?"

"No, I didn't. But Katie's my best friend and she wouldn't lie." Brad thought, she not only would, but she also did.

"Lettie I will let you go. You never talked to me." Brad opened the door and quickly slipped around the back and into the building behind.

CHAPTER 27

$\mathcal{T}$uesday, **September 11, 1992.** Ginny arrived at the office and began calling her witnesses. Her witnesses for Heather were solid. She wasn't too concerned about losing the challenge of Family Services' recent decision regarding Heather receiving custody now.

First, she contacted Gary Benton, who was Billy's sponsor, to make sure he could be available on Friday, possibly all day. She didn't see a need to sit him down and prep him. He said he'd done these types of character witnesses before so they went over things on the phone.

Next, she called Reagan who had already received a heads up Sunday, and they talked a bit. He said he'd like to stop by for a few minutes to get to know her a little better and understand exactly what she was looking for from him. She had already gone over things with Heather and Billy.

She could call Sheriff Reynolds and Billy's boss to the stand, but she didn't see the need. She even wondered what might happen if she called Judge Chadwick to the stand. Probably best to leave that one alone.

Ginny's defense strategy was simple. She would let Family Services present their case. Since they had no reliable local witnesses with any credibility, she wouldn't cross-examine any of them. There was no point in even bothering with their paid professional witnesses since this was a case heard only by the judge.

Reagan stopped in Ginny's office about a half hour later, they chatted for a few minutes, and then got down to the business at hand. Ginny explained, "I'm taking an unusual approach. I explained to the others, I only want you to answer the questions I ask you. No extra information. Answer as simply as you can answer. If I need more, I'll ask another question. The extra information will come on cross-examination. The state Family Services lawyer sees us as a bunch of hicks so we'll play it that way. I will leave a lot of blanks for her to fill in. Every time she asks a question she will hang herself with the information you provide. And each question will tighten the noose. That's pretty much it."

Sounded like a strange approach to Reagan, but he was a preacher, not an attorney.

Vaughan Johnson had pulled the four to midnight shift this week. This gave Brad the cover of darkness. He had contacted the young teen caught parking in the cemetery. Through the conversation, he found out about the rumor that Vaughan had a notebook with names, dates, and blackmail details. He was cooperative since Brad had stopped Vaughan before they became part of the book. The young man emphasized the notebook was the word around school and he wasn't sure if the book existed. If it existed, Brad would find it.

Vaughan lived in an apartment above Sal's Pizza. The stairs were on the back side, so Brad parked nearby and climbed the stairs. Vaughan equipped the door with three locks. Two of them Brad knew he couldn't pick. He could break the glass, but he wasn't ready to let Vaughan know of his real presence and that he was close to pay dirt. He didn't like option number two, but it was all he had. He went back down the stairs and around to the front entrance of Sal's. For a

Tuesday night, Sal's was packed. Good. He nodded hello to Sal as he headed back to the bathroom. He came to a door that could be a closet or the door to the interior stairs. Locked. Old skeleton key. Fifteen seconds and he was on his way up the stairs. The lock at the top took a pick set, but he was in the apartment in less than two minutes. He was pleased to find Vaughan had left the lights on. He looked around before noticing a row of books on the TV console. Books in Vaughan Johnson's apartment seemed as out of place as a stereo system in a deaf man's apartment. He guessed that Deputy Johnson hadn't opened a book since high school so why a whole row of mishmashed books? He read the titles and stopped on the spine of a book entitled, "I Know What You Did." Brad smiled, could this be any easier? He pulled out the book and opened it to discover he had hollowed out the book and it held the notebook. Jackpot. He sat down and browsed name after name. He was particularly interested in what he found concerning Katie. He copied what he found. Next, he looked up Lettie and found, 10/15/1991-Lettie Pike-drinking, fornicating, Baptist. This explained a lot. He put the notebook back in the book and replaced it on the shelf. He locked both the locks and exited by the back delivery door.

CHAPTER 28

riday, September 14, 1992. At 9:30 the bailiff entered the courtroom, "Hear ye! Hear ye! The Family Court of Washington County is now in session. All rise for the Honorable Lloyd Chadwick presiding." Lloyd climbed to his bench and said, "You may be seated."

"The case before us today is Heather Delaney vs. the Washington County Family Services. Heather Delaney is suing for the early return of custody of Sadie Delaney and Jake Delaney." Looking over to the Family Services bench, "Ms. Gates, are you ready to present your case?"

"We are, your honor."

"Ms. Kennedy, are you ready?"

"We are, your honor."

"Ms. Gates, you may present your opening statement to the court."

Ms. Gates began, "You honor, it is the position of the state and the county that early release of the two minor children would be detrimental to their safety and wellbeing. It is our position that Billy Maddox still presents a danger and a threat and that three months of treatment is not nearly enough to evaluate the home situation."

"Thank you, Ms. Gates, and Ms. Kennedy, do you have anything for the court?"

"I do, your honor. Ms. Delaney has cooperated with the Department of Family Services. She has complied with every directive and played by the rules. The Department of Family Services refuses to consider returning her children for at least six months and recently told her they would then seek to place Sadie and Jake in permanent foster care. Your Honor, the issue is Heather's fiancé, Billy Maddox, who we will show is fully rehabilitated and in no way a danger to Heather or her children."

The county called three expert witnesses in the various areas of the rehabilitation rates of abusers and alcoholics.They proceeded with their presentation and most everyone snored. The charts and illustrations were impressive and cost the State Family Services a bundle of money. Finally, an hour and a half later they finished. They then called two of Billy's former drinking buddies. The final witness was Sheriff Tinker Reynolds who was forced to testify about all the arrests and incidents that involved Billy Maddox over the years. This list was long. Each time the Judge called for cross-examination Ms. Kennedy had replied, "No questions at this time, your Honor." When the Judge called for the cross-examination of Tinker Reynolds, Ginny Kennedy replied, "I have one question, your Honor." She got up and walked over to the witness stand.

"Sheriff, the Billy Maddox you gave testimony about. In your opinion, is that the same Billy Maddox that is sitting over there?"

Tinker puffed his stomach up to his chest and leaned forward in his chair and said, "Ma'am, that all depends on what you mean. Is that the body of the Billy Maddox I arrested 18 times in 10 years? If that's the question then, yes. Is the soul in that body the same Billy Maddox? Then, no ma'am, that is not the same Billy Maddox who is here today."

"Thank you, Sheriff, I have no further questions."

"Your Honor, I object. Opinion."

"Duly noted Ms. Gates."

Heather was thinking, aren't you even going to fight back against these bureaucrats? You're supposed to be fighting for my children.

Heather was feeling Ginny was a country lawyer who would get eaten up. The Judge called for a lunch recess and would resume at 1:00 for the plaintiff to plead her case.

Ginny, Reagan, and Heather all met in a private lunch room. Guy Kennedy was the lunch delivery boy. He put the bags on the table and sat down to join them. Heather, who had the most to gain or to lose was visibly upset with the morning proceedings. Without Heather saying a word Ginny looked at her and said, "Everything is going exactly the way I want it to. In Chicago, we do things a little differently, but I adapted to this situation. I have them feeling confident and maybe even cocky. They will slip up. Trust me."

Guy could see Heather wasn't convinced and said, "We came here to help people who couldn't help themselves. We only defend people we believe in. And most importantly, we never lose. Never. You could not have a better lawyer than Ginny. This afternoon will be very interesting. Well, for us anyway."

Heather said, "I hope so." But she wasn't feeling optimistic.

At 1:00 p.m. court resumed. Ginny called Patricia Garcia to the stand. Patricia and Ms. Gates looked at each other in bewilderment. "Ms. Garcia I have only one question for you and it is an easy question which you can answer with a yes or no. Did you tell Heather Delaney that even after six months you would fight against the return of her children?"

"Well, it wasn't exactly..."

"Ms. Garcia, yes or no? I don't care about the wording. Did you tell her you would seek permanent foster care?"

"Yes, I said something like that, but..."

"Thank you, Ms. Garcia. You are excused. No further questions."

She turned to the bench and Judge Chadwick held up his hand as she spoke. "You are dismissed, Ms. Garcia." Ms. Gates felt the hearing changing direction already and was less than pleased that Patricia had ever made a stupid commitment.

Ginny called Gary Benton to the stand. "Mr. Benton, what is your relationship to Billy Maddox?"

Gary remembered; simple one-word answers, "I'm his AA sponsor."

"And Mr. Benton, are you an alcoholic?" "Yes, ma'am, I am."

"Mr. Benton, please tell the court where you work." I work at the First National Bank in Upton."

"Thank you. And how long have you sponsored Billy Maddox?"

"About three months."

"How often does Billy attend meetings?"

"Twice a week."

"Now I realize you don't have all the professional degrees or have conducted the national studies that the experts shared with us this morning, but how would you evaluate Billy Maddox's progress?" Remembering, she said, "In your opinion."

"I would have to say I've never seen a man work through the program so soon and so well."

"Thank you, Mr. Benton, I have no further questions."

Judge Chadwick said, "Ms. Gates, do you wish to cross-examine this witness?"

"Yes, your Honor." She smelled blood in the water and was ready to feast. The thing is, one of the first things they teach you in law school is: Don't ask a witness a question unless you already know the answer. Doris Gates knew nothing about Gary Benton and apparently forgot as she blustered forth.

"Mr. Benton, you stated you were his sponsor and you yourself are an alcoholic, is that correct?"

Gary remembered Ginny's coaching. "When she follows up on the questions I asked, give her as much professional detail as you can get in before she cuts you off."

"Yes ma'am, I've been his sponsor for three months. In my time in AA I've sponsored about 300 individuals. I began drinking when I was thirteen and joined AA at fifteen. I've been sober for 35 years so that gives me some pretty good training and insight." She cut him off. Too much information. She decided she better focus on Billy.

"So you see Billy twice a week at meetings, is that correct?"

"Yes, that is correct. Monday and Wednesday. BUT, I also have breakfast with him on Tuesday and Saturday AND the days I don't see him we talk on the phone." Too much information. Not going well for Doris.

Still not too late to recover. "Mr. Benton, you said you work for the bank in Upton. May I ask your position?" Home run. Arrow through the heart. Strike three, you're out! Oh, Doris, why did you ask that question?

"Well, I graduated in 1984 from Penn State with a dual major in Business Administration and Accounting. I have a Master's in both and I am the President of the First National Bank in Upton. And I might add Billy has worked the program with more determination and sincerity than I have ever seen. Ms. Gates, you don't last long in my field if you can't read people."

She said, "No, further questions your honor." Lloyd gave an under the breath chuckle. Ginny turned in her seat, looked at Heather and beamed from ear to ear.

"Judge, I'd like to call the Reverend Reagan Lamb to the stand."

Reagan stood and moved to the stand and took the oath. "Pastor Lamb, you are Billy and Heather's pastor, is that correct?"

"I am."

"And how long have you known them?"

"I've known Heather and her children for about three years. And Billy for only about three months."

"What did you think of Billy three months ago?"

"Truthfully, he was a vile human being."

"And today?"

"God got a hold of this man in a mighty way. He has been redeemed from sin and death and is a true child of God."

"So your opinion as a religious leader is that Billy Maddox has changed?"

"As the Sheriff said, this is not the same Billy Maddox. He is a new creation."

"Thank you. No further questions."

"Ms. Gates, do you wish to cross?"

"Yes, your Honor, I do." Lloyd was thinking, "I sure hope you know what you're doing lady. I've been where you're going to try to go. Good luck."

"Mr. Lamb, I don't believe in a religion of any type. I've been an atheist, agnostic at best, for forty years. God doesn't change people. I don't think people even need God. I will concede that Jesus was a great teacher, but so were Mohammed and Buddha and the Dalai Lama. And that's about it. So, when referring to Mr. Maddox as being a child of God that makes him a child of nothing. Your testimony has no value in a court of law."

"Ms. Gates, are you asking me to prove that Jesus is who he says he is?"

"If you think you can in under five minutes."

"I'll give it a shot. You said, yourself, that Jesus is a great teacher. And he was, but Ms. Gates did you know he never gave us that option. Never once did Jesus ever claim to be a teacher. People called him rabbi, which means teacher, but he never accepted the title. And yet over and over he refers to himself as the Son of God. He even called himself God when he said he who has seen me has seen the Father. Now it seems, to me, Ms. Gates, you've got a greater decision to make than you've made. Jesus has only given you three choices concerning who he is, and a teacher isn't one. But remember, you said he was a great teacher, so you acknowledge authority in the man. What he claimed was deity so then there are three choices, he's a lunatic right up there with the man who thinks he's a pumpkin. Or he is the greatest liar and deceiver who has ever lived. Or he is Lord as he claimed to be. But please, Ms. Gates, don't give me that nonsense about him being a great teacher... he never gave you that option. But by recognizing him as a great teacher you have recognized the power and authority of the Living God. Any further questions?" Strike two. Rope tightens. Doris, do you really want to face the next batter?

⌢

Ginny decided she didn't need Heather's testimony. Given the stakes, she might be too fragile. She wasn't a believer herself, but she felt Billy Maddox was more than a match for Doris Gates. This woman had been knocked off her game. Last out. Last inning.

Ginny said, "I call Mr. Billy Maddox to the witness stand." Doris salivated as they swore Billy in. "Do you promise to tell the truth, the whole truth, and nothing but the truth?"

Billy said, "Mister, I ain't swearing to nothing until you get me a Bible to put my hand on. And then I plan on swearing it to my God, not you." Judge Chadwick passed his own worn personal Bible to the bailiff. If Doris had noticed she'd be thinking, "This can't be good."

Ginny said, "Billy, are you ready to accept the responsibility to be a husband and father?"

"Ms. Ginny, I've never been more ready for anything in my life. I'm a new creation in Christ Jesus. The old has passed away, it's gone. God said when I received Christ, there was no more condemnation for me."

"Billy, that's enough. No more questions, your Honor."

She looked at Doris Gates as if to say, "Go ahead, I dare you."

She had no choice. This was her last opportunity to win, and she had to break Billy.

"Mr. Maddox, I'd like you to tell me more about being saved and how that makes you fit to be a decent father to Sadie and Jake."

"Well, Ms. Gates, I don't know that I can rightly do that."

Doris was now hopeful of trapping him.

"I've only been a Christian for a few months. I'm what the Bible calls a babe in Christ. I don't fully understand most of what's happened. I'm just beginning to study the Word, so I can't fully explain things like grace and mercy or even really fully understanding that I've been forgiven.

"But I can try to explain it as I see it. Back in the end of May, I got drunk and I beat Heather something fierce. Since that day I haven't had a drink. Until I accepted Christ I still craved it, but I fought it off.

Since receiving Christ I haven't even had the desire to drink. It even smells bad. I haven't been with, or spoken to, any of the drunks you dragged in here to testify agin' me except when they cornered us at the fair. I know I'm an alcoholic and I'm not ashamed. It's no different from being a diabetic. Since May I've laid my hands on Heather often." Pause. "To hold and cuddle her. I realized that until I met Jesus, she was the only person who's ever loved me. And I will spend the rest of my life righting that wrong. I used to work because I had to take care of myself. I've been back to work for nearly three months. I work full time, get benefits, got a raise, and they have promoted me. Most wouldn't consider my job much, but I work hard for an honest day's pay. I can't explain it, but every Friday I come home and hand my paycheck over to Heather and it excites me to do it. See, Ms. Gates, the Bible says a man who doesn't take care of his family is worse than an infidel. Now, I'm not rightly sure what that is, but I don't want to be one." The Judge chuckled. "The first Sunday I went to church it was to please Heather, but now it would take a lot to keep me away. Why, I don't know. I just know I feel better when I come out than when I went in. And I want to get those young-uns back where they belong, in God's house. That day I got up and went forward, I didn't even know I'd done it until I got there and there was Heather right beside me dedicating her life to Christ. When I got up, I asked her to marry me... right there in front of the whole congregation. No, ma'am, that wasn't Billy Maddox in any of these things. That's the power of the Living God at work through His Holy Spirit. You know, Ms. Gates, you ought to try asking Jesus into your life. Might change your outlook and attitude." Out of the park grand slam! And Doris Gates that's strike three, you're out!

Doris went back to her table and mumbled, "No further questions."

~

Lloyd said, "Ordinarily this is where I go back to my chambers and carefully weigh everything and tell you to come back tomorrow and

I'll render my verdict. Ms. Gates, I have to say, I'm wondering how you ever passed the bar."

"I'm ruling on behalf of Heather Delaney. Ms. Garcia you will have those children in the Maddox/Delaney home no later than 4:00 p.m. today. No later than 4:00, is that clear? We are dismissed."

At three fifty-nine Patricia Garcia pulled in and before the engine was off the kids were out and running to the porch. Heather got down on her knees to hug her children and thank God for their return. Billy got a little misty to see the joy in Heather as she hugged her children and wouldn't let go. Pat Garcia was still standing there. Lloyd had come to the house to see if Ms. Garcia was on time. He looked at her and once again said, "Ms. Garcia, you are dismissed." The old hound dog looked at them, gave the tail one thump, and put his head back down... "Oh, were you gone?"

Billy got down on his knees and said, "Guys, I don't know what to say to you. I was a bad person and God is fixing me. I don't expect you to love or trust me yet, but I would like a chance to be a good dad...when you're ready. And in the meantime, I will try to do what a good dad does." They said nothing and he didn't expect they would.

Reagan hugged Billy and said, "Kids rebound fast. They've always wanted a dad and they just don't want to be hurt."

"Yeah, I know. Remember, I've never really had a family. The waiting is killing me."

CHAPTER 29

*M*onday, September 17, 1992. Chad loaded the 'family' into the Tahoe around 5:30 and headed to Upton for a nice dinner. Charlotte was a good cook, but Chad was Chad and felt he was taking advantage of her by showing up for dinner every night. He'd like to hire her a housekeeper and a cook, but he knew how that would go over. So once or twice a week he took everyone out. Tonight they were going to O'Brien's Steak House. There was one thing that was for sure, after a meal there you drove back to Glencoe slowly. You didn't want to lose that steak.

Paul Barnes sat in his chair in a drunken stupor, but Paul was a functional drunk. He sat there and noticed the dead silence and the filth all around him. He knew it was Charlotte's fault it was so filthy. If'n she hadn't run out, there'd be someone to clean. Never thought his daughter could ever be so ungrateful for all he done for her. He missed having Sara around. Without Sara it was way too quiet. She was the only happiness this trailer had seen since Maureen walked out years ago.

Charlotte had always kept the place neat and clean even if Paul refused to buy anything new. The last new thing he bought was a window fan after the AC broke down four years ago. She cleaned up and now he looked at the empty chip bags, beer bottles, and dirty clothes on the floor and he realized Houston had stolen her too. Houston took from him the only things in his life with meaning.

"Those rich people need to be taught a lesson. You can't steal another man's things and get away with it. It ain't right." He didn't care about Micah. He'd lost him. But he had the girls, and he wanted them back. He was losing about $1200 a month without them. He might not get them back, but he could teach them a good lesson. Nobody takes away what belongs to Paul Barnes.

He took two five-gallon gas cans and put them in the back of the old AMC Pacer and headed for town. He drove around the block a couple times until it was dark enough to get to Micah's and Charlotte's house unseen.

The Sheriff had put the word out that he wanted Paul Barnes put away. Everyone feared how he might retaliate if given the opportunity. They had been watching him carefully, but on the closing night of the fair they spread the Sheriff's Office too thin.

Brad was out walking Beasley. Beasley was Beasley, so it was a slow walk. He had a meeting after work and had just gotten out. Since he always took Beasley to work, he'd stop in different areas to walk him. Tonight he wanted to get a closer look at the Bigby House. He walked around the property as much as he could. He noticed that it was as Lettie described, very overgrown. This was one of the few homes that had a front drive with no alley access. As he walked toward the corner he noticed Paul's rusted out Pacer. Even without the rust, the only '76 Pacer in town would stand out. He was about a block away and watched it turn away from him and into the alley behind Pine Street.

Brad said, "Sorry, Beasley, I may have to go back to work." He put Beasley in the car and got a few things out of the trunk. He moved quickly and came from the front side of the house and hid behind Sara's playhouse. Soon Paul came trudging up the path by the garage carrying the two gas cans. This was too obvious. Brad slipped on his ski mask and when Paul was between him and the house, he came up behind him. Now, remember, Paul is a functional drunk and an enormous man. He didn't go down. He turned and swung a gas can at Brad's head. Brad partially blocked it, but it still caught him on the side of the head. He was able to bring his foot up between Paul's legs and nailed him. Paul dropped the cans and grabbed his crotch as he keeled over in pain. When he bent forward Brad brought his knee up into Paul's face and he went down. He took off his ski mask and put a hood over Paul's head and rolled him over. He tightened the hood and put double zip ties on him.

He got in the car and drove to the pay phone outside the Courthouse. "Washington County Sheriff's Office, Deputy Adams speaking. How may I help you, sir or ma'am?' Hmmm... very efficient.

"Deputy Adams, you don't know who I am, but you know me. Here's a chance to make your mark in the department. Behind Micah Barnes house at 315 Pine you will find Paul Barnes zip tied with a mask over his face. There are two gas cans near him with his prints all over them. I caught him before he burned the house down. I suggest you go to the scene and do the things you need to do to make it your arrest. Understand? The Sheriff wants this man put away and this should do it."

He got in the car. "Sorry Beasie, maybe tomorrow."

Deputy Adams was in a quandary. He was alone in the office and sure didn't want to give the arrest to Vaughan Johnson who was on patrol tonight. At that moment Vaughan came in and slammed the door and was about to say something. Adams said, 'Good, just who I wanted to see. Vaughan, you take the desk for about twenty minutes while I take care of something."

"I'm on patrol. What makes you think you can order me around?"

"Uh, maybe because I'm a Corporal and you're not. I'll be back in a few."

Vaughan thought to himself, "Yeah, you're a Corporal and after the election in two years I'll be your boss."

Adams went out, jumped in the patrol car and turned on the siren. When he arrived, he parked out front and left the lights going. He wanted to make sure the neighbors knew he was here. He found Paul lying on the ground, still unconscious with the two gas cans nearby. He quickly cut the zip ties and put them in his pocket. One fell out. He placed the handcuffs on him, untied the hood and rolled him over. He removed the hood and stuck it in his shirt until he could destroy it. Then he slapped Paul's face to wake him.

Paul came to and as he tried to struggle, he discovered he was cuffed. "Who are you?"

"I'm Deputy Sheriff Adams and I caught you trying to burn down your son's and daughter's house."

"I don't think so deputy dawg. The guy that took me down was bigger and stronger than you. It'd take three of you to bring me down."

"Sorry, you're wrong Paul, it was all me. I came up behind you. Ordered you to put the cans down and your hands over your head. You refused and when you turned I hit you with my nightstick and cuffed you. Now we wait for Sheriff Reynolds."

Tink arrived about five minutes later all smiles. "Guess we gotcha, Paul. I told you you'd do something too dumb for even you."

"Yeah, well, you and Deputy Dawg here didn't get me. Someone sucker punched me. I got nothing more to say. I want my court-appointed lawyer."

Tink said, "We'll get you that lawyer, but first we need to get you nice and comfy in your new home." He looked down and saw the zip tie, picked it up and put it in his own pocket and said nothing. He just smiled. Didn't matter to Tink what happened or how. He had Paul Barnes on attempted arson. And Deputy Adam's version of the story was as good as any.

Tink read him his rights, which Paul knew full well, and loaded him in the cruiser. "Too late to get you a lawyer tonight. We'll see what we can do tomorrow. Gonna be hard to find anyone who'd want to represent you though."

CHAPTER 30

riday, September 21, 1992. Four days and Paul was still sitting in his cell. About every half hour he'd yell, "Where's my lawyer? I have my rights you know." It got so bad they finally just closed the door and turned up the radio. The truth was, nobody cared about finding him a lawyer or even recognizing he had rights.

Tinker had requested an arraignment, but they told him the paperwork was improperly filled out and they returned it to his office. Tink went over it three times and couldn't find anything wrong. Then he realized. He wasn't the only one who wanted Paul to pay for what he did to his family. There was nothing wrong with the paperwork. He put it back into the envelope and sent it back to the courthouse. Friday morning he received word from the D.A.'s office. They set the arraignment and charged him with attempted arson, resisting arrest, assaulting an officer, and driving an unregistered vehicle thrown in.

Later in the day, Judge Chadwick's secretary called to let him know that Paul Barnes' request for a Public Defender had somehow been placed in the wrong box and they only now found it.

Tinker went to the cell area to let Paul know he had good news, and he had bad news. "So which do you want first?"

"Since all you've done is mess with me, and deny me my rights, it don't seem that it matters much."

"Now, why would you say something like that? You've got it better in here than in that fire trap, pig pen you call home. I'd think you'd appreciate everything I've done for you. Honestly, I've been trying to find you a defense counsel. Apparently, your request got lost at the courthouse and they just found it. That's the bad news. The good news is your arraignment is Monday at 11:00. More good news, the Judge can force someone to represent you on Monday. And the best news is tomorrow is Saturday. Emma cooks waffles and bacon on Saturday. Paul, this really is your lucky day. So you sit tight. Take a nap. Read the Gideon Bible. You could play checkers against yourself, but you'd probably still lose."

Ever since he'd won over Shirley, she had been playing practical jokes on him. Things would disappear from his office and he'd find them in the strangest places. He had a copy of Rodan's *The Thinker* on a shelf in his office. Last Sunday he had glanced over to the choir area and there was The Thinker sitting on top of the piano. Today was Reagan's day for revenge and he was excited. Today was Operation Shirley. He'd been planning this since he found out Shirley and Langdon were going on a cruise.

Now it was payback time. Shirley fancied herself as somewhat of a period historian and everything in the house had to be in keeping with a period theme or at least period correct. Shirley and Langdon owned one of the older Victorians in the town. Lots of gingerbread, bright Victorian colors, wicker on the wrap-around porch and lots of geraniums and petunias. Inside, the dining room, living room, and parlor were period correct in all the furnishings, artwork, and what was called bric-à-brac. The kitchen was modern and there was a TV room/family room. The library was Langdon's private getaway. Each room upstairs was a trip to another place or time. One bedroom was all Amish. A second was primitive colonial. The third was in the

Mission Period. And Shirley's bedroom was all authentic Duncan Phyfe from the early 1800s.

It was a large home, and Reagan had a whole day's work ahead of him. He stopped by the Greasy Spoon for his usual and then went next door to visit with Wayne. He had to share all the things God had been doing with someone who'd really appreciate what was happening.

Reagan went over to Shirley's about 10:30 and retrieved the hide-a-key from under the geranium pot. What Reagan hadn't realized was that Operation Shirley involved moving and relocating nearly 200 pieces of art and wall decor throughout the house. He had to make sure that every piece did not go with anything else in the room. Just when he'd think he had it right he'd find a piece that might fit that room and have to move two or three more to get a mismatch. He took nearly five hours and no lunch to get it right. The only thing he regretted was he wouldn't see her face.

The thing about a former sociopath is they are still charming when they are no longer behaving with sociopathic tendencies. Such was Billy Maddox. Even when Billy was conning you and taking you for a ride, you still liked him. So it was no surprise that everyone loved the new Billy. The transition from a dysfunctional family to a functioning family went smoothly. It didn't hurt that Sadie and Jake could see that their mother really loved Billy. They could see that she wasn't afraid of him anymore and that made them less afraid. They loved seeing both parents laugh and have fun...that had never happened before. Billy wasn't trying to buy Sadie and Jake's love, but he wanted to make up for four lost years. Being reared the way he was made the emotional part of loving come hard. Billy knew a good dad was a good provider and maybe these things would show he cared. He had cleaned up the whole property and removed anything that was dangerous. He found a good used trampoline and put it where he and Heather could sit and watch from the porch that now had two

210 | R MARSHALL WRIGHT

Adirondack chairs, a repaired post, and the old hound dog. In antici-
pation of the reunion, he'd built a big platform up in the apple tree
and explained about all the expansion plans for future additions. He
even climbed up with them to show them where everything would be.
Thursday evening they'd gone to the Burger Barn and then had ice
cream. Sadie and Jake couldn't remember ever doing any of these
things. So while they weren't being hugged, they were being loved as
best as Billy could for now. They were seeing a very different Billy.

CHAPTER 31

Saturday, September 22, 1992. Saturday morning Billy lay in bed thinking about how his life had changed. He hadn't thought about the guy in the Dew Drop Inn john for a long time. In fact, he still didn't know who the guy was or if he even had a name. This guy sure didn't seem like an angel of God at the time, especially the broken arm thing. He remembered telling Heather that he had a vision and it was like God was standing right behind him. Maybe it was. Billy didn't know much yet about how God works, but he knew he probably couldn't get his attention any other way. He'd sure like to meet that guy and thank him.

He could smell the bacon cooking and knew Heather was in the kitchen. He heard her yell, "Tell your dad breakfast is ready." The only word he heard was "dad" and he felt proud to be what he never had. Suddenly the door burst open and two little feet came pounding across the floor and for a moment he heard nothing until forty-three pounds landed on his chest. Jake said, "Mom said to wake you up for breakfast. Are you awake?" Billy smiled and said, "Oh yeah, I am now." He hugged him.

He got dressed and headed for the table when he heard crashing and banging outside. What a racket. Doors slamming, metal banging, and the sounds of people running around, each with something to say. Billy pulled aside the curtain carefully. He wondered if someone still had a vendetta against him and had gathered a lynch mob in the front yard. He looked out and recognized every face out there including Judge Chadwick, Reagan Lamb, and eight other church members. And none were carrying weapons, but they were armed with ladders, paintbrushes, and lots of cans of yellow paint.

Billy opened the door and just stood there as everyone yelled good morning. The old hound dog never opened his eyes. He'd probably end up gray as they painted the porch floor. The gesture of the people overwhelmed Billy. People he didn't even know just three months ago. People helping and caring about Billy Maddox was a foreign concept to him. He struggled to swallow his pride and just accept that people did things for others because they wanted to. For two months he had wanted to paint the house, but with $500 for paint, he decided there were things his family needed more than a pretty house. Reagan yelled, "Go eat your breakfast and get out of our way, we have work to do."

About three o'clock Saturday afternoon Shirley and Langdon returned from their all-inclusive week in the Caribbean on the island of St. Bart. She was feeling refreshed and invigorated and ready to start on the annual church bazaar. Each church held a Christmas Bazaar and Shirley had headed up the Community Church Bazaar for seventeen years in a row with the help of the Women's Guild members who averaged nearly eighty years old. Shirley was already thinking perhaps she should have planned the vacation for the week after the bazaar to recuperate. But then, she'd miss the accolades that lasted several days and that was really what the bazaar was all about.

Shirley unlocked the house as Langdon dragged in four suitcases, two of which he thought had never been opened. He set them down in the entryway and went to turn on the hot water heater. Shirley went to the hall to check her hair in the big oval mirror she had acquired at a sale outside Upton. She bid way too much, but it was a perfect period piece to hang in the hall. She looked into the mirror, but instead of her reflection, she saw a dog playing poker with a cigar in his mouth. She turned in shock and looked around. Nothing was where it belonged, nothing! She ran upstairs and went room by room. Langdon walked by the staircase. He heard a shriek followed by, "Reagan Lamb, I'll get you for this." Langdon was glad she was upstairs as he roared with laughter. Then he realized, "This could keep her out of my hair for days. Thanks, Pastor."

~

Billy loaded the kids into the GTO about 11:30 and made a run to the new Subway that had opened in the old video store. VHS videos were big business, but Glencoe wasn't ready for three.

Charlie Bailey, who had his hand in about everything in town, had purchased the Subway franchise. Charlie was an entrepreneur and a strong believer who gave God credit for everything he had. He dabbled in anything that might make money, from speculating in real estate, buying land, to investing in a fast food franchise. But one thing Charlie would never do is get involved with anything sleazy or unscrupulous. People jokingly said Charlie owned half of Glencoe. Truth is, he owned a lot of it. Bought it on speculation. Charlie was more of an optimist for the future of Glencoe than most people were. But, his investments had served him well.

Billy got sandwiches and drinks for the work crew and let the kids order what they wanted. They were excited about another new thing they got to do. They walked out. Jake said to Sadie, "I like the new Billy."

She said, "Me, too" and took his hand to cross the street.

The lunch set Billy back a few bucks that he hadn't planned to spend, but it was much cheaper than the paint. He realized it was something he wanted to do and felt good about.

About 4:00 they all stood back and looked at their masterpiece.

Billy now owned the nicest home in the Oaks. Was redevelopment on its way to the Oaks?

CHAPTER 32

*M*onday, September 24, 1992. Paul's arraignment was Monday at 11:00. Allison Dodge was there for the prosecution. This man had been a menace to the community for better than forty years. He never cared who he conned or cheated out of their money. He'd say, "Well, serves them right for being so dang gullible and greedy. They knew who I was." He was one of the biggest scammers in the county welfare system and he knew every legal loophole in the system. Problem was, it was legal. Neighbors all hated him and merchants wanted nothing to do with him.

The Sheriff led Paul in handcuffs and leg shackles just for the effect. He sat him down at the Defense table. There he sat all by himself looking around.

"All rise." Lloyd entered. "Be seated." And we're ready. Judge Chadwick looked over at Paul and said, "Where's your attorney? You aren't representing yourself are you?" Paul just shrugged and looked at the Sheriff.

"Sheriff Reynolds, where is Mr. Barnes' attorney?"

"Well, your Honor, we received word from your office late Friday that the request of counsel had been misplaced. I tried to find someone, but every lawyer I could reach refused to represent him unless compelled by a court order."

The judge asked, "And why wasn't I contacted?"

"Again your Honor, you'd have to ask your secretary. From my perspective, it was the weekend, and I didn't think it was necessary to bother you. Also, I figured you knew. Anyway, he was fine where he was."

"Well, to request bail and set a trial date he needs an attorney. So just march him back to the jail and I'll appoint someone. We'll set arraignment for 2:00 p.m. tomorrow."

Lloyd went back to his chambers and contacted his secretary by intercom. "Ms. Michaels, you and I need to talk, but first please get Ms. Kennedy on the line."

After a couple minutes she was back and said, "Your Honor, I have her on line one" and then she giggled. There was only one line.

Abigail Michaels' husband had a long-standing vendetta with Paul Barnes. About fifteen years ago he bought twenty acres of land from Paul that had belonged to his Pappy. Problem was Paul didn't own the land any longer, but sold it anyway. Paul only spent six months in jail, but Vic Michaels lost his $22,000. Paul was court ordered to pay restitution. You can guess how that went.

He picked up the phone and said, "Good afternoon Ginny. Nice work the other day. Now I have another opportunity for you. I've selected you to defend Paul Barnes. It's an attempted arson case and you will be the court-appointed attorney. Arraignment is tomorrow at two and I'll have the Sheriff drop off all the pertinent information later today."

"But wait a minute, your Honor, we don't do that work. We only defend clients we believe are victims of the system. And I assume Paul Barnes is Micah's father, and if so I want nothing to do with him."

"Ginny, you really have no say in the matter. We do things differently in Washington County than they do in Chicago. The city has both the District Attorney's Office and the Public Defender's Office, as you well know. We don't have that luxury here. We take turns and it's your turn. See you tomorrow."

"But, your Honor?"

"Sorry, no buts, see you at 2:00."

I keep telling you it's a strange little town.

CHAPTER 33

*T*uesday, September 25, 1992. Micah's trial was eight days away and Allison Dodge was feeling good about how things were progressing. This was essentially a "he said/she said" case and those could go either way. Micah had no defense beyond his sister claiming they were together that night, but there was no proof and they wouldn't get a testimony from Paul Barnes now. She knew she didn't have much for the prosecution either, but she felt she had enough. At least she had a reliable witness. Lettie Pike had given a testimony that should be enough for a conviction. And with all poor Maddie Pierce had been through, the jury would be sympathetic to a mother who saw her daughter withdrawing into a shell from all the embarrassment and humiliation.

∼

Guy Kennedy wasn't feeling quite as optimistic. He knew Micah was innocent... that's why he took the case. But with eight days to go, he still couldn't find any way to prove it. Reasonable doubt was the best he had right now. He was good at creating reasonable doubt and had used it effectively in his previous life. This would test if he still had it.

If he could discredit Lettie, that would even the playing field back to she said/he said. You normally don't want the defendant to testify, but this time he might have too. Micah had been a star athlete in the county and he was a nice kid. If he could prep him well enough, not let Allison Dodge rattle him, and then trip up Katie Pierce, he might have a chance. It was a big if, but for now it's all he had.

~

At 2:00 p.m. Ginny Kennedy showed up in the courtroom, but she didn't look happy to be there. She had had time to find out a lot about Paul Barnes and none of it was good. If someone had offered her enough money in her previous life, she might have taken the case no questions asked. Now? Not a chance. She had developed a conscience. But she didn't want to be in contempt by refusing the judge's orders, so here she was. Reluctant, but present.

"Ms. Kennedy, have you looked at the case?"

"I have your honor."

"And how does your client wish to plead?"

"Against my advice, he has instructed me to plead not guilty, and he requests bail to be set."

"Ms. Dodge, bail?"

"Your Honor, no chance, we request he be held without bond. He's not only a flight risk, but he also poses a significant danger to his family and the community."

"Ms. Kennedy?"

"No argument from me, your Honor. She's probably right. He'd take off, and we'd never see him again. Just keep him in jail. Then I'll know where to find him to help with his defense."

Paul jumped in, "Hey, just wait for one cotton picking second. You're my lawyer. Judge says so. You're supposed to be helping me. I want to get out of jail."

"Yeah, and I want to get out of being your lawyer, but I don't see that happening either."

Lloyd banged the gavel, "That's enough, Ms. Kennedy. I'll set a court date and get back to both of you. I'm guessing maybe the middle of October." He looked at Ginny and said, "That should give you plenty of time to prepare your case. We are dismissed." The Bailiff yelled, "All rise," and Judge Chadwick turned and walked out with a big grin.

Ginny looked at Paul and mumbled so he could hear, "What's there to prepare?" Smiled and walked out.

∾

School had been back in session for a week and the weather was unusually warm and neither teachers nor students were happy to be there. Washington was a poor county. The subject of air conditioning came up periodically, but nobody believed it would ever happen and it didn't. Days got long and tempers got short. People were feeling really rutschy by mid-afternoon.

The Pierce-Barnes trial date was approaching and everyone at Glencoe High was talking about it. Two of the stars were there and were actually a distraction to the learning process along with the abominable heat. The principal wondered what the trial would bring in terms of students skipping school for the courtroom. Since the courtroom held only about 75, he decided to just let the chips fall.

∾

Brad stood across the street from the school in the little park that had been created some 100 years earlier. It was constructed in memory of the 14 men and boys from Glencoe who had died in the Civil War. In front of it were three smaller memorials commemorating WWI, WWII, and Korea. There was talk about adding another for Vietnam Veterans, but that hadn't happened yet. The Civil War memorial was a huge boulder standing about six feet high with a copper sculpture of a soldier standing on top. The copper had probably been beautiful, but the sculpture had been green for about 98 of those 100 years. Brad stood behind and to the side of the rock watching to see where Katie and Lettie might go.

The bell rang, the doors flew open, and the building emptied. Lettie appeared to be going to her family's Feed and Grain Store, so Brad followed at a safe distance, not concerned about losing her. There was a small box truck backed up to the loading dock. The rear door was up, and the truck was full. Lettie went into the store and Brad waited. When she came out the back door, she was ready for work and began unloading the truck. Brad went around to the front of the store, entered and then told Ned Pike what he was looking for. He already knew Ned didn't carry it. It was a ploy to ensure Ned was in the store by himself today. With customers coming in and out, Lettie would unload the truck by herself.

Lettie loaded a hand truck with four cartons and wheeled it into the warehouse. Brad went up the side steps of the loading dock and stood just out of view. Lettie returned, pushing the hand truck ahead of her, and entered the back of the truck. Brad quickly moved behind her and once again covered her mouth and put an arm around her waist. "It's just me. Don't panic and I'll let you go as long as you don't turn around. Deal?" "Deal," she said.

"Listen carefully. I know what you did after I left last time. You went right to Katie saying something like, 'We've got to change the story. Because with my statement I didn't see Micah Barnes.' Am I close?" She nodded.

"So tell me the new story. I've got time to listen."

"The only difference is I stayed near the edge of the property and I saw Micah Barnes drive out without Katie. I saw him when he got out, opened the gate and drove off."

"But Lettie, that's not true, is it? You never saw Micah did you?" She shook her head.

"The reason you never saw him is he wasn't there. I know there was someone there. I know Katie was raped. But, Lettie, Katie's been hiding who it is. I'm going to find out why.

"Lettie, it's time to bring this to an end, but it has to be between just us for now. I have the book. I can prove Vaughan Johnson raped

Katie three years ago, and he's been doing it ever since. The rape at the Bigby House? It was Vaughan Johnson."

"I want to see the book. I'm in there too."

"Yes, I saw it... no judgment. He's got a date from last year. His notes say, 'drinking, fornicating,' and then it says 'Baptist.' I'm no dummy, Lettie. I know what he's got on you and why you're scared. I also know what he has on Katie and it's much worse than that. But, listen...I've got the book. Nobody will ever see it because you're all underage and I can keep it sealed. He can't hurt you or anyone else ever again.

"So listen, here is what I need you to do next week"

CHAPTER 34

Sunday, September 30, 1992. It was a beautiful fall morning. Reagan wanted to drive Molly as much as possible before having to put her away for the winter. He convinced Prudy to go for a ride with him in the Miata this morning...top up. He bribed her with lunch across the river and a nice slow ride through the countryside. He wasn't sure about getting her in the car and less sure how he'd get her out.

He was glad there was a diversion scheduled for this Sunday morning. The trial was four days away and feelings and tensions were once again riding high in the town. None of the Pierces were in attendance so he thought that might make things a mite more comfortable. Most everyone seemed to be behaving quite normally. Except for Shirley. She seemed to be a little put out. She sat there shaking her finger at him and mouthing the words, "I'm gonna get you. I'm gonna get you." And while she ran around all morning telling everyone what he'd done, Reagan just shrugged and said, "I have no idea what she's talking about." Everyone thought it was hilarious, and no one deserved it more than Shirley.

Reagan thought the organist didn't sound too bad this morning. Was this a sign he'd been here too long? If she sounded good next week, he'd be sure to have his resignation ready. He stood and moved off the platform. "This morning we have a little surprise for you. Billy and Heather, please come forward." They came up and stood in the center as Reagan shifted to one side. Sadie stood next to Heather holding her hand and on the other side was Jake who reached up, without prompting, and took hold of Billy's hand.

Billy spoke first. "Most of you folks have been real nice to Heather for a few years now. Most likely cause you pitied her being with me." There were nods of agreement and a couple of audible chuckles. He smiled and continued, "And you were right to do so. I was a mean, miserable excuse for a human being and I know it. Last May I began a transformation and when I showed up at church with Heather, I wasn't exactly received with open arms, but I was tolerated and for that I thank you. About a month ago I received Jesus as my Savior and since that time I've been on a wild ride. Many of you were there that Sunday when I asked Heather if she'd marry me and make an honest man out of me." Most of the men again chuckled at that.

Heather said, "Today I'm going to make an honest man out of Billy Maddox and we would like all of you to be a part of it. We invite you to be a part of our wedding. We have consulted with Sadie and Jake and we have their blessing, but most importantly we believe we are doing what God would have us to do. Today, we ask you not to just witness our marriage, but we invite you to be a part of it. We covet your love, your guidance, your wisdom, and even your correction when necessary. Thank you for being here."

Reagan remained to the side as he recited the vows while Billy and Heather looked at each other and four little eyes gazed up. Reagan said, "I now pronounce you husband and wife." And in the loudest voice he had, Jake asked, "Does that mean you're really my daddy? Can we go fishing?" The congregation broke out laughing, but Billy didn't see it as funny...it was a dream come true. He knelt down and said, "Yes it does and yes we can." Billy had never fished in his life.

CHAPTER 35

*M*onday, October 1, 1992. With the trial scheduled to begin in three days, Brad decided he had better start tying up all the loose ends. So far, he'd kept everything to himself. His training taught him that the fewer people involved in an operation, the better. The Navy used to say, during WWII, that loose lips sink ships. Essentially, the more people involved in the planning and execution, the more there was that could potentially go wrong. Lettie was the only one involved now, and he wasn't comfortable with even her knowing. A senior in high school didn't always make your most reliable ally. Two more people needed to know what he had, who so far he'd kept in the dark.

The notebook was key to everything. And Vaughan Johnson thinking the D.A. had a solid case against Micah was the other. Anyone knowing too much too soon, even Tinker or Guy, could tip him off and get the book destroyed. He hoped Lettie felt safe with the new information he'd provided and that she trusted that he knew what he was doing. Today, he'd have to let Tink know what was going on. They had to keep Vaughan under 24-hour surveillance for at least the next three days.

Brad called the Sheriff's Office about 9:15. "Washington County

Sheriff's Office. Deputy Adams speaking. How may I help you, sir or ma'am?"

"Good morning deputy, are you still basking in the glory of that great collar?"

"Yes, sir, thank you very much. It will help with my next evaluation that's for sure. Looks like Barnes will be leaving Glencoe for quite a while. What can I do for you today, sir? Got another one for me?"

"Sorry. You had your turn and we still have to keep Tinker's re-election going strong. Is he there?"

"He went over to the Courthouse to file papers on Paul Barnes. Should be back soon. I can have him call you."

"Deputy, it doesn't work that way. I don't want him to have my number and he doesn't want it. Works better for both of us. When he returns make sure he stays there. I'll call within the hour."

Brad made a list in his head. Never write anything down. When the day comes you forget anything on the list, you're too old for the job. Today, he'd bring the Sheriff on board. Tonight he'd get the note-book...couldn't wait any longer. Tomorrow he'd confer with Guy Kennedy. He'd wait until after jury selection to decide his last moves.

He pulled in next to the pay phone at the IGA and called Tinker. "Washington County Sheriff's Office. Sheriff Reynolds."

"Good morning, my friend. In a couple of days, we will see how Micah's trial turns out. I'm guessing Guy Kennedy is a little more concerned right now than Allison Dodge. And I have to tell you I like it that way."

"Why on earth would you say that? That boy doesn't stand much of a chance if Katie doesn't recant. And right now she's sticking with the story."

"Sheriff, Katie's really scared and I now know why. She's not a bad person. She just doesn't see a way out. She was raped and there is no question about that, but it wasn't Micah. Until recently only Katie knew who the rapist is, and he's been blackmailing her since she was fourteen when he raped her for the first time. I have evidence that Deputy Johnson is who we have been looking for and I'm planning to take him down in front of the whole town, which is what he deserves."

"That won't be necessary. He's sitting out front right now. Let me drag his sorry butt in here right now."

"No, don't do that. I need your help though, but I'm not ready to answer too many questions. I don't want to spook him. He wouldn't get far, but that's not the point. For three years, at least, he's been blackmailing teenagers in this town. He's targeted a lot of girls and blackmails them for sex. He's kept all this information in a notebook and I have it in my possession." Brad wasn't taking any chances. A raid on Vaughan's apartment before he had the book could ruin everything. "The notebook lists the dates, the names, places, and offenses for which he could have arrested them. Most charges wouldn't stick, but kids don't know that. Just their parents and family finding out would be enough in a small town. He's got Katie really good, at least in the mind of a seventeen-year-old who wants to protect her family. She's been willing to drive them away to save them embarrassment. I think the Bible calls it a greater love has no man or woman. She doesn't know someone has lifted her burden, and she's free. She'll know before the trial, but I can't let her know yet...too risky in her delicate emotional state."

"Okay, so what do you need from me? I know I'd take that little weasel down right now."

"That's my point. You can't. He can't know that we know. It's possible he could still get to Katie and Lettie, and maybe even others, and if they refuse to testify, we've got nothing but a bunch of notes. He might even escape prosecution with a slap on the wrist. He's not going anywhere and we need maybe four days."

"I need you to recognize Deputy Johnson's outstanding work and service to the Department. You need to get him on a cushy daytime shift for a few days. He sees himself as an all-powerful authority figure. You need to get him out where he'll strut his stuff for the public. He'll puff up like a peacock. That'll guarantee he won't go anywhere. All he wants is recognition and you need to give it to him."

"You don't know how much it will rile me to do that. Any other way?"

"No, my experience is you put your enemy right out in front

where you can keep an eye on him. You can even jot notes today on how you set up a sting on a deputy suspected of illicit activity within the department. It'll work. That little maniac has a huge ego. He's not going anywhere and you can keep him running all day, so all he wants at night is to get rest. Oh, and you want him to be the deputy in charge of Micah Barnes."

"All right, I'll do it your way just cause I like you. But you better not screw up my re-election. What are you going to be doing?"

"Sheriff, probably best you don't know. A little B&E, extortion, and a little detaining without consent. You know, just the usual."

CHAPTER 36

*T*hursday, October 4, 1992. Deputy Johnson looked a little crisper today. His uniform was cut perfectly and the new black pattern Cordovan shoes glistened. He stood a little taller and a little more full of himself. Tinker Reynolds had finally recognized his value to the force. Daddy would be proud and after the next election, he'd be the new Sheriff. Life was good. He picked up Micah Barnes from the holding area in the Courthouse and ushered him to the courtroom for the jury selection. Vaughan sat Micah down next to Guy Kennedy and then took a seat behind him. He wasn't about to take his eyes off this rapist.

As soon as the deputy was seated, Brad rose and left the courtroom. It was time to visit Vaughan Johnson's personal library and check out a book. Sal didn't open until 11:00, but he had to be there for deliveries. He always left the delivery door ajar using just a brick to keep it from closing. Delivery guys would just yell when they came in. Sal was in the kitchen prepping his fresh ingredients for the day. His lunch crowd was usually pretty good and his eight tables stayed full for about an hour and a half. At night it was his take out and delivery that made him money. The exception was after a high school football or basketball home game and when the pizzeria was slammed.

Brad entered quietly, went to the door and picked the simple lock. The upstairs lock took less time than before and he again stood in Vaughan Johnson's little house of horrors. He entered the living room and came to a dead stop. Oh, this was just too gross, and he wished he had a camera. Vaughan had set up a little 'shrine' to Katie. He hadn't realized Vaughan had singled out Katie with such an obsession. He had several pictures of her. One was a school picture, and he wondered how he got that. One in a skimpy bathing suit taken in her backyard without her knowledge. He had what he assumed was one of her cheerleader Pom Poms. Brad was glad that this would be over quickly. This guy was a sick puppy.

He went to the bookcase and saw an empty spot. Sure enough, 'I Know What You Did' was missing. He checked all the logical hiding places but found nothing. Without the notebook, Micah was finished. Lettie's testimony meant nothing if Katie denied it. He sat on the bed and looked at the clock. The restaurant would open soon. He looked at the spine of the book in front of the clock. It read, 'Oklahoma Raiders: A Story of the Real West'. If that book was from the empty opening in the bookcase, then where was the other book? He went back and read the spines...one by one. A jacket fly read, "Oklahoma Raiders: A Story of the Real West." When he took the cover off, there it was, the hollowed out copy of 'I Know What You Did.' Bingo! He slipped the notebook into his back pocket and left as quickly as he had arrived. He met a delivery man on the way out, said nothing, and disappeared.

It was a strange jury selection. Maybe it was normal for Washington County, but for an attorney from Chicago, it was strange. They needed twelve jurors, and the pool comprised seventeen names. They had called twenty-five, but ten had legal, legitimate reasons to be excused from jury duty. So, after you allow for two alternates that leaves three potential jurors to challenge. In the city, Guy was used to a chess match and if you were good, and Guy was, you get to choose the best available and now he was choosing the best of the worst. He looked at the jury one by one and thought, "I will have to use small words."

The trial date was set for Monday.

CHAPTER 37

riday, October 5, 1992. Guy went into the office at 6 o'clock after a restless night's sleep. He had until Monday to figure out a strategy for defending Micah Barnes. This had never happened to him. He was always prepared for court long before he entered the courtroom. In Chicago, he had teams of people working every angle. Paralegals doing research. Detectives chasing down leads. Paid witnesses and experts at his fingertips. Here they had a secretary who answered phones. She wasn't even a paralegal. A little of Guy's self-confidence was wavering. Every attorney hated 'he said/she said' cases. He particularly hated this one. He kept thinking, "They're just kids." Your client might be innocent, you may even know he or she is innocent, but if the other person is perkier, better looking, or has a nicer smile, your client could go to jail.

This is where he seemed to be and he had no idea who the jury would like better. Three years ago Micah was a star athlete and very popular even though he was from the Oaks. Nice kid. Polite. Had a great personality and a smile to make girls swoon. Everyone liked him because he brought 'winning' to Glencoe High. He was four years older than Katie. Three years ago Katie was just a super fourteen-year-old kid who everybody liked, at least that was the word he had.

But for the last three years, she had been moody, hateful, disrespectful, and the list went on. What would she be like on the stand? He knew that if the jury seemed to believe Lettie then Allison Dodge wouldn't put Katie on the stand. Guy had made an unusual move just in case. He listed Katie as a witness for the defense. That would leave people scratching their heads. If Guy put her on the stand he was taking a huge, unknown risk. Again, the ever true, if you don't know the answer already, don't ask the question. The question was how would Katie come across to the jury and the answer was, he didn't know. He'd put her on the list and would decide later.

He pulled out the list of jurors. This jury selection had been a farce. He had one challenge and used it early. It was a good challenge... even the right challenge. Undoubtedly a person who would vote to convict Micah. It was that obvious. He could read her voice as she answered his questions. The problem is that once you challenged off a juror, you can't go back and say, "I changed my mind, I'd like juror number two back and remove juror number seven." So he was stuck with the rest. He'd like to get the two alternates on the jury but doubted that would happen. If he had the staff, he could perform background checks on jury members, but he didn't. What he had were seven men and five women.

He looked at the list and he wasn't encouraged. He figured the five women had probably made up their minds. Two were prominent women in town. A bank teller who'd been there twenty years and the other the owner of the Economy Store. Both knew the Pierces well. Two he would describe as little old church ladies who'd serve on a jury every day if they could. He was certain they would side with a poor young thing like Katie. Maybe not, but better to work with that assumption for now. The fifth was from the Oaks, and would have been an encouragement to Guy until he found she was the victim of domestic abuse and he had no challenges left. But again, she was from the Oaks and knew Micah better than any of the others.

The men might serve him a little better. Although he lost his number one and two picks by peremptory challenges by the D.A., three of the men had daughters and that could work against him. Two

were businessmen and they might vote politically convenient. The
other two men were blue collar guys and who knows how that
could go.

Guy decided he really didn't have a choice. He'd have to go in blind
and see if he could trip up Lettie. If not, he'd have to put Katie on the
stand, take a huge risk and try to create a reasonable doubt.

Sheriff Reynolds was in his office when Vaughan clocked in. It riled
Tinker, having to watch him strut around like he was the new sheriff
in town. Plus, he had a deputy rebellion on his hands. They could see
Vaughan getting what they knew he didn't deserve, but didn't know
he was about to get what he did deserve. Tinker's hands were tied and
there was nothing he could do to end it. His deputies were giving him
the cold shoulder. It was like, "Sheriff, we have to work for you, but
we don't have to talk to you unless ordered." Whenever one of them
walked into the room Tink could feel the temperature drop. Vaughan
was too full of himself to notice anything different. No one liked him
anyway so ignoring him was the norm. All he saw was he'd won favor
with the Sheriff and it was about time.

Guy went back into his office after lunch, told Sheila he didn't want to
be disturbed and closed the office door. Trouble was, he was already
disturbed. He was one of the best trial lawyers in the United States
and he didn't have a clue how to handle this case. He processed the
what ifs over and over. He kept coming up with the same answers
every time. What bothered him most was he had watched Katie in
court the day he took Micah's case. Every bit of her body language
said he was innocent. He didn't do it.

The phone rang. "Sheila, I told you not to disturb me!" It wasn't
like Guy to be short with anyone.

"I'm sorry, sir, I really am. But there is a man on the line who says he can prove Micah Barnes is innocent. Thought you might want to talk to him."

"I'd talk to the devil himself if I thought it would help Micah. Thanks." He pushed the button for line two and said, "Guy Kennedy here."

"Good afternoon, Counselor. I trust you are doing well?"

"I've seen some better days. How can I help you?"

"I think you may have it wrong Counselor, it's how may I help you? We both know Micah Barnes is innocent, only I can prove it and you can't."

"So, if you have proof why haven't you turned in what you have?"

"I could do that, but it wouldn't be nearly as enjoyable. Let me explain things to you. You and I are essentially in the same business. You defend those who can't defend themselves and usually win. At least that's what they have told me. I avenge those who can't defend themselves and I always win. The differences are you have to work in the confines of the law and your clients know you are working for them. I do whatever it takes and my clients often don't even know I exist. Often, they don't even know they're my clients and they never know who I am. And second, I never want recognition or credit for what I do, because then I can no longer do what I do.

"Let's get back to your problem. One simple yes or no question and remember, the real rapist is going down Monday no matter how you answer. Do you want to get credit for winning the case? Let me give you a hint to the right answer: Sheriff Reynolds is fully on board."

This kind of made Guy feel like the old days he thought he had escaped. He had come to Washington County to be a country lawyer and defend innocent people. So his cautious reply was, "I'll listen to what you have."

"I'll listen," wasn't one of your options. "I've got the proof. The rapist is going down. The Sheriff knows who it is. I can wait until after the trial, doesn't really matter to me, but thought it'd be more fun for you to take him down in the courtroom, in front of the whole town, and get your new office off to a good start. But Micah's your client and you know what's best. So, I guess we're done and you have a good weekend." Brad paused before hanging up.

"Okay, wait. I'm in. I'm just not used to other people making up the rules."

"Okay, then I'm guessing you will not like this, because it's my game and I make the rules. We need to meet face to face because I don't enjoy conversing on the phone. Thing is, you will not see my face. Nobody sees me. We will meet behind the Chevy Dealership tonight at 9 o'clock. You will find a red Cavalier convertible in the back lot and on the antenna will be a hood. You put on the hood and I will join you and walk you to a safe location. Questions? And remember that's rhetorical."

"I guess I'll see you tonight. I hope I don't live to regret this."

"You won't, I assure you. I will give you everything you need to free Micah Barnes."

~

At 2:30 Allison Dodge sat down with Lettie Pike one more time and said, "I am sure we will get a conviction, but I wanted to go over things with you again. You are really the only witness we have. Katie depends on your testimony to send her rapist to jail."

What she was really saying is I'm depending on you to get me a conviction and I really don't care about either of you. Convictions get me re-elected.

Lettie answered, "Ms. Dodge, you can depend on my testimony to send a rapist to jail." Allison missed what she said.

"And, I've decided not to put Katie on the stand. She's too fragile. So, you need to stay calm, sweet, and most of all likable. Can you do that?"

Considering her conversations with the unknown man, she was disliking Allison Dodge. She'd been coached on her testimony and she thought all the D.A. was interested in was winning. All she wanted was a conviction. Lettie reprocessed everything and wondered how

Allison Dodge could not see something was missing. Well, Lettie would play her part but not as the D.A. expected.

～

At 8:55 p.m. Guy arrived at the dealership, parked out front and walked to the rear. He saw what looked like a white surrender flag on the antenna of a red car. The truth was, he wouldn't know a Cavalier from a Cadillac, but he saw the mask. He decided he was right the first time. It was a white flag of surrender and he was being taken prisoner. He walked up to the car, removed the hood, and placed it on his head. Point of no return.

Brad could sense his uncertainty as he stiffened when Brad touched his elbow to guide him. They went around the back of a white windowless cargo van.

"I'm sorry that everything I do seems like part of a covert operation, but I've been doing things this way for years and it just seems to work. I'll tell you what I've got." He told him about Deputy Johnson, the book, how Tinker and Deputy Johnson's "special assignment" fit in. Most importantly how Lettie's cross-examination would go. And hopefully, Lettie's testimony would free Katie to tell the truth.

Brad explained, "Net result. You and the Sheriff get credit for finding the rapist. Allison Dodge sees she needs to do her due diligence and remember the Constitution promises innocent until proven guilty. Katie is released from her physical and mental bondage. Hopefully, her family can heal. Micah goes free and he and his family can start living again. And me? I can retire. I'm getting too old for this stuff. I've been neglecting my family way too long." He gave him a manila 8x10 envelope with the clasp in place and sealed tightly with tape. "Here's the proof. I've highlighted the most important information on copies. The notebook is in there. Vaughan's handwriting was verified by a handwriting analysis expert. And most importantly, I've promised the people involved that the Judge will seal the evidence. Guy, you've got to make that happen."

"Wait a minute. How did you get this? If it was obtained illegally, the judge will have to let him go."

"It seems Deputy Adams found it under the seat of the cruiser when he took it to the car wash. Not to worry, Counselor, I'm thorough." He told him to wait one full minute before removing the mask and slipped away.

CHAPTER 38

*S*aturday, October 6, 1992. Katie hadn't come out of her room in three days. Maddie blamed Adam more than ever. Even Katie not speaking to her was his fault. "Adam, she's your daughter, do something!"

"Now suddenly she's my daughter?" Adam stared in disbelief. "Exactly what do you think I can do? Grab her by the hair and pull her out? You've spent the last year trying to be her friend rather than her mother. What did you expect? Anytime I've said no to her, you turn around and give her permission. She won't listen to anything I have to say, but you think I can go in there and undo the mess you've helped create."

"Adam Pierce, how dare you talk like that? If you'd been there for her three years ago, like I've been, we wouldn't be in this mess."

"Are you kidding me? If I'd been there like you've been there, we might be grandparents by now! How do you think it helps to be her buddy when what she needs is her mother? Don't you get it at all? There has been something wrong and has been for a long time, something you and I know nothing about. And whatever it is, it didn't begin at the Lazy Daisy or even when Micah, quote, "raped her." Whatever happened, happened three years before that. Maddie, I still don't believe Micah raped her. I won't say they haven't had sex, but he never raped her. I forbade her to see him because I saw something you didn't see. I guess I should have said something, and for that I'm sorry, but I thought it was just teenage hormones. It would pass. Maddie, she loves that boy! That's why none of this makes sense. She can't come to you and talk about it even though you think you opened the communication door. She won't come to me because I forbade her love. It's like if she destroys him then she'll destroy her feelings. I don't know if that makes any sense. But apparently, it makes sense to her. Maddie, she is in mourning. I know Monday could be the most horrible day this family has ever had and certainly the worst day for her. We could both lose a daughter forever. Our daughter could destroy her life by doing what she thinks is the right thing to do. And, I don't know why. Maddie, we need God in our lives more than ever. The Bible says, "With God all things are possible." Maddie, we have no place else to turn. I don't want to lose you or Katie. Will you pray with me for a miracle?" Reluctantly she assented, and he took her hand and walked to the door of Katie's room and poured out his heart to God for fifteen minutes.

Adam was sorry now he had bumped out the wall in Katie's room and put in an en-suite bath. But at least he still had a key to her room. He prayed, "O Lord guide me," as he slipped the key in and opened the door.

As he approached the bed Katie jumped off and ran at him yelling, "I hate you! I hate you! I hate you!" She pounded her fists against his chest and Adam just let her go. She was hurting him, but the hurt inside her was far greater than any pain she inflicted on him. When she tired the pounding slowed down, and he put his arms around her. She tried to pull away, but he wouldn't let her. He pulled tighter. No matter what she said or did he refused to let go. Finally, the struggling ceased, and he held her. He prayed, "Father, you hold us in your arms as a shepherd holds a sheep who was lost, but is found. Lord Jesus, this is my little girl. She is hurt and I don't know how to fix it. She's shut me out and maybe it's all my fault. You loved the world enough to let your son die for our sins and Father I would gladly die for Katie right now if it would heal her brokenness. I would give up everything I have if she could find joy in you. You have revealed to me that there is more here than I can know or perhaps ever understand. But two things you've shown me she can't deny. Micah Barnes did not rape her. Lord, I believe her. I believe my Katie was raped. With all my heart I trust and I believe her, she's not lying to me. But what you revealed to me, reveal to my precious Katie. Let her know it's okay to follow her heart. Don't let her destroy or abandon the most important person in her life." He gently released her. She drew back several inches and he looked in her eyes, "Katie, I love you. Come back to me."

He let his eyes drop as he moved to the door. From behind him, "Daddy, I love you." With God all things are possible!

CHAPTER 39

Sunday, October 7, 1992. Adam and Maddie were finally talking without yelling and accusations. They were far from family healing, but the sincerity of Adam's prayer outside Katie's door had softened her heart. Maddie knew the only place to turn was the open arms of God. She was ready to go back to church. Adam grabbed his Bible and keys and opened the front door. Maddie went out and Adam turned to close the door. "Wait for me. I'm coming too!" Adam looked at Maddie and Maddie looked at Adam. Neither said it, both thought it.

~

Chad pulled the Tahoe into the alley and up to Micah's house. Charlotte and Sara came out and got in the car. "Where's Micah?"

"He said he wasn't going today. He's been down since Friday. He said he sat there looking over at Katie and couldn't believe she was doing this to him. He said he was glad this Jesus stuff worked out well for me, but it wasn't working for him. I didn't know what to say, so I told him we'd save him a seat if he changed his mind."

244 | R MARSHALL WRIGHT

~

Reagan came through the side door and walked right past the first chair to the second. Ouch, someone finally changed the chairs and didn't tell him. Not a good start. Kind of a different angle from here as he began his Sunday scan of the congregation.

With the trial one day away this could be the last time he'd see some of these people. He hoped it wouldn't, but this could tear this congregation apart. He'd deliberately chosen a passage on forgiveness.

As he gazed around the sanctuary, he noticed that Katie was sitting with her parents in the 'family pew'. He was both pleased and mystified at her presence. At least they were there as a family and that was something that hadn't happened for weeks.

He noticed that Mr. and Mrs. Maddox were there with Jake next to Billy. The two seemed to be inseparable. He wished he could use Jake as a sermon illustration this morning. Here was the perfect model of showing forgiveness. And a small child shall lead them. How true. A child, even after being hurt, will go to his father and hold up his or her arms to be lifted up and held. Reagan thought, why can't adults do the same thing? What happened to us?

Chad and Charlotte were there and you would be hard pressed to slide a sheet of paper between them. But even though they were in love, Chad accepted that Micah came first right now. They had their whole lives ahead of them, but right now no one knew what the future held for Micah. Reagan was used to seeing Micah sitting next to Charlotte, but today the seat was empty. Micah had not yet come to Christ, but Reagan believed it was only a matter of time. Chad's male Christian influence was ever present and Charlotte consistently encouraged him to walk with Christ. To trust God. But that's hard for an unbeliever who sees nothing good happening in their life. Reagan thought, "O Lord if only he could see, as we have seen, what you're doing. And I am mindful of what you're doing that I don't see."

The organist stopped, or finished, the Prelude, depending on how you viewed it. She hit one of those awful organ notes that happens to amateurs and it sounded like total discord. Reagan was reassured, he wouldn't have to resign. But he sure wished she would. He stood and gave his traditional thank you for her fine selection and wondered how many members must think every time he does that, "Reagan Lamb is tone deaf!" After giving the announcements and the morning Call to Worship he announced the Opening Song, 'How Great Thou Art.' Every so often we need a reminder.

As they sang the third verse, Micah Barnes walked in hesitantly. It seemed like he was trying to go back out, but his feet kept moving forward. When he arrived at the pew, the usual seating arrangement wasn't available. Normally he'd sit on one side of Charlotte and Chad on the other. Someone was sitting next to Charlotte. Chad noticed him first and immediately stepped out of the pew so Micah could be next to Charlotte. They finished and everyone was seated. Then it happened.

Micah saw the Pierce family. He immediately started to rise and felt a hand on his knee forcing him back down. Chad leaned over, "This is God's House. He's in control Micah. Let it play out." He remembered hearing Chad speak those same words the first Sunday they'd met. "Let it play out."

During prayer time God took over again and there was no mention made of the trial and yet you knew it was foremost on everyone's mind. During the time of silent prayer, Reagan was sure God was bombarded. At least he knew he was bombarding him.

He moved to the pulpit and began with an illustration. "The great Vince Lombardi was hired to coach the Green Bay Packers. The team was storied with excellence and championships but had fallen on hard times. Vince called his first team meeting and when he stood to address them he had one hand behind his back. He introduced himself and said he was there to build a great team. He complimented the players on their individual abilities including a young Bart Starr. He then said great players alone don't make great teams. It takes the basics and going back to the fundamentals. Today we are going back to the basics. He pulled his hand out from behind him and said, 'Gentlemen, this is a football.'

"I tell you that story because sometimes we forget the simplest basics of the Christian faith and we need to go back to them. It's all about love. More specifically, God's love for us. Loving God, loving others, loving yourself. The Bible says we love because he first loved us. It was freely given to us, it was demonstrated to us, but we cannot do it until we first accept it...

"Jesus taught there are two great laws. All the rest hinge on these two alone. The first is the first. It's first for a reason. If it isn't first, there is no second. You can't do the second without the first. Impossible. Can't be done.

"The first is to love the Lord your God with all your heart, all your mind, and all your strength. Simply stated. You are to love God first with everything you have. Nothing held back. Ever. You can't do that unless you have received Jesus Christ into your life...

"The second, Jesus said, is like unto the first. You are to love your neighbor as yourself. Jesus clarified this to an expert in the law when he asked, "Who is my neighbor," and Jesus told the Parable of the Good Samaritan. It clearly points to my neighbor as anyone. I'm to love all people as God has loved me. I'm to love all people as I love myself and I can't love myself until I obey the first commandment!...

"When we love God we forgive as he has forgiven us. That doesn't mean they become our best friend. It means that God has freed us from the burden of carrying all that hate that keeps us from connecting with him...

"Forgiveness doesn't always come easy. When asked how often he needed to forgive his brother, the man suggested seven. It seemed reasonable to him to forgive someone seven times. Jesus said, no that's not enough. If you are truly mine, you will forgive him 70 times 7. That's 490. And if you can forgive someone that many times you are where our God expects us to be. Told you it wasn't easy...

"It begins with loving God, accepting Christ, loving yourself, loving others, and offering forgiveness. Every time you pray the Lord's Prayer you pray to God that he will forgive you of your sins in exactly the same way you forgive people who sin against you! Think about where that puts you in your relationship to God right now. Is it where you want it to be?

"Some of you sitting here this morning have never taken that all-important step of giving up control of your life and giving your life to Christ. Some of you at one time repented, you invited Christ in; you knew the joy and peace he brings. And then, somewhere, sometime you took back control of your life. Let me ask, how's that working out for you? I know there are several of you who have recently found the joy of a new life in Christ. You have seen what happens in a God-controlled life. Some of you have recently rediscovered the joy of Christ and the difference he makes. You're here. Show of hands, how many of you never, ever want to go back again?"

Reagan was aghast as hands went up. Billy stood up and said, "I'm a brand new creation in Christ. I never want to go back. I was dead, but now I'm more alive than I've ever been." The most prominent raised hand was Judge Lloyd Chadwick, front and center. Behind him was Adam Pierce. Heather had her hand held high as she held Billy's hand with the other. Charlotte, after seeing Billy stand, also stood, but her hand was not raised. Her arms were outstretched toward heaven as a child seeks to be held by a loving father. Other hands were raised. The time had come.

"The Apostle Paul had been a Pharisee named Saul. Taught by the most prominent Jewish scholar of all time. He was a "Jews Jew" steeped in the law and tradition. He had a writ to capture and kill Christians. On the Road to Damascus, he encountered Jesus Christ and God got hold of him and transformed his life. He wrote to the Christians in Ephesus: in Chapter 3 beginning with verse 14 When I think of all this, I fall to my knees and pray to the Father, 15 the Creator of everything in heaven and on earth. 16 I pray that from his glorious, unlimited resources he will empower you with inner strength through his Spirit. 17 Then Christ will make his home in your hearts as you trust in him. Your roots will grow down into God's love and keep you strong. 18 And may you have the power to understand, as all God's people should, how wide, how long, how high, and how deep his love is. 19 May you experience the love of Christ, though it is too great to understand fully. Then you will be made complete with all the fullness of life and power that comes from God.

20 Now all glory to God, who is able, through his mighty power at work within us, to accomplish infinitely more than we might ask or think. **21** Glory to him in the church and in Christ Jesus through all generations forever and ever! Amen. (Living Bible)

"I invite you to come before the throne of Grace. Receive forgiveness and new life in Christ. It's yours for the taking. It's free, and it's eternal." Reagan stopped, and the organist began softly playing Amazing Grace. It was a miracle. It was beautiful, and he bet she was under the power and control of the Holy Spirit because no way could she play that well.

People got up and came forward led by Shirley Langford of all people. The Elders and Deacons came to the front sides ready to pray with people. Charlotte saw Micah squirm in his seat and look very uncomfortable. Chad whispered to him, "Let it play out." Micah got up to walk to the front. Charlotte stood to follow and Chad said, "Pretty Lady, God's in control. He doesn't need you," and she sat down and took his hand.

As he walked by the third pew, Katie turned her head and saw him for the first time. Their eyes met, but Micah kept walking until he reached the Communion Rail and knelt between two others. Judge Chadwick moved over and knelt on Micah's right side to pray with him.

Maddie was so torn in every direction she didn't know what to do. The message hit home. For years she had known great joy in Christ . When did it disappear? Where did it go? She couldn't hate Micah for accepting Christ, but how do you forgive the person who raped your little girl? Could even God do that? She felt Adam put his arm around her and pull her close. She cried.

The whole congregation watched as Katie Pierce rose and moved to the center aisle. She never took her eyes off Micah as she took ten steps to the front and stood close enough to reach out and touch him. She squeezed into the small space between him and the woman on his left. She knelt down. Neither looked, but Micah remembered the smell of her hair and his heart beat faster. Looking straight ahead she bowed her head and reached out to the Communion Rail and put her hand on top of his. He felt the warmth of her hand and froze. She prayed, softly and quietly, "God, I'm sorry. Please forgive me. I don't know what to say. I want Jesus in my life. Help me set things right. Give me another chance. And Father, I selfishly ask you to make Micah feel for me what I feel for him." Micah was dumbfounded by what he heard. Could it be? Katie continued. "When he discovers the truth don't let him hate me as I have hated myself for three years. God, I need the power of the Holy Spirit in my life. I now turn myself over to you wholly and completely." She turned to Micah. "Tomorrow's the day. Micah Barnes, I love you more than life itself." She rose and ran out of the church. Adam left Maddie sitting as he ran after her.

~

Micah was trying to figure out what happened as they left the church. Chad said, "We need to talk about it, Micah. Something beyond explanation appears to have happened, but you need to let us in."

Micah picked up Sara as they walked over and sat under the huge maple showing off its fall wardrobe. They sat as Micah gathered his thoughts. "Chad, I think it just played out. You've tried to show me signs all along. Things that only God could do. But I couldn't get my head around a God who really cares about me. There was no evidence to show he did. Today I saw it. Pastor Reagan spoke to my heart with a message from God. I had no choice but to respond. Then Katie came forward and when she put her hand on mine, inside I lost it. I was a helpless child. Every feeling I ever had for her came rushing back. What she is or would do to me didn't matter. I just loved her. She prayed to God that I would feel about her as she felt about me. It was strange because then she prayed that when I find out the truth, I wouldn't hate her. And before she ran off, she whispered in my ear."

Charlotte was on pins and needles, "What did she say?"

She said, "Tomorrow is the day. Micah Barnes, I love you more than life itself."

Chad looked at him, "You really don't know what happened, do you? God promised to everyone who's in Christ, all things will work to good for those that love him and are called to serve him. Micah, are you ready to serve God for the rest of your life?"

"Yes, Sir, I believe I am."

"Then just let it play out. Just let it play out. You'll have your answers soon enough."

~

Brad sat back, stunned and amazed at what transpired as he watched. He thought, "Who would ever believe the Holy Spirit would ever come back to this place?" It seemed to him the Holy Spirit had left years ago, long before Reagan came. It appeared no one had missed him. "Wow! This throws a whole new light on tomorrow. Tomorrow will not go the way I planned. It will go the way you planned, Lord."

Today many people were set free, but two in particular. Tomorrow would set more people free as they watched a miracle unfold. Well, one wouldn't be set free.

~

Adam finally caught up to Katie a couple blocks away and walked beside her. After a few minutes, he asked, "Why did you run out?" Then he said nothing.

"Daddy, my life is such a mess. I'm so confused as to what is happening. I invited Jesus into my life because I know I've done some awful things. Maybe others can and will forgive me for what I've done, but without God, I can't forgive myself. I've hurt so many people over the last three years. I've hurt people I love because I thought I was protecting them. I've made a mess of everything. Now I need to make it right.

"When you held me and prayed yesterday, it seemed like God was speaking. You said things you couldn't possibly know unless God told you. And I didn't feel any condemnation as you prayed. I didn't sleep much last night. For three years I've denied what happened. For three years I've denied my feelings and blamed myself. I haven't been able to love anyone and I haven't felt worthy of being loved.

"When Micah stopped at the Lazy Daisy, I didn't hate him for what he did to me. I hated him for what he was doing... he loved me when I didn't deserve to be loved. I could see how much he cared. More than any boy has ever cared. You had forbidden me to see him, but that didn't matter. I had forbidden myself to see him anymore because my feelings for him were wrong; I wasn't worthy of him. Is that freaky strange or what? I wasn't worthy of Micah Barnes! When Micah went forward this morning something happened. I saw that God loved him and I wanted God to love me. I went forward and when I knelt, I put my hand on his and I could feel what you prayed, but so much more happened. I asked God to accept me and help me straighten out this mess. I prayed for strength to do what needs to be done. A burden was lifted. I felt free. Free enough to tell Micah I loved him more than life itself. Daddy, I love Micah Barnes and I want to be with him. I looked at Charlotte and Chad and, in Chad, I see a guy who doesn't care where she came from, doesn't care who she was, doesn't care what anyone in the town thinks. He only cares what God thinks. I want to be Chad Houston. I'm young, I know, but if God is part of this it can't be wrong.

"And yes, you were right. I was raped three years ago, and it has happened several times since, by the same person."

She wept as Adam put his arm around her and they continued to walk as she gathered herself together. "I had just turned fourteen and just started dating. I'm not going to tell you the whole story right now. It'll all come out tomorrow. I've got to do it my way. I've got to claim victory over what was done to me. You're my daddy, and I know you want to avenge me, but you've got to trust me." She gave a faint smile. "That's been hard for the last three years. This guy has been black-mailing me about things he said he knows about you and mom. Things he said would destroy the family and the business. Said he had proof and witnesses, and if I ever told anyone he'd reveal it all. Some-how, in my mind, I had to protect the family, but all I did was destroy everything. You and mom hate each other. You've hated me. And mom, she's been too blind to see."

Adam quietly said, "Katie, I could never hate you."

They came to a stop and Adam turned and faced her. "Wow, so much to say and yet I feel I shouldn't say anything. First, mom and I will be just fine. Second, thank you for finally trusting me. Third, if God is bringing you and Micah together, who am I to interfere? Fourth, I will let you handle it your way. Let's find mom. She needs to know this too."

Judge Lloyd Chadwick, who'd been on the other side of Micah had great hearing and heard everything. He walked out of church scratching his head, "Tomorrow will be very interesting."

CHAPTER 40

*M*onday, October 7, 1992. At 8:30 Chad walked Micah into the Courthouse holding area and turned him over to Deputy Johnson. He was once again in the Sheriff's custody and in the presence of the next Washington County Sheriff, according to Vaughan Johnson. After Chad left, Vaughan started in with the taunting. "After today there will be one less Oakie for us to worry about, boy. What were you thinking? Thought you could rape a pretty young thing like Katie and get away with it? We gotcha and you're going away for a long time Oakie."

～

Upstairs Lloyd Chadwick waited in his chambers for the two attorneys. He waited, and he prayed and asked God to give him more wisdom than he'd ever possessed. Allison and Guy met in the hall and just looked at each other. She then said, "If you're asking for a last-minute plea deal, it ain't going to happen."

"Ms. Dodge, you got this one all wrong. I thought you set this up. You know I'll crush your witness and Micah will walk." A little false bravado peeking through. Both were now wondering what was going on.

They knocked and were admitted. Neither was offered a seat because the meeting wouldn't last long. The Judge said, "Either of you have anything you want to say before we begin the trial? Now would be a good time if you know something I don't know."

The District Attorney looked perplexed at the comment. Guy knew he had a surprise, but what the Judge was asking sounded strange to him too. Both nodded and said nothing. "Okay, then let's go get started. I'll see you in a few."

Vaughan Johnson had never looked finer as he marched Micah to the defendant's table and sat him down using the full authority of his position. Then he went behind the bar and sat directly behind him. He thought, "This will be good."

Guy came in with an armload of papers and sat next to Micah and said, "Good morning." He assured him everything would be all right, but to his surprise, Micah said, "You're right Mr. Kennedy, God's in control now. It will be great."

Katie and her parents came in and took their seats. Allison sat next to Katie and said, "It's almost over. We will put him away."

Katie said, "I hope so. It will be the happiest day of my life." The D.A. couldn't quite get her head around that comment. She knew Katie wanted Micah put away, but really? That badly?

The bailiff called the court to order and announced the Judge with "All rise, the Honorable Lloyd Chadwick presiding." The Judge seated everyone and turned to the jury. He thanked them and then read what was expected of them. He then asked each attorney if they were ready and called for opening statements.

· The District Attorney looked over the jury and began. "It's really quite a simple case. Micah Barnes, over the age of eighteen, raped Katie Pierce who was under the age of eighteen. It is a case of statutory rape. We have two witnesses. Katie herself will tell you the humiliation and pain she has suffered because of this animal's violent attack upon her…"

"Stop! Stop! Judge, you need to stop her now! Make her stop! None of it's true."

The courtroom was flooded with murmuring and Allison Dodge was obviously thrown off. It was already going so well as she was about to paint the picture she wanted the jury to see.

Judge Chadwick banged his gavel several times. "Order in the court. Order." The room quieted down as the Judge spoke. "Ms. Dodge, for the time being, you may take your seat and we'll get back to you. Miss Pierce, you are very much out of order and I could hold you in contempt for your outburst in my courtroom. But I'll let it slide. You stopped your attorney right in the middle of her opening statement which has never happened in my courtroom before. You have my curiosity up. Why would you disrupt my court? Do you perhaps have something you'd like to say?"

A very soft-spoken Katie Pierce stood up and said, "Yes, your honor I have much to say to the court right now."

"Miss Pierce, would you come up to the witness stand? Bailiff, please swear in the witness."

Vaughan Johnson wasn't the brightest deputy that Tink had ever had. In fact, if it hadn't been for the influence of his father and small county politics he'd never have been part of the Sheriff's Department. But, he was smart enough to know that when Tink came down the aisle and sat next to him and Corporal Adams entered from the other side and sat down on the other side that this might not be his best day.

After being sworn in the Judge said, "Remember, Miss Pierce, you are under oath. So, what do you have to say?"

"Your Honor, the first thing I want to say is Micah Barnes never raped me." Gasps and cheers.

The gavel came down. All it took was one bang and there was silence.

"I lied and I'll take what's coming. Micah has never touched me or harmed me except for the incident at the Lazy Daisy. I hope Micah loves me, and I know I love him. That part's hard to explain, but I will if I must. I'm ready to face the consequences for my actions, and I deserve what I get."

She continued, "Three years ago someone raped me. I was fourteen years old. I was out with a boy on a group date to a football game. We sneaked off from the group and went down behind the locker room. We were kissing and stuff and he put his hand up under my blouse. I knew I should stop him, but I didn't. He unbuttoned my blouse, and I didn't stop that either. I don't know what would have happened, but a Sheriff's deputy came around the corner and caught us. We were both terrified and didn't want our parents to find out because I knew I'd be grounded for a long time. He took our names and let us go. A few weeks went by and my parents said nothing so I thought everything was okay. In October I was at a dance and the same deputy cornered me in the hall. He said he hadn't reported me to my parents and if I was nice to him they'd never need to know what I did. He tried to kiss me and I pushed him away and ran back into the gym. A few days later he stopped me on the street. He was on duty. He said he'd meet me Saturday night at the park and we'd go someplace special where we could be alone. I said no. He then pulled out a list of things he said he knew, and could prove, about my family and it would all go public if I didn't do what he wanted. I read it and I believed it."

Charlotte held onto Chad tightly as she realized Micah was going to be exonerated. Her baby brother, who was much like her son for years, was now free to live his own life. That meant she could now think about herself and her future. Katie had professed her love for Micah and Charlotte was sure Micah loved her.

Maddie was sobbing violently and holding onto Adam so hard it hurt. How could she have been so blind? How could she not see the signs? Reflecting immediately on each time Katie had been the worst and knowing it was after a rape. She'd done nothing to help her child.

Micah was shocked at what he heard and put his head on the table. He wanted to block his ears and refuse to listen. Wow! Here he was being a gentleman and respecting her. He thought she was pure. Now she says she loves him while another guy was having sex with her. He understood it was rape, but she could have fought him. She could have gone to her father, the police, even to him. But she didn't.

Vaughan knew where this was going, he was safe. She already brought false rape charges against Micah so her credibility was shot. It was back to he said/she said, and he was a law enforcement officer. There wasn't a shred of proof he ever touched her. No one ever saw them together.

Guy knew he possessed the loaded weapon.

Tink didn't get to be Sheriff for fifty years by being stupid. The day Brad called him, he'd called and asked Judge Chadwick for an open-ended search warrant for Vaughan Johnson's apartment. He knew Brad would never use it, but he had it in his pocket and marked it as of the date it was used...the same date Brad broke in. He had the notes from the beginning of his "investigation" into corruption in his department. It was now his arrest, and he felt good.

She continued, "I didn't see an option or way out. I met him that night, and he raped me the first time."

Micah was thinking, first time! How many other times that you did nothing about?

Katie spoke, "This continued on about twice a year for the last three years, but it stops now. Today. Here."

Judge Chadwick asked, "Katie, is this person in the courtroom?"

She stood and pointed at Vaughan Johnson who at first glared at her with a look to kill, but he felt Tink's hand tighten on his arm. He yelled out, "You haven't got a shred of proof. It's your word against mine. We already know you accuse guys of rape to get your way."

Lloyd banged the gavel several times.

"Deputy Johnson you'll be quiet or I'll have you removed. You'll get your turn." Asking what he assumed was a rhetorical question, "Does anyone have any proof? Katie, do you have anything to prove what you're saying is true?" She shook her head. She had nothing. No proof whatsoever, only those horrible photos indelibly etched in her mind. She suddenly realized he might just get away with it. Her word against his. Guy Kennedy broke her train of thought.

He stood. "Your Honor, I have in my possession Deputy Johnson's personal blackmail notebook that he's been compiling and using for the last three years. It goes back to shortly after he joined the department. It's got handwritten names, dates, and notes. It has been verified by writing analysis. He's been blackmailing teens in town for three years. I was going to present it as evidence during the trial, but now seems as good a time as any." Allison Dodge's initial reaction was that it hadn't been entered during discovery, but that was moot now.

"I knew someone broke into my apartment. That was an illegal search. That was personal property removed illegally."

Tink stood, "I believe he may be referring to this search warrant you signed last week, your Honor. Deputy Adams and I found the notebook in a hollowed-out book entitled, "I Know What You Did." Quite an appropriate hiding spot. I have had Deputy Johnson under surveillance for several days. Vaughan Johnson, you are under arrest for the multiple rapes of Katie Pierce." He Mirandaized him on the spot and removed him from the room.

Brad sat there, pleased as he could be. Sheriff Reynolds still had it. Covered every base and better than he had. "Yeah, I'm not as good as I used to be."

Judge Chadwick looked at Micah. "The charges against you are dismissed, Mr. Barnes. Miss Pierce, you and I will need to talk in the next few days. You will be doing a lot of community service. Ladies and gentlemen of the unneeded jury I thank you for your service. Case dismissed." The Judge stood, the bailiff called, "All rise." Lloyd left and as soon as his back was to the courtroom a big broad smile crossed his face.

After the room cleared Chad made the first move. Micah still sat at the table, head down, even as several people gathered to congratulate him. While many assumed he was just overwhelmed, it wasn't that at all. What was there to congratulate? He had won nothing. If anything, he lost his dream. Yes, Katie had set him free, but at what cost to their relationship? He couldn't be with her now. Vaughan Johnson had ruined her. His mind went where he didn't want to go, "Why God? Why did you bring us so close only to tear us apart? What kind of cruel joke are you playing?"

Chad suggested that they go for an early lunch and then go home and relax by his pool. Too cold to swim even though it was heated, but it was a beautiful fall day to sit outside. They got in the Tahoe, stopped to pick up Sara from the sitter, and headed for Angie's. Charlotte and Chad were excited and eager to talk, but Micah was in a deep funk. Every time they'd ask what's wrong he mumbled and kept his head down. He nibbled at his food and pushed it around on his plate. Chad paid the bill, and they went home in silence.

Micah was the first one out of the car, and without saying a word, he wandered off on the grounds. Charlotte was really concerned now because nothing made sense. He should be excited. For the first time in his life, he was free and had a chance to do something with his life. She put Sara down for a nap and joined Chad on the patio. The sun was bright, the house blocked the breeze, and it felt good to sit and soak in the rays.

"Where's Micah?"

Chad said, "Out there somewhere."

Charlotte said, "What's going on? I don't understand it. He should be happier than he's ever been, but you'd think his childhood pet had just died by the way he's acting. He was so worried yesterday and then today Katie set him free. He got what he's wanted for months and now it's like he doesn't want it."

Chad let her go until she was talked out. "I think I know what's going on. God's working in his life, but he can't see it. Sometimes God calls us to do things that just don't make sense. It doesn't seem like something God would call us to do and yet he does. We don't understand that everything God does brings glory to him, not us. Jesus said to become the greatest you have to become the least. The world doesn't understand that. Micah is wrestling with God. Maybe he needs a referee." He got up, kissed her on the forehead and headed out onto the grounds.

As he walked through the gardens, the hundreds of mums were

coming into full bloom and the leaves on the fruit trees were turning. Apples hung from the fully loaded trees and Chad picked two as he walked by. Micah sat on the edge of a clearing that gave a view of the hills beyond. Chad sat down beside him and offered him an apple, "Here, you need this. You haven't eaten all day." Micah took the apple but just held it in his hand as he looked to the hills.

Chad said, "Who's winning?"

Micah just turned and looked at him with a perplexed expression on his face. "Huh?"

"I asked who's winning? You've been wrestling with God for several hours now and I asked who's winning? You or God?" No answer. "Okay, so that question is too hard. I asked you yesterday if you were ready to serve God for the rest of your life. What did you tell me?"

"I told you I was."

"So are you serving God right now or are you fighting him with every breath in your being? What is God asking you to do that scares you so much?"

Micah said, "I think he's trying to tell me to take Katie and love her. But after he's shown me these things about her, how can I do it?"

"Micah, you can't do it, but God can. Let me tell you a couple of stories. The Bible is full of flawed people who tried to fight God. It's full of fallen women whom God reached out and redeemed: Rahab, Gomer, Mary Magdalene: but there are two Jesus set free that stand out. You were in church the Sunday Reagan talked about the woman caught in adultery. They were ready to stone her and what did Jesus say?"

Micah said, "Let him who is without sin cast the first stone."

"Yes, and one by one they walked away. And when Jesus asked her where are those who would condemn you? She said they're gone. He replied that he didn't condemn her either and told her to go and sin no more. And don't forget the woman at the well. Jesus pointed out to her she'd had five husbands, but he realized it wasn't all her fault. Long story short. He forgave her.

"The other story is about a guy who moved to a certain town. He was a man who'd like to think he follows God's leading most of the time. He met a lady and God said this is who I have chosen for you. He found out the lady was on welfare. She came from the wrong part of town. Her family life was terrible except for a brother who loved her dearly. She was an unwed mother with an illegitimate child. But God had said, 'This is the woman I've chosen for you.' Micah, do I need to go any further with this story?"

"No, I think I have the picture." Micah sat there and stared at the apple and after a bite turned to Chad and said, "Thanks for being here. I look forward to being your brother-in-law." He stood up and took a big bite out of the apple and turned toward the house. As he walked by Charlotte he said, "Talk to you later, Sis, I've got something to take care of now."

Chad returned to the patio with a big smile on his face and a fresh apple in his hand. Charlotte was seated on the lounge and Chad sat down in the chair next to her. She said, "Micah sure looked like a man on a mission. What did you say to him?"

"I told you I thought he was wrestling with God. Well, it seems now the score is God one and Micah nothing. He didn't seem to understand that submission to God means his will in your life, not yours. God knows when it's a match made in heaven." With that, he dropped down on one knee and said, "Charlotte Barnes, God brought you into my life and you have made me the luckiest man in the world. Will you and your family, but mostly you, marry me?" Finally free to live her own life she said, "Yes, God, I will marry the man you've chosen for me." He handed her the freshly picked apple. "This will have to do until we go to Clark's and pick out a diamond."

The phone rang and Chad said, "Could be important. Could be Micah. I better go answer."

Charlotte reflected on her life. Some would say it was a fairytale type of story with Cinderella and Prince Charming. And while it was beyond anything she could have imagined the day her mother walked out it was no fairytale. Born into an abusive home. Her mother walked out in the middle of the night. A teen forced to take care of her little brother. Dreams of college dashed by a spiteful father. A dead-end job at eighteen. An unwanted pregnancy at nineteen. Another generation on welfare. Imprisoned by life and the Oaks. An encounter with Reagan Lamb that changed her life. Receiving Christ. Dedicating her life and her baby to God. Brother accused of rape. Pain, agony. Trusting God is in control. An encounter with a stranger on June 2nd. Love at first sight. Discover he's a multimillionaire, and she's on welfare. Run, as fast as you can. Be pursued by the hound of heaven who'll never let go. It's not a fairytale, it's a God thing. And how often has it happened and people miss it? We may not see God raising the physically dead, but he raises the spiritually dead. He had with Billy Maddox.

Billy Maddox was at work when he heard what had happened. Billy and Heather were pulling their married life together. They were working with Reagan to start outreach ministries to the Oaks. They found an old building and Reagan signed a contract to rent it for practically nothing. Reagan knew that only Oakies, with the help of God, could reach other Oakies. Truth be told, there was no more famous Oakie than Billy Maddox, except for Paul Barnes who was sitting in jail. And all the Oaks knew of the miracle story of Charlotte Barnes and after things calmed down Reagan hoped to involve her in this ministry too.

Heather was the real organizing force in the community. Her and Billy's testimony had spread far and wide in a short period. It started when Wayne Miller had asked them to come and share their story. They had been in most of the churches and were sharing their vision with others. A loosely knit non-profit developed with Heather heading it. The first thing they did was to establish a thrift store. That was followed by a food pantry. They envisioned a program to help pay for medicine. Heather was in charge of volunteers running the program. Most of the volunteers were people who had at one time been part of the welfare system because it was hard to pull the wool over the eyes of those who had been wool pullers themselves.

Heather and Billy had met with Ginny Kennedy and Ginny agreed to handle the adoption process that would make them a one name family. Billy realized that as husband and father he had greater responsibilities than restoring a GTO that would take money he didn't have. The Chevy dealer gave Billy a really good deal, realizing that it was a restorable classic. Billy Maddox, of all people, drove out in a low mileage 1989 Dodge Minivan. With windows that worked!

Billy was now head of airport maintenance and received another raise. Apparently, Chad couldn't fully retire and indirectly was bringing air traffic into Washington County. It wasn't likely that there would ever be an international airport, but business was good.

Micah knocked on the Pierces' front door. This was a first. He and Katie were never where her father might see or know. He waited, not knowing what to expect, but he kept saying over and over. "I want to be your servant," Adam answered the door. Micah gulped, "Sir, may I please speak to Katie?"

Adam said, "Well, it's about time. Where have you been? Katie's been crying her eyes out and was terrified you weren't coming. Come in, but let me say one thing. Never hurt my little girl."

"Sir, I couldn't, I wouldn't. Even when she accused me, I still loved her. It really upset me this morning after what she revealed in court, even if it was the truth, and I had a pity party. I wasn't thinking about what happened to Katie for three years. I only thought of what happened to me this morning."

Adam led him to the library, opened the door and softly said, "Katie, someone to see you."

Micah entered and stood before her, shuffling his feet. They spoke no words as she patted the cushion next to her. He sat. She took his hand in hers and he felt the sparks flying. He pulled his hand away, and she looked at him with disappointment. He took both hands and gently placed one on each cheek as he drew her in and kissed her with his first ever kiss of love.

Katie said, "I prayed you'd love me as I love you and that when you found out the truth, you wouldn't hate me."

"Katie, I loved you long before you ever loved me. I was a boy chasing a dream of a lifetime with a girl I didn't deserve. You and I come from two different worlds and I wanted to give you everything, but I had nothing to give. When I saw you with Billy Lee and that Mustang I lost it. My dream exploded in a million pieces. I knew I could never give you those things.

"In the courtroom this morning I felt like I was the victim, not you. In my dream, I would be your first and only. And then I wasn't, and I hurt so much I can't explain it. I was so selfish in my thinking. I never thought about what you've been through or how you felt. I went to my pity party without a date and yelled at God for what he'd done to me. Chad found me. He asked if I had yielded to God? We talked, and he showed me how wrong I was. I believe God has chosen you for me. I beg for your forgiveness and ask you to help me to be good enough to deserve you. Katie, I want to start over. Hi, I'm Micah Barnes and I'd like to take you out to dinner tomorrow night."

"I'm pleased to meet you Micah and I would enjoy that."

Micah added, "I sure hope my sister lets me take her Grand Am. You deserve better than my truck."

CHAPTER 41

$\mathcal{W}$ednesday, October 10, 1992. Charlotte wanted a simple church wedding. She and Chad had discussed this several times, and the topic was nearly worn out. Chad insisted that she could have the wedding of her dreams. No budget. Charlotte kept telling him a simple church wedding was the wedding of her dreams. As a child, she had read all the fairytale princess stories that make up a young girl's dreams. And the day her mother walked out her dream world ended and reality set in. So her dream became a small church wedding with a man who would love and cherish her. Until a year ago she didn't even have a church and who wanted to marry a welfare mother with a one-year-old? The dream she'd felt would never happen was becoming a reality. It was more important to her than Chad could ever understand.

Chad finally gave up, well, sort of, and let her plan the wedding. They asked Reagan to marry them and reserved the fellowship hall and asked the senior ladies guild to cater. Chad told her he'd work with the ladies and take care of the reception.

Chad always cringed at some choices she made. Such a simple person, so unassuming, and yet so elegant. She went to the Economy Store to order her wedding dress. He could have flown her to New

York, Chicago or even Paris to pick out a gown. She went to the Economy Store. The owner tried to show her catalogs and explained she could alter anything in the store. Charlotte wanted nothing to do with that. Then she showed her the rack of several dresses she kept on hand. Charlotte looked at them, noting the prices of $660-$800. Charlotte had had so little for so long that an extravagance of paying $600 for a dress you'd wear once made no sense. She moved to the rack of inexpensive evening gowns, and much to the disdain of the owner chose an off-white dress with a price tag of $99.99. It was the most expensive dress she'd ever owned. She told Chad about the purchase and he said, "I guess we'll need to sell the house to pay for it." He followed with a smile and wondered how God had given him such a woman. She could have everything but wanted nothing.

The guest list was short. They offered a general invitation to the congregation, but only a few received invitations she had printed at the Lighthouse. The only invitation Chad sent was to his former partner and his plus one, whoever that might be at the time of the wedding. He had no family. A few cousins he'd met once or twice, but wouldn't bother to invite. They mailed out several local invitations. Judge Chadwick, the Kennedy's, Tinker and Emma, Adam and Maddie Pierce, since it looked like they'd be family soon. Katie received her own but felt very much a part of the wedding party. They sent a special invitation to Billy and Heather and family. They had not yet announced their heavy support of the new ministry, but would soon. On the bottom of each invitation, they requested that attendees give gifts to "Project New Hope," the name given to the Oaks ministry.

Charlotte talked to Chad about some of her childhood friends. "I have mixed feelings. They were an important part of my life for seventeen years. They were always there for me when Daddy went on a rampage. They are good people, but frankly, they will not be too well received at our wedding. Some of them might even end up being downright embarrassing."

"Charlotte, you wouldn't even be asking me about this unless it was important to you for them to be there. Look at us. Do we really care what people think? They aren't the ones we are trying to impress, are they?" About twenty Oakie families received personal invitations to the Houston/Barnes wedding on October 27, 1992.

Even the wedding party was going to be small. Charlotte asked Prudy, a very, very, pregnant Prudy to be her Maid of Honor since she and Reagan had been so important in her life. Sara would be the Flower Girl. Whether she'd walk down the aisle was yet to be determined. Micah, bless his heart, pulled double duty. He would be Chad's Best Man, a job he didn't feel worthy of performing. But in addition, he'd walk his sister down the aisle on her wedding day. The greatest honor of his life.

CHAPTER 42

*T*uesday, October 16, 1992. Paul sat in his cell, mad at the world. It appeared he had no redeeming qualities at all. If he ever did, they were gone now. He cussed out everyone including God. He blamed Micah and Charlotte for his present predicament. And mostly he blamed that rich boy from Californ-i-a.

Paul was like the man in the story of a young pastor assigned to a country church and when the meanest, the most hate-filled man in the county died he was asked to do the funeral. He had pre-arranged his funeral since no one would give him one. He had one request. The preacher would get an honorarium of $500, if he said something nice about him. The young pastor anguished over this for three days. He asked all over town, but no one could think of anything nice to say about him. The day of the funeral, the place was packed anticipating if the young pastor had found anything nice to say. He went to the lectern and said, "Today we gather to say goodbye and good riddance to John Wallace. The only good thing we can say about John is that his brother was worse."

You couldn't even say that about Paul Barnes, he didn't have a brother. The day they moved him into the cell he threw the Gideon Bible under the cot. There it remained. Billy thought maybe he could get through to him since they went way back, but Paul just ridiculed Billy's faith. Billy wasn't deterred and went back again, but Paul refused to see him. Reagan, because of his relationship with Micah and Charlotte, had visited and tried to talk with him. The small talk went okay, but at the mention of God, Paul yelled and swore and started after him as Reagan yelled for help. At the sight of Deputy Adams, with a weapon drawn, Paul backed away. Reagan told Wayne about the encounter at breakfast the next morning. Wayne, just because he's Wayne, went to talk with him. Wayne was ready and started the visit from the safe side of the bars. Paul picked up a handful of leftover mashed potatoes and threw them at him. Mean through and through. Even Charlotte had stopped by on two occasions, but he refused to see her. Micah said, "He's my father and I will pray for him, but I won't go see him."

The day before the trial, Ginny Kennedy stopped by to visit her 'client'. Paul was smart enough to see that she was the only chance he had of not doing hard time. He put on his best face as he said, "Good morning, Counselor, are we ready?"

Ginny said, "I'm ready. I hope you are." Paul's flag hasn't gone all the way up the pole for a long time. He thought this was a good comment. She asked if he had questions. He replied, "Not if you've got it covered."

She said, "Paul, your case has had my undivided attention," then she walked away and whispered, "for thirty seconds."

CHAPTER 43

*W*ednesday, October 17, 1992. Court convened and the Honorable Lloyd Chadwick was presiding. The District Attorney, Allison Dodge, was ready for some blood. It was re-election time, and she needed a win. She called Corporal Adams who testified as to what happened. It didn't appear that Ginny had changed her courtroom tactics. On cross-examination, she said, "No questions." Allison called Tinker as a witness and again on the cross, Ginny said, "No questions." Next, they called the gas station attendant who remembered Paul's Pacer and him filling the cans. Again Ginny said, "No questions." The prosecutor rested her case and they took a short break.

Paul asked Ginny, "What's going on? Why didn't you cross-examine? Adams wasn't the guy who took me down. And no one saw me at the gas station because the cans were already full."

"Look, Paul, I'm your attorney and I know what I'm doing. I got it covered."

Judge Chadwick turned to Ginny, "Counselor, you may present your defense."

Ginny stood and looked at the District Attorney, then the Judge, then the jury and finally at Paul, "Your Honor, I have nothing. Abso-

lutely, nothing. There's a witness, but Paul didn't see him, can't identify him. So I have nothing. The defense rests."

Paul's face exploded into a rage as he lunged at Ginny Kennedy. He
forgot. His feet were shackled, and he fell on his face. The verdict was
guaranteed from the git-go, but this clinched it. Paul would probably
get an appeal at some point, but it was good enough for everybody in
town. He'd be gone for a long time. Sheriff Reynolds said he'd get him
and he did. Brad was happy with the outcome. Corporal Adams
would probably get a promotion. And Micah and Charlotte no longer
feared retribution from their father.

After a year passed, the Barnes property was sold for taxes. Micah
bought it just in case. His father had a lot of schemes but he never
knew if any paid off. He knew that every so often he'd flash money
around, but Paul would never give up the system for the occasional
cash he flaunted. Micah spent evenings and weekends demolishing
the property piece by piece. He'd put the junk out by the gate for trash
pickup and nobody ever took anything. It was all junk. After several
months he decided there wasn't anything and the most valuable thing
on the property was the old Winnebago. One day he decided to throw
out the filthy, dilapidated furniture. He realized it made no sense that
his father kept that disgusting overstuffed, now understaffed, chair.
He took out his knife and cut the cushion and dug. He pulled out a
little over $300,000. His father had been literally sitting on $300,000
for years. It was now his. He and Katie had $300,000 dollars. He
offered half to Charlotte who refused to even talk about it. She didn't
need it. She had more money than the Glencoe First National Bank.
Well, we are getting way ahead of ourselves.

CHAPTER 44

Saturday, October 27, 1992. On Saturday afternoon at 1:30 there were about ninety people gathered in the sanctuary of Community Church. They waited and Charlotte looked around and thought *"this is perfect."* It was exactly what she wanted, a small wedding with a few friends. She was pleased to see several Oakie's in attendance. Even from the back, she could pick them out. She had requested the ushers seat people as a congregation so Oakie's sat next to prominent members of the community.

Charlotte thought, "If these people are my friends then they have to accept not only who I am, but where I came from." What had Chad said, "The key to everything is never forget your roots? It keeps you grounded. It humbles you to remember where you came from. And it reminds you where you may not want to go." For the first time, she was proud of her roots. It made her who she'd become.

Chad realized that if he had fallen in love and married in Southern California, this wedding would feature a cast of dozens and thousands in attendance. Glitz and glamor. The bride wouldn't be wearing a $99.99 dress from the Economy Store and he wouldn't dress in a Men's Wearhouse suit. He looked at the congregation assembled here and thought, she's right again, it's perfect. These are the people who are most important in our lives. These are people who love us for who we are and not what they can get. Suddenly, a totally unexpected thought came to Chad. Totally un-wedding related, "God, you want me to do it, don't you? I know she would be happier. It's not who we are, is it? Let's talk about it later."

Charlotte had peeked in the direction of the Fellowship Hall and didn't see what she expected nor did she see any food in the kitchen. Too late to ask Chad. He was with the pastor, but knowing her 'husband,' he had something up his sleeve. Charlotte again had insisted on the church organist even though Reagan assured her she could bring in who she wanted. Charlotte said, "No. That's who I want. She's part of my life. She may not be great, but she's part of the church family." Kind of made Reagan feel a little guilty about some things he'd thought over the last three years. A little guilty, but not a lot guilty. Out of the mouths of Christian babes...isn't that the expression? Something like that. Well, the organist began and Charlotte smiled, it sounded wonderful. She and Micah took their places at the back and waited with Sara and her basket of rose petals.

The Wedding March began and Chad and Reagan entered. Chad nodded at Sara who stood there looking panicky. He knelt down and held out his arms and whispered loudly, "Come to daddy." She dropped the basket and ran to his waiting arms. Charlotte looked at Micah and said, "That's exactly what I want to do right now."

Micah smiled, "My dear sister, you will. When you reach the front, you will have run to the arms God has provided for your life."

"Micah Barnes, I love you. When did you get so wise?" The organist hit the high crescendo, and she walked down the aisle.

Micah took Charlotte's hand and placed her hand in Chad's and stepped to the side. Sara had the best view in the place from her daddy's arms. When Reagan reached the part of the ceremony for each to give their vows, he announced they'd written their own. Chad began...

"On June 3rd I walked into this church for the first time. When I saw you I recognized you as the girl who had given me directions the day before. I was lost. That day I moved over next to you and offered you directions. I took your hand to comfort you and God said, "Chad Houston, this is the woman I have chosen for you. Take her as your wife." I was found. Charlotte Barnes today I take you as my wife to complete me and make me whole. I promise you I will love you even with the last breath I take and no one will ever hurt you again. All that I am and all that I have, I give you this day...my pretty lady".

It took a while for Charlotte to compose herself. "Chad Houston, I've never told you this before because I didn't want you to get a swollen head. The day I gave you directions I assumed I'd never see you again. You turned around in that big expensive car that had no place in the Oaks...(they both laughed at their inside joke)...You didn't know I was a baby Christian who was trusting God for all things. As you drove away I said, 'God, that is the most beautiful man I have ever seen. Why can't I have a man like that?' I believe Jesus told his disciples, 'You have not, because you ask not.' I asked and God has given. I fought your love for a long time because I wasn't like you. I didn't believe God could or would give a girl like me a guy like you. But you showed me we are much alike. Chad Houston, I take you as my husband and I will never let you down or let you go. I love God with all my heart, soul, and strength, but you come in a close second."

Reagan pronounced them husband and wife and introduced Mr. and Mrs. Chad Houston to the congregation. Some softly applauded politely. Others clapped, cheered, whistled, and even stomped their feet. Lloyd Chadwick, front and center, joined the crowd, and he too clapped and stomped his feet. Who'd have thought? The judge brought the two sides of town together, for a couple hours anyway.

After the roar died down and before leaving the platform Chad made an announcement. "There has been a slight change in the reception location. It will not be held in the Fellowship Hall as originally planned by my beautiful bride. It's still catered by the wonderful ladies of the church but will be held in our home in one hour. I have seating for one hundred and twenty five. Please join us for a surprise you'll never forget. And listen, if you meet any friends along the way, bring them too. We've got plenty of room and lots of food."

As they recessed up the aisle Charlotte Houston said, "What have you done?"

He smiled, "You'll see."

They allowed time for the guests to arrive and then pulled up to the front of the mansion and the sixteen-foot tall oak doors. Valets were everywhere and a 'butler' was serving as a doorman. He held the door as they entered and climbed the circular staircase to the ballroom.

As they entered Charlotte saw the beautiful, tastefully decorated room. The head table was straight ahead and the wedding party was standing waiting for someone to announce their entrance. She saw their seats and smiled as she took note. Chad had placed a high chair between them. Ten person round tables were arranged around the ballroom. In the middle was the dance floor and to her right was an eight-piece combo. The bandleader took the mike and announced the arrival and entrance of the bride and groom and for the second time today clapping, foot stomping, and whistling erupted. The ballroom was filled with sounds that had probably never been heard in there before.

After dinner and toasts, the first dance was announced. As Chad and Charlotte took center stage the combo played the sweet strains of 'more than the greatest love the world has ever known...more than this love I give to you my own.'

After a half an hour Chad noticed that while some guests were enjoying the combo, the others, not so much. Chad took the mike and asked for the guests' attention. "I promised you a surprise and a surprise you shall have. Charlotte my dearest, I want to say in the most positive, loving, and complimentary way I can, you are the simplest and most uncomplicated woman I've ever known. I could give you everything, but you ask for nothing. But, I need an honest answer from you right now. If you could have any performer in the world sing to you today, who would it be? Think carefully because it's too late to change."

Charlotte looked and said, "Josh Turner?"

He pointed to the now closed doors, "Ladies and gentlemen, Mr.

Josh Turner!" The doors opened and while this had been going on the combo had turned country and the instruments all changed and the most exciting day of Charlotte Barnes Houston's life got better as Josh came forward and sang to her, 'Would You Go With Me." The reception lasted well into the evening as the celebration continued. The whole world for the taking, but Charlotte chose the Jersey Shore for her honeymoon. It's where she'd wanted to go since she was a little girl.

CHAPTER 45

*S*unday, November 18, 1992. Not counting vacations, for the first time in three years, Reagan Lamb wasn't present for Sunday worship. Prudy went into labor about two in the morning and off they went to Upton at an urgent, but safe, speed. No Molly for this trip. Baby Reagan was born Sunday at 1:46 in the afternoon and weighed in at a hefty seven pounds, nine ounces, and twenty inches long, although Reagan thought he looked much taller.

As Prudy lay asleep in the birthing suite, Reagan sat quietly holding his son. He tried to imagine his father ever holding him. Maybe it had happened, but try as hard as he might, the picture wouldn't focus. He pondered how life might have been with a father who loved him, but even more, he wondered what it would have been like if his father had only loved his mother. He looked at little Reagan and said, "You'll be loved every day of your life and I promise I'll never stop loving your mother." Prudy heard every word.

Reagan had been at Community Church for four years now and witnessed God do the impossible. Billy Maddox got saved. He got really saved. Who would ever have thought that could happen? Even more, he was a great dad and a loving husband. Shirley Comstock, his biggest nemesis, had become his biggest booster. He had witnessed the re-dedication of Lloyd Chadwick. He had been a part of God's plan for Charlotte Barnes and had seen Micah come to Christ. He had witnessed Katie Pierce set free from her bondage and God heal Adam and Maddie's marriage. So much had happened in the last nine months and his life had changed in so many ways. It was time to finish letting go of the past. If so many around him could put their total faith in God it was time for him to let it go. Move on.

The next day the three of them returned home and the constant parade of visitors began. Baby gifts, food, and flowers. Reagan had never been this happy. As he held his son he never stopped smiling at Prudence Lamb.

Christmas Eve 1992. As Reagan retold the Christmas story, he held baby Reagan in his arms. He stood silently as the congregation lit their candles. His mind whirled as he thought over the last years. "The child in the manger and the child in my arms have transformed my life forever. For God so loved me, that he sent his only son that if I believe in him I shall not perish, but I will receive eternal life. And not only did he send his son for me, but allowed his one and only son's blood to be shed for me, Reagan Lamb." Reagan, as much as anyone, knew that he had never done enough to earn God's grace and more than that. He didn't deserve it. Yes, grace like a river flows.

EPILOGUE

*T*hings don't really change all that much in a small town. Glencoe is no exception. The truth is sometimes you totally miss those small things if you aren't paying attention. Nineteen-ninety-two had been an unusual year in Glencoe. A lot of big changes and a lot of drama, but now everyone was ready for things to calm down with the dawning of the new year.

* * *

Billy and Heather Maddox continued their work with Project New Hope as they watched it grow and bring new hope to dozens of families. The Board of Elders asked Billy to enter deacon training in further effort to really become Glencoe Community Church. And in July, the court granted Billy his request to adopt Sadie and Jake much to the children's great joy. Billy was proving to be a role model father. At the final hearing Jake said, "He's the bestest dad ever. He takes me fishing and I know he hates fishing."

* * *

Becky Walsh saw the writing on the wall. The church was computerizing, and she wasn't. That didn't mean the Becky News Network shut down, she just had to find some new sources. She never figured out what happened to all that coffee.

* * *

Tinker Reynolds was once again re-elected, to no one's surprise, since he ran unopposed. It had been a great year for the Sheriff's Department. They hired a new deputy. With the assistance of Mike Pembly and Billy Maddox, Tinker had intentionally reached out to the Oaks to find a new deputy, and they found a great young prospect. Emma sat in church alone, the election was over. She went to all the garage sales in the spring. It was time to redecorate the jail.

* * *

Bill Bemis passed away in April. Few people could have told you his or his twin brother's name. They were just the old guys who looked like Tweedle Dum and Tweedle Dee who came into town every morning in an old truck. No one seemed to know for sure where they lived. It was way up a hollow somewhere. Supposedly, when their mom died, they put her in the freezer on the front porch next to their rockers, but no one knew for sure. Reagan was asked to do the funeral. He was pleased to do it. They'd never met, but Bill was a close friend.

* * *

Wayne Miller and Reagan continued their relationship through prayer and weekly Bible Study until Reagan left after ten years at Community Church. Wayne would remain in Glencoe several years after Reagan left, but found no one to replace his great friend.

* * *

In September the county was shocked. Judge Lloyd Chadwick announced he was retiring from the bench. He had adjudicated the county bench for seven years and felt it was time to do something else. He became chairman of the board for Project New Hope and spent countless hours giving free legal advice and volunteering, but mostly he loved working with the youth. Maybe he could help save the next generation.

* * *

Allison Dodge had been re-elected, but was planning to run for the seat of Washington County Judge when the special election was announced. Guy Kennedy gave a serious thought of running against her. She had no mercy in her soul and as Lloyd had shown, justice needed to be tempered with mercy.

* * *

Ginny was becoming known as a fierce women's and children's rights advocate. They didn't make much money. Didn't need it. Nobody ever found out who they had been. Ginny sure was busy. Still had no answering machine.

* * *

Shirley Comstock finally came around. Years later when Reagan accepted a call to another church, Shirley was the first to say, "Tell me it's not true. What can we do to get you to stay?" Who was this woman and what had she done with Shirley? Langdon found his calling as Reagan developed The Caring Ministry designed to let the elderly and those in the church know they were never forgotten.

* * *

Adam and Mattie Pierce began marital counseling in January, along with Katie, who was getting the help she had needed for three years. Each month Adam and Maddie became closer. The message Reagan had given resonated in her soul. 'Some of you knew the joy of knowing Christ, but somewhere you lost it." She was finding it again.

* * *

Micah and Katie announced their engagement in May just before Katie's graduation. They got married in early October uniting what had been the Hatfields and the McCoys. But they didn't move into Micah's house. Instead, they moved into the mansion. After experiencing God's grace in his own life Lloyd Chadwick had dismissed all charges against Micah and Katie.

It's one of those long stories that is somehow an unexplainable God thing. At the wedding, a year ago, Chad received a message from God. That house would never make Charlotte happy. In fact, that great big house would only make her miserable. So without telling her, he decided to sell it. In a town like Glencoe it was an albatross around his neck. It was a great buy, but he hadn't considered resale.

In August Micah had found the $300,000 dollars and Chad had an idea. He got together with Micah and Katie. "What are your plans after you get married?" Like most young couples they hadn't really thought beyond wedded bliss.

Micah said, "Well, I'll keep working at the lumberyard for the time being. I'm hoping Mr. Pierce will offer me a job in the store, but he hasn't said nothing yet."

Katie said, "I'm clerking at the store, so between us and with a house that's paid for we'll be fine. And we have $300,000 dollars." They both grinned.

"Exactly. Micah, have I given you good advice? When you've listened, which wasn't always, how's it worked out?"

Micah agreed. "Chad, you've got a great business mind. You wouldn't be where you are at your age unless you knew what you were talking about. So, what are you suggesting?"

"I want your house." Chad saw the look on Micah's face. "Now, hear me out. Charlotte would never say it, but I know she hates living in the mansion and I know she loves your bungalow. What I'm suggesting is that we swap houses, even up. You turn the mansion into a bed-and-breakfast and let Katie run it. Micah, you need to quit your job now and enroll in fall courses, even before you get married. You're smart and you don't need to work right now. Make the $300,000 work for you. Get a business degree to show Adam you're worthy of taking over the family business. Remember, when you first dated Katie it was your dream. God is making it come true. Katie, you need to finish your education too. If you enjoy running a B&B, maybe a degree in Hospitality Management."

The wedding was a much grander affair than Chad and Charlotte's. The church was packed. Chad was the Best Man and Charlotte was the Matron of Honor. Lettie Pike was her Maid of Honor. She had six attendants and you get the picture.

When they left the reception Chad drove up High Street but didn't turn on Broad Street. When he went by the turn Charlotte asked, "Where are we going?" Chad simply said, "Home" and turned into the alleyway before Pine. They got out of the car and Sara ran for her playhouse.

"Okay, so what's going on?" Chad took her by the hand and walked around to the front and opened the door. Everywhere she looked was their furniture. Chad said, "I hope you like it...it's your new home."

Charlotte turned and hugged him and said, "It's exactly what I wanted. How did you know?"

Chad smiled again, "It was pretty obvious." Then he explained the whole thing including the sneaky four hour move.

* * *

Brad went into retirement. For months he had wrestled with what was being preached at Community Church versus what he'd been practicing. He was good at what he did and being an Angel of Justice for the helpless gave him great personal satisfaction, but spiritually it left him empty. On the one hand, he believed he pleased God, but on the other he felt God was not pleased. He knew he had to change his life. One evening he sat on the couch with Beasley in his lap and reflected on his life. Where it had been, where it was now, but most importantly where it was going. No matter what he'd done, God remained faithful and blessed him. "Beasie, it's time for us to do more for the Kingdom of God than what we've done. It's time for me to seek God's will for my life rather than assume God's will for my life."

* * *

When he was nine months of age, Reagan and Prudy offered their child and their lives in total dedication to God. They had been Christians for a long time. Now it was time to be more. The last year had shown them the awesome power of God in all the miracles he had performed in so many lives. How could they not give him everything? They decided they wanted a public ceremony and arranged with Micah and Katie to use the gardens of the Bed and Breakfast for the dedication setting.

Over one hundred people gathered as Reagan, Prudy and the baby arrived. Reagan walked in proudly carrying his son and Prudy held the leash of their dog as they moved into place and stood before Wayne Miller. Reagan wouldn't have had anyone but Wayne preside at this wonderful occasion. Wayne took the child from Reagan and held him toward heaven and said, "What name is given to this child?"

Reagan said, "He shall be called Reagan Bradley Lamb, Junior." He proudly turned to those gathered and said, "But we will call him Brad." And Beasley pranced around proudly at the dedication of his little human.

SYNOPSIS OF WHEN THE RIVER RUNS DRY

We return to the strange little town of Glencoe with another story of redemption, grace, and second chances. God's grace flowed forth like a raging river. Lives were touched, and families were changed, and one man was at the center of it all. Did the grace of God suddenly stop flowing when tragedy struck Glencoe? And what do Reagan Lamb, Kyle Shaw, Marisa Fields, and Jenny Wade have in common? All of their lives had been devastated in some way. Each of them watched their dream of living happily ever after disappear into the mess of their lives. Although feeling alone and abandoned, God was still at work in their lives, intertwining their lives to the lives of other Glencoe residents we've already met. As one chapter of their lives ends, a new one begins if they are open to God's leading. God shows each one of them that he's still writing their stories.

ABOUT THE AUTHOR

My name is Richard Marshall Wright. My middle name is my mother's mothers maiden name. Since there are already authors named Richard Wright I chose to go with R. Marshall Wright, which I have discovered can be confusing.

I graduated from the University of Maine in Orono, Maine in 1969 and Drew Theological School in Madison, New Jersey in1972. I'm a retired U.S. Army Chaplain and served 23 years Active and Reserve. I'm also a retired pastor and an evangelical Christian. Like many others, I've always wanted to be a writer, kept saying I was going to write, but never did until about two years ago. It would be nice to write the next great American novel, but I will probably never do that. But I will continue to write Christian fiction, hopefully with some twists along the way. If one person says "Hey, that's a pretty good book," then I'm happy.

I've been married to my fabulous wife, Lynn, for fifty years. We feel we have been truly blessed in that we are able to spend our summers on a lake in Michigan and our winters in Florida. We have two children and five grandchildren. Marnie is married to Arick and is the eldest and has been a stay at home mom rearing three active boys...Luke, Levi, and Loden. She holds a Masters degree from Northwestern in communications and is also a writer. Trevor is married to Lori and is a successful pastor in Findlay, Ohio. His two are Emma, who is the oldest grandchild and the only girl, and her brother Cole. We are extremely proud of everyone in my family.

ALSO BY R MARSHALL WRIGHT

Grace Like a River Flows (Book One)
When the River Runs Dry (Book Two)
Finding Grace (Book Three)
When Grace Came Down (Book Four)

The Lonely Seagull (Book One)
For the Love of Grace (Book Two)

Laura, Don't Run!

When Grace Came Down (A Christmas Story)

https://www.amazon.com/author/rmarshallwright

Made in United States
North Haven, CT
04 September 2023

41124603R00178